Miryam's Guest House

The large house in the leafy London suburb, empty, derelict, and with its garden a wilderness, always 'looked haunted' to the Anglican priest who tells this story. But really it was haunted only by his memories of things that had happened there in the lively, exuberant, but already threatened years of the 'Twenties', after the First World War. In those days it was a guest house which its hostess, Miryam Davids, liked to think was inhabited only by 'gentlefolk', but in fact contained a remarkably odd assortment of guests.

One of them was the Rev Hugh Fields, returned from the war, after serving first as a chaplain and then as a ranker in the trenches. He had come to a room in Miryam's house, after deciding to withdraw from an active ministry and give himself to much study, in the hope of rebuilding a faith which had once been his but which had been left by the war in grave disarray. His aim was to write a book which would rebuild the faith for himself and for others.

Then to the house came two young lovers, Siward and Theresa Bartleby, newly wed, deeply in love, and typical representatives of the 'Bright Young Things' of the Twenties, believing in little but the pursuit of gaiety and happiness. They attach themselves to the Rev Hugh partly because he is the only youthful one among the guests and partly because, calling him their Resident Padre, they can use him as a vessel for their doubts and difficulties and dreams. So deeply do his desires become interwoven with theirs that he is able to write in one place: 'Siward and Terry; I really don't know if the story I have to tell is their story or mine.'

BOOKS BY ERNEST RAYMOND

NOVELS
A London Gallery *comprising:*

We, the Accused
The Marsh
Gentle Greaves
The Witness of Canon Welcome
A Chorus Ending
The Kilburn Tale
Child of Norman's End
For Them That Trespass
A Georgian Love Story

Was There Love Once?
The Corporal of the Guard
A Song of the Tide
The Chalice and the Sword
To the Wood No More
The Lord of Wensley
The Old June Weather
The City and the Dream
Our Late Member

Other Novels

The Bethany Road
The Mountain Farm
The Tree of Heaven
One of Our Brethren
Late in the Day
Mr. Olim
The Chatelaine
The Visit of Brother Ives
The Quiet Shore
The Nameless Places
Tell England
A Family that Was
A Jesting Army

Mary Leith
Morris in the Dance
The Old Tree Blossomed
Don John's Mountain Home
The Five Sons of Le Faber
The Last to Rest
Newtimber Lane
The Miracle of Brean
Rossenal
Damascus Gate
Wanderlight
Daphne Bruno I
Daphne Bruno II

BIOGRAPHIES, ETC.

The Story of My Days (Autobiography I)
Please You Draw Near (Autobiography II)
Good Morning, Good People (Autobiography III)
Paris, City of Enchantment
Two Gentlemen of Rome (The Story of Keats and Shelley)
In the Steps of St. Francis
In the Steps of the Brontës

ESSAYS, ETC.

Through Literature to Life
The Shout of the King
Back to Humanity (with Patrick Raymond)

PLAYS

The Berg
The Multabello Road

Miryam's Guest House

A NOVEL

by

ERNEST RAYMOND

CASSELL · LONDON

CASSELL & COMPANY LTD
35 RED LION SQUARE, LONDON WC1 4SG
Sydney, Auckland, Toronto
Johannesburg

First published 1973

ISBN 0 304 29185 4

Printed in Great Britain
by The Anchor Press Ltd,
and bound by Wm. Brendon & Son Ltd,
both of Tiptree, Essex

F. 173

Contents

The House that Looked Haunted

To me the house looked haunted. It was the last in a terrace of nine houses and the only one unoccupied. Why it had been left empty for several years I do not know. Probably an inheritor of the house, living elsewhere and knowing that the terrace was scheduled for demolition one day, had decided that in these years of monstrously inflated prices it was not worth the cost of redecorating within and without so as to let it to a tenant. In a few years he would be given an inflated sum for the ground on which it stood.

Meanwhile the occupiers in the other eight houses remained *in situ* with curtains in their windows, paint on their window frames, and their small front gardens trimmed and tidy. This helped to give the single empty house at the top of the terrace its mien of dereliction and decay.

Once they were nine tall Victorian houses with a white stucco rendering of their semi-basement and entrance floor, while all above this stucco facing, three floors of it, was London grey-brick. It was only this house whose stucco, unloved and untended, was scabrous and suppurating. The London brick above it was a cinder-grey after a century of smuts flying from London's chimneys; its windows, wide and spacious, were dingy and blank; the front garden was a jungle of high weeds; and the privet hedge, once only breast-high, had grown nearly as high as a prison wall. The gravel drive, matted with grass and moss, was almost as much a green wilderness as the old lawn at its side; but perhaps the most drear and downcast feature of all was the ivy creeper from the side wall which had invaded the pillared portico and formed a dense and drooping canopy over it; almost a weeping canopy.

No doubt it was only to me that the house looked haunted. To others it looked disowned and abandoned; but I—I had lived there for ten crucial years more than fifty years ago when it was Miryam Davids' guest house (her euphemism for a boarding house) and I had shared in a tragedy there.

The street in which it still stands has the pleasant name of Christian Street, an apt name too when I was housed there, for I was then a young clergyman in the Archdeaconry of Middlesex which in those days embraced the whole of London north of the river and included in its embrace no less than ninety-one rural deaneries and two-hundred-and-one parishes. And that's the only hint I shall give you as to the whereabouts of our Christian Street, so that you may have all the difficulties in the world if you seek to find this house. Our Christian Street, so far as I can see, is too small to be gazetted in any atlas of London. There is a Christian Street gazetted in Stepney, but thank God ours was not there.

I walked up that weedy drive and climbing on to a paling before the semi-basement, looked through the bay window on the entrance floor, comforted to think that the high wall of overgrown privets was concealing from anyone walking up Christian Street this unseemly behaviour in a tall ecclesiastic of venerable years, in his clerical black and with a clerical dog-collar. I am taller than most and could reach with one hand the brickwork above the bay window. The window revealed a large room behind it, empty, dust-blown and dishevelled, with its wall-paper hanging in dog-ears; but for a moment I recalled its past. I saw again the heavy mahogany furniture, the large side-board with its high over-mantel, the long dining-table with all its leaves in place, so that all Miryam's guests could be seated around it. This re-created day must have been in the early twenties, just after the First War when such furnishings were already becoming outmoded, but they suited Miryam well because at sixty years of age she was still living comfortably housed in the past, unaware that the last few terrible years had decimated her world. Apart from Miryam's large figure at the head of her table, I saw three women and three men (one of whom was myself) sitting at meat along with 'The Two Young Things', newly wed and newly arrived : Siward Bartleby and Theresa O'Neale; Siward and Terry in all the gaiety of their youth and in all the first glory of their married state; two of 'The Bright Young Things', as the lively youngsters of these post-war years, hungry for everything life could offer, were calling themselves. Siward and Terry; I really don't know whether the story I have to tell is their story or mine.

The Prophet's Chamber
on the Wall

When I had finished gazing through the window for a picture of
the past like a magic-lantern's slide, I left the garden and walked
down Christian Street again to its junction with a broad road.
This was no main street but wide and busy enough to be called
a lateral highway, so (to cover my traces) I will call it only
'Linden Highway' because of some tall and towering lime-trees
that graced its side-walks here and there. Now, because Christian
Street was such a small side-street, and a cul-de-sac at that (I
perceive I must take care or I shall be revealing too much), I was
able to walk a few yards along this highway to look across the
back-gardens of Christian Street and see the high back-wall of
Miryam's house. My eyes sought and rested on the two windows
of her top back-room. Behind those twin windows was the ample
chamber which had been mine, and in which the memorable
things had happened. No possibility today of climbing to look
through *those* windows and fill the empty room behind them with
scenes of the past; I could only stand on the pavement and stare
up at the two windows visible above a garden that was now but a
wasteland of overgrown shrubs and tall draggle-tail trees.

Miryam Davids had been a regular, devoted, and (in my view)
rather foolish member of our congregation, her 'faith' being no
more than a credulity incapable of questioning the dogmas learnt
in childhood and warmly intolerant about them: but she was
good-hearted, extremely sentimental, and well able to idolise a
fresh young deacon twenty-three years old and looking, I daresay,
about nineteen. When I first came to the parish as a deacon, my
first lodging had been unsatisfactory, and Miryam, in an expan-
sive and sentimental hour, said, 'You shall come to me. You shall
have the splendid room at the top of my house. It's a large room
designed no doubt for a staff of servants, two at least and a
tweenie, so there's plenty of space for your books and your desk

and chairs for your visitors; and Willy and I'll put a curtain round the bed. It shall be your room always. Come and go as you like. It'll be there waiting for you. And you can have all your meals with us, so what could be better?'

At this point, abounding with gratitude, I took to calling her *sub rosa* 'The Shunamite Woman', a title easily understood by my vicar and fellow curate, and by the many people who, fifty years ago, read their Bibles regularly. It is possible, however, that a reader of today will have little or no acquaintance with the Bible and will need an elucidation. So let me deliver to him a few verses from the fourth chapter of the Second Book of Kings; perhaps amending the translation here and there in the modern fashion : 'And it fell on a day that Elisha passed to Shunem where was a great woman; and she constrained him to eat bread. And she said unto her husband, "Willy, Behold now, I perceive that this is a holy man of God which passeth by us continually, so let us make him a chamber, I pray thee, on the wall; let us set for him there a bed, and a table, and a stool, and a candlestick; and it shall be, when he cometh to us, that he shall turn in thither." And it fell on a day that he came thither, and he turned into the chamber and lay there. And he said to Gehazi his servant, "Call this Shunamite". And when he had called her, she stood before him. And he said unto him, "Say now unto her, 'Behold now thou hast been careful for us with all this care; what is to be done for thee?' " And Gehazi answered, "Verily she hath no child and her husband is old. . . ." '

Now quite a little of this was appropriate to Miryam, for it came to pass that two years later, after I had been priested for a year, behold, I was sent off to the war as a chaplain on Gallipoli, and before I departed she said, 'I shall keep your room for you, so that whenever you come on leave, or when you come back to us for good, it'll be there for you, and if I allow any stranger to occupy it in your absence, he will have to understand that he must treat your books which are now innumerable—how any-body can need and read so many books I can't imagine—and your cupboards and your desk drawers with the utmost respect, and be ready to move into some other room if you want to come home for a while. Because this is your home.'

Then again she was certainly a 'great woman' in one sense; not in the Bible sense, not in sheep and goats and she-asses, but in bosom and hips and thighs; her husband was now an old man, twenty years older than she, and withal a rather wicked old man, I thought, with a wealth of knowledge and mischief in naughty old eyes, 'Uncle Willy' as we called him; she had no apparent children, but into this matter we shall probe later; and, lastly, that top upper-room which she had provided and kept for a holy man of God (myself, no other) could well be styled a chamber on the wall.

My vicar preferred to call it 'My Prophet's Chamber'.

But what sort of prophet came back to it from the War?

3

What Sort of Prophet?

Well, his name was the Reverend Hugh Macnaughtan Fields, but since the vulgar invariably omitted any Christian names or initials between the holy title and the surname, I was known to most as 'The Reverend Fields'; though why the vulgar or illiterate persisted in saying 'Rev Fields' but never dropped into saying 'Sir French' or 'Sir Haig' or 'Sir Jones' or 'Sir Robinson' I have never understood. One struggling humorist began calling me 'Mr Glebe' since a glebe was the land attached to a church and could be referred to felicitously as 'reverend fields'; but this jest, being hardly an uproarious one at the best of times, did not survive, and 'The Rev Fields' I remained.

And in the first days of 1917 this Rev Fields was on a little troopship bucketing through the Mediterranean from Alexandria to Marseilles. Chaplains in the First World War were allowed to volunteer for one year of service with the forces and then, unless they decided to prolong their service, to return to their parishes. I after some months on Gallipoli and a year in the desert of Sinai had decided to abandon my commission and come home, but I was not returning to my parish. A year amid the horrors of war had brought wide awake the too simple mind of a fervent young Anglo-Catholic and set him thinking as never before. In this 1917 I must have been twenty-seven and it amazes me now to recall how it was not till this my twenty-eighth year that I began profoundly to think. Amazing because, on the face of it, my academic career had been distinguished. When, long years afterwards it was recorded in *Who's Who,* it read very pleasantly—at least to myself studying it: a scholarship from Winchester to New College, a First Class in Mods, Greats, and Theology, with a fellowship to complete the flattering picture. But love can batten down thought, and my love for the Oxford Movement and for its bright issue, our old *Ecclesia Anglicana* in resplendent Anglo-Catholic robes, had flourished unabated from my days in Oxford to my days in Gallipoli and the first of my days in Sinai.

But one day, deep in my thoughts among the rolling sand-dunes of Sinai, I knew that my priesthood would have to halt. Not to cease, but, as it were, to halt and stand marking time. Or, in a better figure, to retreat. To negotiate a strategic retreat to a position where the enemy could be better contained and better attacked. Deciding on this, I suddenly thought, with some satisfaction, that the British possess a remarkable—even a glorious—talent for retreating. Consider how many of our most belauded operations have been retreats. At this hour of my life our famous retreat from Mons was still fresh in my mind; I had myself been on Gallipoli when the retreat from Suvla Bay and Anzac into the Aegean Sea was achieved without the loss of a single man (or so they put it); a few weeks later I had played my part in the no less brilliantly successful retreat from Cape Helles into the same Aegean; three years later in the war I played precisely the same part in a splendidly organised retreat from the Baku peninsula into the safety of the Caspian; and if I wanted further support for my notion that not once or twice in our rough island-story some fine retreating was the way to glory, I had only to remember Sir John Moore's retreat to Corunna where he was buried and 'left alone in his glory', or Wellington's retreats from Torres Vedras in the Peninsular War, and from Quatre Bras to the admirable hills and hollows of Waterloo.

And now, fifty years afterwards I can add to my list of such glorious memories the most celebrated of all : Dunkirk.

So my return in that little bucketing trooper was not without its recollections of Sir John Moore and the Iron Duke. My faith in God had not trembled at all; it has always been for me less an emotional than an intellectual base for any conceivable interpretation of the universe—however veiled in a mystery far beyond human understanding. But I could no longer preach from the pulpit, or teach confirmation children, with the old certainty such dogmas as the Virgin Birth, or the physical Resurrection or, most fundamental of all, the Divine Sonship of Jesus, the young man from Nazareth. Nor could I any longer believe happily in the 'creative' miracles such as the feeding of the five thousand. All these matters I must take into a private wilderness and there struggle to see if I could recover, as I longed to do, a sufficient faith in them all—or ar least in the Divine Sonship.

But this was not the only decision that I was carrying home

with me in the troopship. In March of the previous year, when the war was going badly enough, Parliament had introduced conscription for single men between the ages of eighteen and forty-one, and I had now decided that successful work by a chaplain among fighting men was all too difficult and I could do quite as effective a job, and possibly a better one, by serving side by side with lads who had been forced by law to cohabit with death in the trenches. I was coming home to ask my Bishop's consent to my volunteering at once as a combatant soldier, uncommissioned. I would tell him that, though I could not for the present teach or preach any more, I would maintain my priesthood so far as to help our brigade chaplain whenever he set up his communion table in some green field or ruined hut.

§

Let me tell you one story to expound the difficulty which I, for my part, had found in attempting a ministry at the front—other padres may have been more successful. When we had got ourselves off Gallipoli and were encamped in Sinai I suggested to my Brigadier that I should try the experiment of having a voluntary instead of a compulsory church parade. I told him that I thought an enforced religious devotion—if such words could be applied to thousands of tough men marched, paraded and ordered to pray—was self-defeating. The Brigadier was obviously shaken by this novel and most irregular suggestion, but, a kindly man, said, 'Well . . . well . . . I don't know . . . still . . . try it for once, padre. . . . But just supposing you don't get anybody there. I promise you *I'll* turn up, but you won't like having to pray and preach and sing hymns alone with me.'

'No, a few will certainly come, sir,' I assured him for his comfort. 'I know one or two quite devout lads'; and gratefully I went to the regimental sergeant-majors in their tents and told them that only volunteers were to come to my church parade next Sunday. There were only three R.S.M.s, as we had been stripped of one of our battalions. Well, two of them looked, if somewhat shocked, relieved, but the third R.S.M. was an Irishman and a Catholic, and as Irish and Catholic as a Catholic Irishman could be. Moreover he was a sergeant-major of the old terrifying pattern, as loud in voice as he was rich in invective. He was manifestly disturbed by this hitherto unheard-of suggestion, but what could he do but utter as if they were the last words of resignation, 'Well, if that's what you're afther sayin', sor . . .' though the real words in his mind were, I am sure, something more like, 'Holy Mary, Mother o' God, the holy Apostles Peter and Paul, and all the Saints, pray for us. . . .'

And on the Sunday morning he 'fell in' the whole of his battalion, company by company; and when he could bring himself to speak—instead of doing as the other R.S.M.s had done and calling for those who would wish to go and pray—he, a man of warm religion, willingly accepting the disciplines of an authoritarian Church, 'fell out' not those men who wanted to go to church but those unholy and despicable ones who didn't. He bellowed out, with a strong distaste, 'The Holy Man says that only those who want to are to go to church parade. So fall out, those who *don't* want to. Come on! Jump to it. You hear what I say. Fall out, those who don't want to and stand here in front of me.'

Perhaps ten or a dozen heroes, out of some four hundred men, fell out of the ranks and stood—anxiously, I do not doubt—in front of their R.S.M. with the whole of their battalion in formal array behind them.

The R.S.M. looked at them, hostility aglow in his eyes; then, deciding that so small a number was not worth consideration, roared at them, 'Ey! *Here!* Fall in agen, you bloody heathens! And go to church as good bloody Chris-chens shud.'

Without hesitation, and very smartly, they fell in again, each to his own company.

Thus it came about that this church parade of mine was in its appearance something that was a joke against me throughout my chaplaincy, and something that has never been seen in the British Army before or since : a three-sided square with two sides composed of a few volunteers from two battalions, and the third a magnificent assembly, rank behind rank, company behind company, of a whole battalion marched to its Anglican worship by its R.S.M., a good Catholic.

§

Ours was a merry and ebullient fellowship on that tossing troopship, but since she was only a small white liner, built by Greeks, I think, and made sufficiently narrow in the beam to negotiate that high-walled drain, the Corinth Canal, it held but one battalion of our brigade and the officers and men of the First Field Ambulance, with sundry oddments from other brigades or divisions. There was one shy and lonely figure among us, a middle-aged chaplain, with hair thin and grey, eyes older than his years, and a figure not fat but fleshy enough to have a double chin—in brief, an unsoldierly figure in a khaki uniform. He was the Rev Stephen Burrell from a General Hospital in Alexandria, who, unlike me, was really returning after a year's service to his parish in Kent. A shy scholar and Fellow from Oriel, whose Common Room was still haunted by the shades of Keble and Pusey, and the sad shade of Newman—Oriel, the very source and wine-press of Anglo-Catholicity—he was almost inevitably a follower of them, and he suggested to me that we should say our divine offices, Matins and Evensong, daily together in his cabin or mine. This would be possible, because as captains both, we had single cabins in this small ship. I did not like to tell him that I had long forgone this daily devotion prescribed for Anglican clergy, so we fell into the pious habit of saying the offices in one cabin or the other, while the ship in a turbulent winter sea rolled and pitched, so that, swaying beside each other, we read versicles, responses, psalms, lessons and prayers for the King's Majesty, the Royal Family, the Clergy and People.

One day, after such an uneasy and swaying Matins in my cabin he asked shyly, 'Would you do me a great kindness, Fields?' He had not yet overcome his shyness to the extent of calling me Hugh.

'Why, of course, Steve.'

'I'm afraid it's rather a delicate subject——'

'Never mind. Fire away.'

'It's—it's just that I've been terribly bound up since before leaving Alexandria. It's nine days—if you'll forgive my mentioning it—since. . .'

'Since what?'

'Since I had a motion.'

'Nine days! Good lord!'

'Yes, and I'm wondering if you'd ask one of these M.O.s of the First Field Ambulance—I don't know any of them, and I shouldn't care to ask them myself—if he'd mix me some sort of—' he halted before the impolite word—'aperient.'

'Oh, that's easy enough. He'll give you a Number Nine.' The Number Nine pill was, naturally, the Army's panacea for most ailments.

'Oh, but that'd be no good. I've had heaps of them, without any effect. I shall need something stronger.'

'Nine days. That must be a record. I'll certainly ask Snooty Collins to mix you something. You know Snooty, don't you, Lieut Collins, R.A.M.C.?'

'No, I don't know any of them. But he wouldn't mind, would he?'

'Of course not. He'll look after you like a mother.'

So I went to Snooty, a pleasant young doctor, qualified for only a year or two and then sent straight to us on Gallipoli. I said, 'Snooty, Padre Burrell, C.F., is in a parlous state and in need of urgent help.' And I outlined the deplorable symptom. Nine days. 'Surely that's a record?'

'Lord, no. He'll survive. Tell him that in a year or two he'll be as good a man as ever he was. Meantime, a Number Nine or two——'

'Oh, no, it's something far beyond the reach of a Number Nine, so for heaven's sake mix him a real juicy purgative.'

'You bet I will. Where shall I give it to him? Or perhaps I'd better hand it to you to give to him, if he's all that embarrassed.'

'Yes, yes,' I agreed. 'Give it to me and I'll put it into his cabin.'

Needless to say, Snooty, romping about the ship, forgot all about this promise and later that day Padre Burrell sought me out to learn if any rescue was in sight.

I hurried to Snooty's cabin, found him there and reproached him for neglect of duty and 'infamous conduct in a professional sense'. 'A little longer and your patient'll be dead.'

He apologised humbly and in less than ten minutes came to my cabin bringing a medicine bottle filled with a villainous-looking concoction, white and thick and apparently clouding the bottle to its neck.

'That looks as though it ought to do the trick,' I said.

'That'll do it,' he assured me, and went off to play quoits.

I took it to the padre's cabin but he was not there. Probably, a conscientious man, he was doing his usual lonely circumambulation of the deck, so I placed the bottle in one of the two receptacles for tooth glasses above his wash-basin.

His walk round the deck took a long time for the little ship was pitching and rolling and he was probably as determined to do his daily thirty rounds as to say his daily offices. When he returned to his cabin, it was to see that the bottle had somehow leapt from its enclosure and burst in a horrid messy whiteness on the floor.

He came to me in distress, saying he didn't like to give trouble or be a nuisance to anyone; but I went straight to Snooty who was still trying to play quoits on a rocking deck and said, 'Snooty, look here : you got your time-fuse wrong in that ghastly concoction. It detonated in the cabin instead of in the padre.'

A mishap of so diverting a character reached the ears of every officer in the ship and, for all I know, most of the Other Ranks and the crew. It reached our second-in-command, Major Liveday, a short and plump little man well enough named because he had a lively humour and the reputation of being a 'live wire' on any day of the week, in trenches or out of them.

'What!' he exclaimed when he heard the story. 'This is monstrous. We can't have this sort of thing going on. Culpable carelessness. Nothing less. Endangering the ship. Padre Fields is quite right in his accusations against Snooty—I mean Lieut Collins, R.A.M.C. A severe reprimand is not enough. It's clearly a case for a court-martial. Yes, a Field General Court-Martial—though how it can be a Field General on board a ship in a damned awful sea I don't know. But let that pass. Tell Snooty—I mean the Accused—that I'm shocked beyond measure. And that he's under open arrest and will be court-martialled tomorrow. In the Dining Saloon. Yes, the Dining Saloon after lunch. Have him closely watched so that he doesn't go over the side. And obviously Padre Fields must be the Prosecutor.'

Whether Major Liveday, who was only second-in-command, would have had the authority, in other than farcical circumstances, to order a court-martial I don't know. Our C.O., Col Chatwind, was on board and enjoying the joke but probably thought it wiser for a commanding officer to take no part in such frivolous proceedings; and moreover that he had no such talent as his Major in conducting a mock court-martial, so he would be content to sit in the audience, grinning.

To me Major Liveday just said enthusiastically, 'Padre, we're court-martialling Snooty tomorrow and since it's on your evidence that he'll be found guilty—I mean, that the case to be heard against him will depend on your evidence—you must be the Prosecutor. You see that, don't you?'

I said 'Yes, sir,' and that nothing would give me greater pleasure than to prosecute Lieut Collins for— for—

'Yes, what for? We must be clear what the indictment is, if that's what it's called. Look, padre, Harry Howden is a barrister in his private life, so get him to frame a charge or charges properly. He must be well used to doing this sort of thing. Dig him out, and tell him he's under orders to phrase a charge in proper legal terms and to let me have it this evening. We must do everything in an orderly manner. Nothing slovenly or slap-dash.'

I found Lieut Harry Howden in the Card Room on the promenade deck, and when he was free to speak with me I gave him his orders. He showed himself as pleased with his assignment as I was with mine. His young round face suggested that he was but a newly-fledged barrister, apprenticed perhaps for a year to some active junior, studying under him and devilling for him. Probably he'd never had more than a dock brief or a brief marked at the lowest figure of one guinea. 'Oh yes,' he said, 'I'll do that. Tell me exactly what happened. We must do this by the book.'

I told him all and he said heartily, 'Okay. Leave it to me. I shall enjoy this. I think there'd better be more than one charge so that we can be sure of getting a guilty verdict. I suppose your old padre realises that he'll have to give the principal evidence.'

'I don't think he'll like doing that. He's a shy old thing and slightly afraid of you all. You're all too young for him.'

'Can't help that. Duty's duty. Can't have him dodging the column. Go and tell him to prepare his evidence. Perhaps he could pray for the necessary courage, or something. Now I'll get down to it. Leave it to me.'

And so pleased was he with his brief that he drew up an appalling array of charges. He read them out to me as a poet might read his favourite poems. 'Listen, padre, the charges against the Accused will be as follows : one, gross dereliction of duty; two, conspiring to create a public mischief; three, conduct to the prejudice of good order and discipline; four, dumb insolence before a superior officer—I'm not so confident about this one, but the old padre *is* a captain and Snooty only a two-loot and there was no word spoken between them; five, possessing an offensive weapon with a view to endangering life; six, possessing an instrument with intent to produce an explosion at sea; seven, but I'm not altogether happy about this one either, administering a destructive substance with intent to murder; and, finally, in case any of these fail to stick, conduct unbecoming to an officer and a gentleman. I think all those ought to please the Major, don't you? And we're bound to get a verdict on one of them.'

'On four or five of them,' I assured him. '*I* am the Prosecutor.'

He added proudly, consulting his sheet, 'I thought of including "conspiracy to debauch and corrupt the morals of a liege subject of Our Sovereign Lord the King", but I feared that this might be a non-starter; I couldn't quite see how the morals of the old padre came into the business; or who was a fellow-conspirator with him . . . unless it was you.'

'No, no; leave that one out,' I agreed. 'A Prosecutor can't be one of the Accused.' (I was to learn better than this, later on.)

By two o'clock in the afternoon the Dining Saloon was filled with nearly all the army officers aboard and with several of the ship's officers too. This being the Officers' Mess there were no Other Ranks present apart from the Mess servants who rejoiced in their privileged position, and most of the Saloon stewards to whom none of us could say nay. The room greatly crowded, Major Liveday made his entry in a remarkable fur-collared, fur-cuffed, fur-lined coat; whether he thought that this—in a heated room—made him look more like a High Court Judge or a Court-Martial President, none of us has ever known, but this formal, if grinning entry—or perhaps the fur coat—was greatly applauded by all. He sat himself at the Captain's seat at the Captain's table where four other officers of the Court were already awaiting him. In addition to them a young officer, fresh from school and probably nineteen, was nominally the Deputy Judge Advocate. No one ever looked less like one.

Now entered the Accused with his Escort. To the most boisterous cheers of the afternoon.

Major Liveday, a President gratified by this more-than-capacity audience, offered everyone a welcome. 'Gentlemen, I am glad to see so many of you here. You will have the opportunity of learning that Military Law, like British Law, is the fairest in the world, always open to the public unless the safety of the State is involved, when it would of necessity be conducted *in camera*. I have given great consideration to this case and decided that the State is not endangered by it, so you are all very welcome.' He turned to the Accused. 'Lieutenant Collins, do you object to any officers of this Court?'

'No, sir. Delighted to see them.'

'Good. You are charged with——' strictly, I imagine, the Deputy Judge Advocate should have read the charges, but the Major was not going to deny himself this office. He had rightly guessed that each of the charges, as announced, would be greeted with loud cheers from every part of the room, loud clapping, loud stamping, and other demonstrations ill-suited to a court-martial. The one that got the loudest ovation was the last and simplest : conduct unbecoming to an officer and gentleman.

The Accused, by the way, stood to the right of the Captain's table, and from here he applauded several of the charges as heartily as anybody else.

'It is possible,' continued the President, 'that the Accused will not be found guilty on all these charges but only on three or four of them. And there may of course be other aspects of his alleged criminality which we shall not be asked to assess because they have not been specified in these indictments—possibly to lessen the labours of the Court.' Here he dropped—or forgot—his legal jargon and called on me to prosecute. 'Now come on, Rev Fields. Do your stuff. Let him have it.'

'May it please the Court,' I began, having read plenty of trials; and the President said 'Golly !', surprised by this fine opening.

I told my story and concluded my speech with a prepared joke which got more laughter than it deserved, the audience being ready to laugh at anything. When the laughter had subsided, the Major said, 'Well, Rev Fields has done his stuff very efficiently, you'll agree. I might perhaps fault him in that, according to the book, he should "bring out everything possible in favour of the Accused"—if he can think of anything. This he has failed to do, and doubtless because he couldn't discover anything, so we shall have to wait to hear what the Prisoner's Friend has to say. But I pity him his task. Now the chief witness for the Prosecution is the Rev Burrell. Come on, Padre Burrell. We are all anxious to hear from you.'

Universal cheers for this all-important witness.

But a difficulty here. The witness must swear to give true evidence; and nobody in the whole room possessed a Bible. The witness offered to go and fetch his. The Major called the whole assembly a congregation of barbarians and allowed his Prisoner to swear by Almighty God, imagining he had a testament in his hand.

Padre Burrell was the surprise of this whole affair. Whether it was that, after being a stranger to all, he was happy to be welcomed in this fashion as one of them, or whether it was that behind his shyness and solitariness there lay a native wit and gaiety (had he not been long ago a scholar of Oriel?) my memory after all these years will not allow me to decide : all I know is that he was the success of the afternoon.

With a nervous grin he began by saying, 'I have heard all that my learned friend, counsel for the prosecution, has put before you, and my first observation must be that, instead of acting as Prosecutor, he should be standing alongside the Accused as an accessory before the fact—'

Uproar of applause.

'—since it was he who instigated the Accused to prefabricate this atrocious mixture; and to be an accessory before the fact, my lord—'

'There are no lords here,' interrupted the Major. 'Thank God.'

'I beg your pardon. To be an accessory before the fact, Mr President, is, as I understand the law, to be equally guilty with the principal of this particular felony.'

'Good heavens! Is that so?' asked the President.

But here I rose. 'Mr President; if what my learned friend—I mean, the present witness—has just said is correct, I submit, with great respect, that he also is an accessory before the fact since it was he who counselled and procured me to induce the Prisoner to commit this felony—or, rather, these many felonies with which he is charged. I know some law too.'

Further and mounting applause for me.

'Oh, come off it, padre!' protested the Major. 'For the Lord's sake, shut up. We can't have three Accused and two of them sky-pilots. You padres are a terrible lot. Oblige me by sitting down.'

I bowed. 'I sit down, Mr President. But under protest.'

'Damn "under protest". I'm not sure that it isn't contempt of court. Isn't that so, Mr Judge Advocate?'

The late schoolboy had no reply to this. 'I'm afraid I don't know, sir.'

'But, God help us, it's your business to guide us all. Well, I rule that the padre's protest is wholly inadmissible. Now, Rev Budley —Burrell, I mean—tell us exactly what Padre Fields asked the Accused to do.'

'I only know,' answered the witness, 'what he told me he had said. I can only give it to you, so to say, in *oratio obliqua*, not in *oratio recta.*'

The Major stared at him in bewildered ignorance, and looked all round the room as if for help from the audience, amid their delighted laughter. Whatever school had trained Major Liveday to be a live wire in the New Armies it was clearly not a classical school. He appealed for help. 'Is there any gentleman in the audience who is prepared to tell me what on earth the padre is talking about? In what language is this distinguished witness speaking. Italian, is it?'

'No, sir. Latin.' The distinguished witness himself was the first to offer aid. 'You are probably mixing up *oratio obliqua* and *oratio recta* with *oratorio.*'

'I'm doing nothing of the sort. I'm not mixing any damn thing with any other damn thing,' said the President.

'Then you differ from Mr Snooty, the Accused,' submitted the witness with a disarming smile. 'He was careful to distinguish between the two.'

This apt rejoinder got its meed of laughter and applause.

The Major, since he was coming off second-best in this encounter, immediately pronounced, 'I must remind you, reverend sir, that your sole business is to give evidence against the Accused and not to stand there criticising the Judge. Am I right, Mr Deputy Judge Advocate? Should he make comments like that?'

The schoolboy Advocate had learned his part by now. 'No, sir. The comment was wholly inadmissible.'

'There you are, Mr Burrell. Now behave yourself. Meanwhile will *someone* tell me what the padre has been trying to say with his *oratio this* and *oratio that*?'

A scholar among us rose and expounded. '*Oratio obliqua*, sir, is conversation recorded to the witness. *Oratio recta* would be the actual words spoken.'

'Go on!' exclaimed the Major, and 'Good Lord! Is that so? But, anyway, what the hell's the difference?'

'It's "hearsay evidence",' the irrepressible witness explained, 'and therefore, in the excellent words of the Deputy Judge Advocate, "wholly inadmissible".'

'Hear, hear,' came from several in the audience, probably anxious to show that they too knew something of the law.

'I'm not allowing any "hear, hears". This is not a session in Parliament or a political meeting. It's a solemn court of law.'

It was as he said this that the President observed for the first time that many in the room were smoking cigarettes, pipes or cigars, and decided this should surely have been disallowed in a solemn Court-Martial. So he thought for a while, and then said, 'Gentlemen, you may smoke'; taking out his own cigar case, putting one in his mouth, and offering one to the Prisoner at his side. Who accepted it gratefully, as well as a box of matches from the President.

Both cigars alight, the President resumed, 'Now, for pity's sake, Rev Burrell, proceed with your evidence against the Accused.'

'My evidence is simple enough, sir. It is that no blame whatever attaches to the Accused.'

'Then what the devil are you doing there as the prosecution's chief witness?'

'I am following your instructions, my lord, when you so rightly said that the prosecution must bring out anything in favour of the Accused. And I can't think of anything more in his favour than that he should be wholly innocent.'

I seized upon this reply to let loose on the court a pretty phrase which I had sometimes met in my reading of famous trials. 'Clearly I must ask your leave, sir, to treat this witness as a hostile witness.'

The Major dropped both hands to his sides in a gesture of despair. 'What is *he* talking about now? Is he talking any sense, Judge Advocate?'

'Excellent sense . . . I think,' said the Judge Advocate, after thought.

'I don't understand how we can have hostile people in a court of law, but if you say so—deal with him as you like, Mr Prosecutor.'

I thereupon asked this troublesome witness, 'If you say that no blame attaches to the Prisoner, whom, may I ask, would you accuse?'

'No one, sir. Neither the prisoner, nor you as an accessory

—though if he's in the dock you ought to be there too—nor indeed the ship itself, but the sea.'

'The *what?*' An appeal from the President.

'The sea, sir. The *mare infidum*.' Obviously pleased with the success of his *oratios* he was in the mood to produce articles of the same kind from his classical storeroom. *'Et ventosum'*.

'In the name of God . . . ? What language is the padre using now? Is it bad language? If so, I won't have bad language in my court.'

'The treacherous sea,' explained the witness. 'Plato. The windy sea. Horace.'

'Horace who?'

'Quintus Horatius Flaccus.'

'Oh, my God . . . oh lord . . . would it be possible for this witness to stand down in favour of someone who talks English?'

I could not immediately, for laughter, tell my fellow padre to stand down, so he proceeded to address the court.

'The gravamen of the offence is——'

'The *what* of the offence?' demanded the President.

'The gravamen, the substance of the accusation, is surely no more than this : who flung this noisome bottle—or this hand-grenade or whatever you like to call it—from my tooth-glass receptacle on to the floor of my cabin; and my submission, with great respect, is that no living person did so, but that the sea, which was pitching and plunging abominably, most certainly did. I accuse the Mediterranean Sea.' And he added another item from his classical store. *'Mare Nostrum.'*

The President shrugged, spread two hopeless hands and said to me, 'Put him down. We can't have a court-martial with only the sea as the Accused. And in Latin.'

'But Bill Hudson, sir, the Prisoner's Friend,' I pointed out, 'is entitled to speak now.'

'Christ, is he? Oh yes, of course he is. Well, Bill, come along. Fall to. You're entitled to cross-examine this extraordinary witness as much as you like.'

But Bill Hudson of 'A' Company, hardly rising from his chair at a table, said, 'I have no desire to do so, sir. He has said everything that I could have extracted in favour of my client, and indeed quite a lot that I shouldn't have thought of. I will content myself with thanking him.'

'Well, well, I suppose that's in order. But this is certainly the most extraordinary court-martial I've ever heard of—the Prisoner's Friend congratulating the Prosecutor on his principal witness. Put your witness down, Padre Fields; we've had quite enough from you padres.'

I waved my disastrous witness away, and he withdrew with a formal bow to the Court, as it might be to the Holy Table, which no one else had thought of doing so far. Generous applause accompanied him all the way to his chair.

As I had no other witness I could call, I said, 'The People rest' —not that this was a proper remark in a British court but that it was a phrase which always delighted me in American trials.

The President gaped at me in astonishment. 'The People do what?'

'Rest, sir. The Prosecution kind of represents the People.'

'In Christian English you mean that the Prosecution has said all it wants to say?'

'Yes, sir; and leaves it to the other guys to get on with it.'

The Major, after his discomfiture by the retiring witness, was palpably resolved to display some knowledge (probably acquired last night) and rebuild his reputation as an able judge. He addressed the Accused, 'Now look here, Snooty : you can either give evidence on oath in which case you can be cross-examined, or you can make a statement not on oath. Which would you prefer to do, Mr Prisoner?'

'I would wish to make a statement on the bloodiest oath imaginable that I agree with everything the prosecution witness has said. In other words, that there's no case against me on any of these idiotic charges, and that the whole court-martial has been a lot of footling nonsense—with great respect to you, sir. I now suggest that it is your business to pronounce this as your decision.'

'Don't you start teaching me my business. The Court is now closed that it may consider its verdict. This may be difficult so I think it would be apposite for those stewards there—who have profited, I hope, by this demonstration that British Military Law is the fairest in the world—if they would bring to each member of the Court a whisky, the cost to be debited to the President. Oh, yes, and one to the Prisoner, with the compliments and good wishes of the President.'

Then the five members of the Court got into a huddle, mimed

a chattering and a chaffering together over their whiskies, after which the Major hammered on the table for silence and announced, 'After the most careful and protracted deliberation we have found the prisoner guilty on all counts, but I am advised that there could be a plea in mitigation, which could be followed by a recommendation to mercy.' (Cries of 'Oh, no.') 'So some evidence of the Prisoner's character, please, Mr Adjutant.'

The Adjutant's evidence was terse. 'Pretty abominable, I should say. On the whole. Yes.' Cheers of approval.

'Yes, I thought as much.' And the court began whispering again; but the President in due course pronounced, 'The penalty for all these grave offences being serious, and we being men of notable magnanimity, and the Accused being young and foolish, we have decided to take the plea in mitigation as read and to allow the recommendation to mercy to go through.'

Universal protests, several boos, and a voice, 'He should have been sentenced to drinks all round, at the least.'

And thus in some such general din, and general movement, this court-martial came to an untimely and untidy close.

§

Next morning, soon after the winter dawn, when the sun was just above the easterly hills of Provence, our little white ship sailed into the port of Marseilles. It went weaving past the rock-based Château d'If and the Comte de Monte-Cristo's little islands, Ratonneau and Pomègues, towards the harbour. On a western hill, and on the apex of her great church, the statue of Notre Dame de la Garde, with arms outspread, looked down upon our entry to bless it. The ship tied up at the Quai de l'Europe in the new harbour.

Our Army in the First War could easily occupy a whole day in getting one battalion off a ship and on to a quay; and it was in the late winter afternoon, when the lights on the opposite Quai St Etienne were already shivering deep in the sheltered water, that all our lively throng which had rejoiced in their mock court-martial stepped ashore, most of them, including the merry Major, to die.

The Ypres Salient, the Third Battle of Ypres, and Passchendaele awaited them.

4

'17 to '20

Before the Great Men in the War Office had fully absorbed a situation so unusual as that of a chaplain wishing to resign his commission and to enlist in the ranks; before they had resolved, among their other military preoccupations, how to deal with so abnormal a phenomenon, three months of another year passed and I was still with my brigade on the Somme, being moved from Beaumont Hamel to Beaucourt-sur-Ancre, and then forward from Miraumont to Le Sars, because in February the whole German line retreated to a new and easier position in front of Bapaume.

Thus I was able at times to wander over that dreadful battle-field which was now no more than a vast green plain over-arched by the sky's whole dome; empty, quiet and serene. It was bisected by the Bapaume Road straight as a tautened rope and I could not hold myself from walking up and down that silent road, with the world's first tanks lying beside it disabled and derelict, while on its either flank among the grass and weeds whole villages such as Martinpuich or Courcelette were no more than piles of rubble and dust. Out of these waste-heaps rose little graveyard crosses of wood saying Martinpuich, Courcelette, Pozières.

It was while I was at Le Sars that I received my orders to return home, and it was in my dug-out there one day that I lay on my chicken-wire bunk—the dug-out was no more than a little room hewn out of the high north bank of the Eaucourt l'Abbay road. Along its roof, six feet below the earth floor, you could see the snapped roots of the shrubs and young trees that topped the bank. In this capacious dug-out, which I called The Presbytery, I lay like a fox in its earth—except that I lolled on the sagging bunk reading a letter from Miryam whom I'd apprised of my early return.

As I have told you, Miryam, that devoted churchgoer (which is not quite the same as 'devout'), was capable of extreme senti-

mentalities and perhaps the most extreme was her adoration of
her late young curate, the Rev Fields. Her letter was as full of
goodwill as it was empty of commas and other elucidatory stops,
though here and there a dash like a crack in a roof let in a
gentle light. I read :

'Dear Mr Fields It's wonderful to think you will be coming back to
your room sacred to you after nearly two years it's been occupied often
in your absence how could I afford in these days to keep it empty but
everyone has been ordered to be very careful about your books and
everything so it will be just as you left it I am so glad you think of it
as your home so is Willy—'

This I doubted. I couldn't imagine Willy caring a damn one
way or the other whether I came or went—

'—I told the Vicar on Sunday after church and he said I must kill
the fatted calf which doesn't seem very sensible because I said I was
sure you haven't been wasting your substance in riotous living or feeding swine with husks whatever they are the Vicar laughed but would
you believe it when I told Willy what I had said he couldn't remember
where it all came from he's a naughty old man never reading the Bible
at all or coming with me to church Hyacinth of course is still with us
I don't know what I should do without her you can't imagine how
awful things have been here. We've had air-raids not with Zeppelins
but with air-machines quite a few people have been killed Once last
year we watched a fight between one of our splendid boys and the
wicked German I don't know which won but I agree with Willy that
its time we took some reprisals against German submarine prisoners we
have got it'd teach them a lesson not to sink our merchant ships—'

Yes, dear Auntie Miryam (so I now called her, and Willy,
Uncle Willy) but what's to stop the Germans instantly taking
reprisals against *our* prisoners off the ships that are blockading
them and trying to starve them. Use your loaf, dear Auntie
Miryam. And persuade Uncle Willy to use his, a good loaf once
upon a time.

'—Food is getting more and more difficult to get and they say we
are soon to be rationed with ration books so I don't know where the
fatted calf will come from as I said to Willy but I'll try to make a special feast for you its almost impossible to get servants they are all

23

making munitions at absurd prices what I should do without Hyacinth as my right hand I don't know—its wonderful your having some leave at last I do hope you will spend most of it with us Yours v. sincerely Auntie Miryam.'

As to this name 'Miryam' : Auntie Miryam's father had been a poor parson but a rich Hebrew scholar and, knowing that the unvowelled Hebrew letters of the famous name were M-R-Y-M (as witness the lovely 'Mary', historically the same name) insisted that his daughter's name should be spelt with a 'y'—to the great discomfort and confusion of most people for ever after. And Auntie Miryam, who loved her 'y', would be impatient and grumpy—'Why can't people ever get a name right?'—if anyone —friend, baker, banker or grocer—addressed a letter to her with an 'i' instead of the 'y'.

'There was nothing my father didn't know about Hebrew,' she would brag. 'He was one of the great scholars of his day'—all of which was quite a little in the mist on the far side of truth. There were times when I've wondered how so fine a scholar could have sired a woman, friendly and loyal, no doubt, and abundantly churchy, but naturally rather stupid.

I was reading her letter a second time when Sam Chambers, the Adjutant of the battalion with whom I messed, burst into my dug-out holding a sheaf of papers in his hand.

'Dammit, padre,' he said, 'when the hell do you leave us? For heaven's sake don't go at once. Here's a whole dossier of papers that have been travelling from Brigade to Division, to Corps and to the War House wanting to know why, in Alexandria before you got on to Gallipoli nearly two years ago, you buried a Private Andrew McKinley in an area reserved for commissioned officers. You seem to have buried him on the wrong side of the pathway in the cemetery. It was very wrong of you. Surely you know that in the British Army there's a hell of a gulf fixed between Officers and Other Ranks—in this case, a wide pathway. Your comment, please. Quickly, instead of loafing on that bed at this time of the day. What did you go and do that there for?'

'I've no memory of the burial at all. I was new to the business then, and probably just did what the corporal in charge of the burial party told me.'

'Well, who the hell was he?'

'Haven't the faintest idea. He's probably dead by now or a lieutenant colonel.'

'No, for God's sake come up with something better than that, or this bundle of bumph will go on its travels again and be back with us some time next year. Or the year after. And in the meantime there's a war going on.'

'But surely there's a perfectly simple solution,' I said.

'Not in the Army, lad. Nothing's simple in the Army.'

'My idea solves the whole damn thing in a minute.'

'Nothing in the Army's solved in a minute. And if it's something quite small like this it takes years and years. But what's your idea, any old how?'

'Simple enough. Give the good private a posthumous commission and have it gazetted a week before his burial.'

The Adjutant's eyes gleamed with pleasure. 'Splendid, padre! Splendid idea. Solves everything, as you say. I'll submit it as your suggestion and send it on its way home to the War House.'

That was my last act as a chaplain and I always tell it with pride because I think of it as one of my few successes. Sam, months afterwards, wrote and told me that the High-ups had allowed themselves a smile at my suggestion, and had resolved to leave the private in peace where he lay, without even removing his offending rank from his headstone; but they had instructed Brigade to warn the chaplain in question that he was not to do this sort of thing again.

Which, of course, I was no longer in a position to do.

And the war went on.

I was given three weeks' extended leave—'to put my affairs in order'—before I reported to a Recruiting Depôt for enlistment in Andrew McKinley's rank of full private.

I had not been on leave since 1915, and I have to confess that in the train from Folkestone to Victoria I was thinking that with all my equipment hanging over my uniform—water-bottle, mess tin, gas mask, haversack—and with the historic mud of the Somme still on my puttees and boots, I should be regarded as one of our heroes from the war. But it fell out differently. On the top of the stairway at Victoria Underground Station I was stopped in my tracks by something I'd never seen before nor expected to see now : at the bottom of the stairway by the barrier stood a woman ticket-collector. In a ticket-collector's uniform with a peaked cap, metal buttons, and a long skirt. I stood gaping. It was I who admired her with her uniform and clippers, not she who admired me with my battle equipment and my mud. All she said, as she saw me standing up there, motionless and stupefied, was 'Well, are yer comin' dahn or aren't yer? What I meanter say is, make up yer mind, for Cry-sake.'

I descended humbly, though hurt as well as surprised by this welcome so short in feminine charm.

But of course Victoria Station had now endured three years of muddied khaki coming down its stairs.

To a certain extent the lady's curt and unfriendly question has always symbolised for me the State's hesitations about my desire to come down the steep stairway from a captain's rank to that of the humblest combatant rank in the Army.

Later from—well, never mind where—I took a taxi to Christian Street and found my large upper room—the Prophet's Chamber on the wall—swept, cleaned, and garnished for me, with a vase of daffodils and narcissi on my desk to assure me of Miryam's—and perhaps Willy's—affectionate welcome.

My interview with my Bishop in his palace at Fulham was neither brief nor easy. It was early evening, and he was splendid in full purple uniform with medals and orders on his breast, because he had to attend, a little later, some tremendous State occasion. But, as ever, his face above all this grandeur was benign and welcoming. (There were those who called it saintly. Any saintliness in the face was the more remarkable for the worldly episcopal purple with its many stars and state decorations.) Shaking his head, he resisted my request with the familiar words, 'The hand that holds the chalice mustn't hold the gun.' To this I responded, 'I know, my lord, that that's what is usually said but I can't escape from my conviction—or what seems like a conviction—that my task is to do what all the other fellows, old and young, are being ordered to do. I hope I may never have to kill, but honestly, my lord, it seems to me far more a matter of suffering *with* them in the trenches and of taking my chance of death with them than of killing with them.'

'A chaplain risks death too.'

'Not in the same way, my lord. I've been a chaplain with a front-line unit now for two years. I've always tried to get round among the boys in their trench bays, but this is seldom more than

a parochial visit. One is too often far behind them in the compara-
tive safety of Battalion Headquarters or on the Quarter-master's
Dump.'

The Bishop thought long, and we argued further. I told him
that I would not conceal from my brothers-in-arms that I was a
priest in Orders; I would do all I could to help our chaplain,
even, if it were possible, preaching to little gatherings about my
unshakeable belief in God, and certainly helping him sometimes
when he was celebrating Holy Communion. At this stage I said
nothing to the Bishop about the trembling of my faith in the
Christological dogmas and my desire after the war to retreat into
a private wilderness and there worry out these doubts alone,
longing, longing, to find and possess the old faith again. All this
was for the future. I did dare to say to him that my urge to be
with the boys in their humble ranks was seeming to me almost as
clearly a Call, as my original Call to offer myself as a candidate
for Holy Orders.

There was a very long silence after this and then I saw the
Bishop, after fingering the pectoral cross on his breast, make a
tiny sign of the Cross above it, which told me that he had been
praying in the silence and that his secret prayer was at an end. He
said, 'I have found it very difficult to know what I ought to say
to you and I pray God that my counsel now will be in accordance
with his will. I have decided that all I can say is "Go the way your
conscience seems to be directing you, dear boy, and my son in
Christ. You have my consent and my blessing".' He blessed me,
making the sign of the Cross towards me. 'And my prayers. May
God go with you all the way.'

§

In fact my three weeks' extended leave was eroded by a sudden
order to report to a regimental barracks for training on the
generous expanses of Woodenham Plain. Here I learned for the
first time, though I had been in the Army two years, how to form
fours, how to handle a rifle, how to slope, order, trail and present arms; how to crawl on the grass like a death-adder with a
Lewis gun for my fang; how to dismantle a Lewis gun into all
its many parts and then to reassemble them into a perfect weapon. I may say that no one in the Army was ever more surprised

than I was, when I had reassembled the weapon and the damned thing *worked*.

Six months of training and I was sent, not to France as I had supposed but to India and thence to the 39th Brigade in Mesopotamia, so that I saw but little fighting : one battle at Kirkuk in 'Messpot' and then, after crossing the Persian uplands a battle on the Baku peninsula where I got slightly wounded in face and shoulder. I don't know that in all the war I killed anyone; possibly not, because I was just about the worst shot in my battalion; but I do know that, as I have told you, I spent the last days of the war—when all the Allied armies were advancing to victory everywhere—retreating with my brigade in excellent order from the Turks outside Baku, and seeking safety in ships on the Caspian Sea.

Two months in North Persia as an occupying army known as Norperforce, and then it was Eleven Hours on the Eleventh Day of the Eleventh Month. All hostilities ceased everywhere, and I was both delighted and surprised to find myself alive as a competent corporal on full pay.

5

Round Miryam's Table

In the first months of peace the War Office or the Ministry of
Labour or the Home Office or the Lord-Knows-Who had formed
'Demobilisation Lists', stating the order in which professional
men, artisans and others could be got out of the Army and into
civilian life for the health of the country's economy. I seem to
remember that miners and teachers came first and poets last—a
natural arrangement for a country that treats none of its literary
practitioners as important until they are safely dead. Where anyone so incomprehensible as a curate turned corporal should figure
in these lists I have never known. Fairly low, I imagine, because
I was not demobilised till the first months of 1920.

But it doesn't matter because it is with a date in 1923—or was
it 1924—that I have now to deal : a day when all Miryam's guests
were seated round her long mahogany table. Three years or more
had I lived in my Prophet's Chamber, serving no church as a
curate and doing no more priestly work than to help my late
Vicar in administering the chalice on the great feasts. My heart,
however bewildered my head, was still in love with the idea of
Anglo-Catholicity, and since I now had a small income be-
queathed to me by the best of godfathers, I was giving all my time,
as I had long wished to do, to study and serious reading because
I had an ambition to write a work of deep scholarship which would
set forth the terms for a happy marriage between the High
Churchmanship of the Anglican Communion and the Higher
Criticism emanating from Harnack and the Tübingen school in
Germany; from, say, Fathers Loisy and Tyrrell late of the Roman
obedience; and from the great English bishops, Lightfoot, Hort,
Westcott and Gore. Gore was very much my man : a High Anglican who had founded a Community of fully professed religious
at Mirfield but yet accepted the Higher Criticism of the Scriptures.

Enormous the task if I was to tread in the tracks of these great
intellects, and so far I was happy with little more than the
epigraph for my book. It came from Father Tyrrell and seemed

as precise and apt as epigraph could be. 'What Christ freed us from was not externalism but its abuse; not the letter but its oppression of the spirit; not ritual but ritualism; not the priesthood but sacerdotalism; not the Altar but the exploitation of the altar.'

Here was everything I wanted to say, for my heart was longing to persuade my head into keeping—and my readers' heads into keeping—the old doctrines, the old priesthood, the old traditional and beautiful rituals distilled from the art and love of twenty centuries, and an Altar where Calvary's sacrifice was still pleaded on behalf of the world—all this for my *Ecclesia Anglicana* with none of the oppressions, intolerances, and censorships, the many new *de fide* doctrines (as they appeared to me) imposed on the Roman Faithful. All the vestments of the Mediaeval Church, its ceremonial, its songs, its Gregorian chants, but none of its superstitions and still less of its anathemas. Without the Incarnation there could be—well, nothing that I loved and longed for : no Church, no sacraments, no beauty of ceremonial, no warrant for the great Passions of Bach with their haunting Chorales, no Mass in B minor, no Palestrina Masses, no Handel's *Messiah*.

Round Miryam's table then, on this occasion in '23, or '24, the company was not large; there were still two empty places for 'The Two Young Things' who would arrive tomorrow. Miryam sat at the table's top and though it was not a narrow table her broad figure filled it well. Willy sat on her left, myself on her right, Hyacinth Wilberforce next to me, Hetty McGee next to Willy and—the very monument of a buxom, dynamic and dominating woman—Mrs Jane Julia Pemberton at the table's foot. Here, as with cocktail parties today, some of the guests have been introduced to you only by name, and you are left wondering who, in fact, and what, in hell, they are. For the present I must leave Hetty McGee and Jane Julia Pemberton as merely two voices at the table, Jane Julia's deep, almost masculine, voice sorting well with her aquiline nose and imperious manner; two persons still shrouded in the veils of your ignorance—though, when I come to think of it, this is no way to treat so formidable a lady as Jane Julia Pemberton—'Jane Julia', as she always was to me.

'Uncle Willy' was Miryam's only and recent husband, though

she was his second wife. He was an old man so heavy in build and protuberant in belly that he couldn't have sat comfortably between the table's top and the sideboard, though why he didn't occupy the table's foot is perhaps explicable only by the fact that it was inconceivable to put so impressive a character as Jane Julia among the lesser people at the sides. Willy, over eighty and long retired from some undefined position in the Empire and Oriental Shipping Company had, as I have hinted earlier, such wicked and mischievous old eyes that I have always suspected that he had been notably more than an *homme moyen sensuel* during his eighty years; that, in truth, he had lived voluptuously, untroubled by his conscience, and to the utmost of his vigour all the time. And with me it was a suspicion amounting to belief that it had been Willy's vigour that accounted for the presence of Hyacinth. In short, that, some thirty years before, while his first wife was still alive, he had lived a little vigorously with Miryam while she had been the young and comely maiden who could still be imagined as long buried in her now corpulent mass, and as having long abandoned the attempt to get out. Miryam always said of Hyacinth, 'I adopted her when she was a child after my fiancé died and long before I married Willy, because I so wanted someone to love and care for,' but, knowing my Miryam, I knew that despite her regular churchgoing she could tell such lies as occasions required; and I had never fully believed that her tale of a fiancé was more than a nice, sweet, sentimental fiction with possibly a small basis in fact. The story, sweetly sentimental too, of her adoption of Hyacinth as 'the dearest of little babies' could not be disproved in these years that cover our story, because it was not till two or three years later that the Adoption of Children Act must have obliged her to tell a court the truth of a *de facto* adoption.

I wish I had been there to hear.

A further guess of mine was that Willy, as merry as he was roguish, had suggested the surname Wilberforce for Hyacinth, his daughter, because its overtones were those of religion and piety, the great Wilberforce having been the most famous of the saintly 'Clapham Sect', the destroyer of slavery, and the author of *A Practical View of Christianity*.

I was the more inclined to this suspicion because, though Willy had long abandoned any desire for goodness in himself, he was capable of applauding one or two examples of it in others, and he loved to tell the story—I must have heard him tell it twenty times—of that tremendous day in the House of Commons when, in 1807, the bill for the abolition of slavery was passed and every man in the House rose to his feet to give Wilberforce round after round of cheers—every man except one, Wilberforce himself, who sat bent over his seat with his face in his hands and the tears pouring down his face.

The tears would be almost in Willy's eyes and voice as he told this favourite tale.

But sometimes I would wonder whether, when considering the name Wilberforce for Hyacinth he had weighed it in the balance with Wesley. Had not Wesley written to Wilberforce on his battle against international slavery, 'Unless God has raised you up for this very thing you will be worn out by men and devils, but if God be with you, who can be against you?'

Willy loved to tell us this bit too.

'Hyacinth is a fraud,' he informed me on this occasion when we were alone together at the dining table waiting for the women who were still gossiping in the large room called the Lounge. For a moment I thought he might be going to tell me the real truth about her birth and begetting. But no. 'She's an awful fraud. It amuses me to listen to her when she's talking to some real expert in art or music or literature. She talks about "adoring" whatever he admires, when actually she knows next to nothing about it, and she never realises that sooner or later he'll see that hers is all a put-up show. I never put up that sort of play-acting myself because I know that, sooner or later, I'll say something that'll reveal my real ignorance. At other times I can lie with the best if necessary—saving your presence, Hugh—but never when I know I'm certain to be found out. Do you ever lie, Hugh?'

'Well, I can't say I never have.'

'Of course not. One can't get through life without an adequate supply of lies. But poor Hyacinth—she's a good well-meaning girl, but a born humbug without the skill to conceal the fact.'

All this was true enough, if ruthlessly stated, because Hyacinth was just a prim, proper, conventional and conforming young woman. She was as inveterate a churchgoer as Miryam—her mother?—but I could see that her churchgoing had a value above Miryam's and made demands on her life that were far more exacting. She would never have lied as easily as Miryam was ready to do when the proprieties required it of her, but, as Willy had said, in matters of literature and music and art Hyacinth was a natural hypocrite and *poseuse,* pretending to knowledge and 'adorations' that were largely bogus. It was all part of her need to conform : she must appear to think and feel and admire whatever I or the Vicar or the organist or Sir Tom Hapwell, the church-warden, thought she ought to think and feel and admire.

While Willy and I were discussing Hyacinth our Perce Bywater entered. You shall have a full introduction to Perce. There had been some hesitation in Miryam before he became one of her guests. He was one of the many assistants at Groves the Chemists' vast emporium in our High Street. He was thus, alas, in trade, and therefore in Miryam's view not a gentleman; and she'd had to think twice and again before accepting him as a guest. This was at just about the same time as she was arranging my Prophet's Chamber for me—in the last years before the war. No difficulty about me : a parson and inevitably a gentleman. Now, Groves the Chemists, besides selling medicines and toothpaste, had long counters displaying stationery and books and post-cards and 'fancy goods'; but Miryam, badly wanting at this time another regular paying guest, chose to forget this. 'My idea was always to take in nothing but gentlefolk,' she said to me. 'I don't really like having anyone in trade among my guests. But you'll admit that a chemist is hardly a tradesman like other shop-keepers. They are almost gentlemen, aren't they? Rather like doctors. I mean, it's almost a learned profession, isn't it?'

In imagination I saw Perce behind his stationery counter selling cards and fountain-pens and sticking-gum and blotting-paper, but, delighting to help him and Miryam both, I said, truthfully enough, 'Miryam dear, I should think a fully trained chemist has scientific qualifications far above mine.'

'You really think so?' asked the doubtful lady.

'I do. There are chemists and chemists; some of the most famous men in history have been chemists, Lavoisier and Faraday and Cavendish and Dalton,' I said, and decided that I was in no position to criticise Miryam as a fluent and skilful liar when an occasion asked for it.

'You really think Mrs Pemberton and Hetty McGee will approve?'

'I'm sure Hetty won't mind, and I should refuse to be bullied by Jane Julia. It's your house. Not hers.'

'Well, I hope you're right,' she said. 'He seems a decent young man.'

A decent young man, and almost a gentleman he certainly was, even if occasionally he mislaid an aspirate. He had a special difficulty with my name, and I can only spell his rendering of 'Hugh' as 'You'. But surely there was an excuse for this. After all, the whole English-speaking world is in two minds as to whether to sound the 'h' in the word 'humour' or to drop it. Consider the disparate views of the dictionaries : one spelling the word phonetically as '*ūmer*', another as '*hūmer*'. Perce chose to drop the 'h' before 'Hugh', and he would greet me sometimes with, 'Morning, You. How's things going with you, You?'

There was less excuse for his management of the 'u' vowel sound in all words—though the whole American continent inclines to support him in this practice. He always spoke of a dook and of Irish stoo, and he would say, 'In a libellous case like that one would certainly be entitled to soo. Don't you think so, You?' My only other criticism of him was the zephyr of peppermint which enfolded me when he and I were in a full discussion—but here again he seemed to have the support of the whole western hemisphere in this devotion to chewing gum. At one time I kept a box of peppermint creams, swallowing one if I foresaw a long talk with Perce; and the prophylaxis was complete.

So the three men, myself, Uncle Willy, and Perce Bywater, had now arrived at their places round the dining table; the four women, Miryam, Jane Julia, Hyacinth, and Hetty McGee, still delayed.

§

But at last all four appeared, and Miryam began ladling out the soup from a huge tureen, while Emmeline, the old parlourmaid, waited to deliver their plates to the guests. Emmeline, still in a long skirt, apron and cap, looked, as did so much of the house's furniture, like a relic of the years before 1914. Emmeline's wear, pink in the daytime and severely black-and-white for dinner, showed that Miryam was still unaware that an old comfortable world had been collapsing around her during four years of war.

'It's all settled,' said Miryam, supplying soup to the first plate.

'*What*'s settled?' demanded the deep, semi-masculine voice of Jane Julia.

'The two newly-weds are really coming. They are arriving to-morrow. Coming straight from their honeymoon in Brittany.'

'Oh, I *do* think it's wonderful, having two newly-weds coming,' said Emmeline, pausing over this statement of her satisfaction before placing the first soup-plate in front of Willy. Emmeline never hesitated to take her part in the talk round the table if it interested her. She would stand with an undelivered dish, contributing an opinion while those still unserved beat impatient fingers on the tablecloth. Nor did she acknowledge any precedence for ladies or seniors : she went round the table beginning with Willy and so coming at last to me, when the soup or the dish had been somewhat chilled by her halts as she offered the company her sentiments. As with King Arthur's Table Round, all in her view were equals.

'Yes,' continued Miryam. 'And they're two delightful young people, he twenty-three, she twenty. And he's Oxford and all that. Went back to his college after serving a year in the war.'

'*What* college?' came from Jane Julia's deep imperious voice.

'Oh, I don't know what college.' True enough, Miryam didn't know one college from another.

'It wouldn't be my college by any chance?' I ventured. 'New College?'

'Oh, no. It's an old college. He told Willy what it was.'

'Wadham,' Willy provided, lapping up a spoonful of soup before any others were served.

Quickly resenting Miryam's assumptions that New College didn't compare with others for antiquity, I told her that New College was founded in 1379; Wadham not till sixteen-hundred-and-something.

'Oh, I *do* like Oxford and Cambridge men,' said Emmeline, halting between Hetty McGee and Jane Julia. 'Though I'm Cambridge myself, because light blue's always been my favourite colour.'

I was now getting exercised about the temperature of my soup. There was still Perce Bywater to be served.

'I can beat Wadham too,' Willy declaimed. 'Jesus beats Wadham easily. 1571.'

'So awkward Willy's college having a name like that,' Miryam suggested. 'One's almost afraid to mention it. One feels one's being profane.'

'*I* don't,' Willy assured us, tapping his breast. 'I was at Jesus from 1864. What's more I nearly rowed for Jesus.' This was probably a lie, or at least a generous exaggeration.

'Oh, do be quiet, Willy,' Miryam appealed. 'It doesn't sound nice to ordinary people.'

'No, fancy giving a college a name like that,' said Emmeline, pausing over Perce. 'One wonders how they come to do it.'

Mischievously, to shock the women, including Emmeline, Willy said, 'I well remember Jesus bumping Magdalen and Keble and St John's. The rowing push when I was up were a terrific crowd. Giants most of them. Jesus ought to have gone to the head of the river.'

Here Hetty McGee disposed of this general embarrassment by asking Miryam, 'What's the young man's name?'

'Siward. Siward Bartleby.'

' "Siward"? What a funny name. I've never heard of it before.' The first words from Hyacinth.

'Nothing funny about it at all,' said Willy, promptly snubbing her. 'There are lots of Siwards in history.' This no doubt was a fact, for he may have been a bad old man, but he'd taken a good degree in Classical Mods and History.

'Yes, Siward Bartleby,' Miryam repeated, probably because she wanted to add, 'He's related to Lord Bartleby. A nephew.' Obviously there'd been no such difficulty about this young man as there had been about Perce, the chemist in his shop.

'Oh, I'm *longing* to see them both,' said Emmeline, pausing to announce this desire before bringing me my soup. 'I never seen 'em when they come. The master let them in, didn't you, sir? Oh, I'm so glad they're coming to us.'

'And what about the girl? Is she a duke's daughter?' That deep Jane Julian voice was often tart and faintly contemptuous.

'No, but an archdeacon's.' Miryam said it proudly. 'The Archdeacon of Norbury. Archdeacon O'Neale. It was the dear Vicar who suggested they came to us when they couldn't find a home. The housing shortage is just awful.'

'I never know what an archdeacon is,' Emmeline confessed, withholding my soup till she should be informed.

'Half-way between a vicar and a bishop, Emmeline,' said Willy, 'and wearing gaiters.'

'A bishop! Well, I never did! Oh I do hope he comes and sees us. And I can't help feeling glad there was no houses,' she confessed, standing quite still with my portion of soup, while my fingers tapped impatiently. 'I'm sure it's very wrong of me but it'll be so nice to have some young people here—not that the Rev Fields and Mr Bywater are all that old. But they ain't twenty and twenty-three, like. I mean it'll be nice to have some truly young people.'

' "The sweet breath of youth", Emmeline,' Willy offered as a suitable comment.

'What say, sir?'

He repeated his words to Emmeline, who, bemused, answered, 'Yurse . . . yurse, I s'pose them words are just about what I mean. You can't get away from it. There's something sweet about youth. Yurse.'

At which point I got my soup.

'What's his job, this young feller?' asked Perce. 'Has he one?'

'Oh yes,' the enthusiastic Miryam replied. 'Quite an important job, I think, in this broadcasting business.'

It was always clear to me that Perce Bywater had a sense of inferiority in the company of Oxford graduates like myself and Willy and of a woman like Jane Julia who was the widow of a Rear-Admiral Pemberton. So now, as a businessman who, unlike the ladies, would know what was afoot in the world of business, he supplied, 'The British Broadcasting Company, commonly known as the B.B.C. Their headquarters are at Savoy 'Ill.' He turned to me. 'That's so, isn't it, You?'

'I haven't the faintest idea where they live,' I said.

'Well, I'd say he was damned lucky to get a job with them,' said Willy, while Miryam cast an unquiet glance at Jane Julia who surely wouldn't approve of swear words. 'Now, Willy, really!' she reproved him, and then returned to her enthusiasm. 'He told me that he had no difficulty in getting taken on to be trained in broadcasting because he was an Oxford man.'

Willy improved on this, considering it to be his field. 'A graduate with a second-class honours degree. Not bad, so he got taken on as a trainee.'

'Yes, but he's now got a full-time job, he says, in what they call Programme Output. He's thrilled with it; says he'll have to deal with news and talks and plays and things. That should interest you, Hetty. Perhaps you'll be able to help him.'

This was a generous remark to Hetty McGee, an actress of some small prominence in her day, but long forgotten and unwanted.

'Oh, how wonderful,' said Emmeline, who was now clearing away our soup plates. 'And will he have to do any broadcasting his'self? Wouldn't it be wonderful to hear someone from this very house speaking on the wy'less? My sister and her hubby have a set and say it's wonderful. They say you can have every window tight shut and still hear the voices or the music through the walls. You can hardly believe it, can you? Sometimes I reely don't know what the world's coming to, like.'

This long contribution to the table talk accounted for all our plates, and she had to leave this satisfying causerie while she carried them to the kitchen. But she comforted us for her temporary absence from the symposium by the words, 'I won't be a minute. Just 'arf a mo'.'

'Tell us more about the girl,' Willy requested, more interested in young females than in wireless sets.

'She's rather lovely, I thought,' Miryam declared.

'So did I,' said Willy.

'Yes, I'd call her beautiful, but what surprised me was that she was far more eager and witty and lively than you'd expect from a blonde.'

'Why, what's wrong with blondes?' objected Willy. 'I've seen some Swedish blondes who'd——'

'Never mind about your Swedish beauties. I'm talking about English blondes. It's almost a commonplace that they tend to be duller and emptier than brunettes.'

'They tend to be nothing of the sort,' interrupted Willy, who clearly had no objection to blondes. And spoke, maybe, from experience of them during eighty years.

'Well, anyhow, this girl, blonde or not, is a radiant young creature; there's no other word for it.'

'Yes, I thought that,' Willy agreed.

And I put in, merely for the sake of talk, 'I can hardly wait to see her.'

'Of course she's not all that blonde,' Miryam corrected, as if trying to find an explanation for the girl's unexpected vivacity. 'Something between blonde and auburn. Her hair's shingled as you can imagine but it's been well done and suits her, but what pleased me more than her pretty face was her figure. She wore the usual idiotic boyish dress which tries to hide everything a girl's got, but I could imagine the breast and waist and hips behind it; and the short skirt showed really lovely legs.'

'Yes, he's certainly a damned lucky young fellow,' mused Willy, and I could guess that his thoughts at this moment were far from the B.B.C.

'Here we are,' announced Emmeline, entering with a steak-and-kidney pie on a tray. 'Everything comes to 'im 'oo waits.' Not an aptly encouraging slogan because she'd returned very quickly from the kitchen; it was more a desire to comfort them for any loss they had sustained by the departure of one of their more prominent conversationalists. 'There you are 'm.' And pie-dish and plates went down before Miryam, with Emmeline standing at her side ready to dispense our portions.

'Meanwhile,' asked Jane Julia, 'who and what is this Lord Bartleby?' She asked it in a tone that suggested she was never one greatly impressed by a title.

'Probably the son of his father,' Willy offered, ready, as ever, to damp down Jane Julia with any facetiousness. ('There's one person in this house,' he would say, 'who's not going to be bullied, chastised, purged, or purified by old Mother Pemberton. I've no intention of ever being laid out by your old Pemberton steamroller. . . . That old battering-ram.')

'Really, Willy!' Miryam rebuked him.

'That much I had imagined,' Jane Julia averred, haughtily disposing of his witticism. 'I hoped for a more informative answer than that.'

Perce, ever trying to hold his own in company superior to himself, provided a quick answer. Impressed yesterday by the advent of a lord's nephew, reported to him by Miryam, he had researched in a *Who's Who* on the book counter at Groves'. 'He is Lord Grafton Bartleby, second viscount, principal shareholder, and lately chairman of IPAF, Mrs Pemberton.'

'IPAF?' This query which Perce desired (having the information) came from more than one of us.

'Imperial and Allied Foods, Limited,' he supplied.

'*What?*' exclaimed Miryam, pausing in her task of allocating portions of pie.

'IPAF,' Perce repeated. 'I suppose they're easily the biggest grocers in the world.'

Miryam went silent. The word 'grocer', like the touch of a sorcerer's wand, had struck her dumb.

I knew what she was thinking. Once, long before this, speaking to me of the famous Viscount Cowdray, head of Weatman Pearson's, the public works contractors who had established a vast oil business in Mexico, and in their time constructed such huge engineering enterprises as the Blackwall Tunnel and the Blue Nile Dam; of this Lord Cowdray, master of splendid castles and the lovely Cowdray Park in Sussex, millionaire and Chairman of the Air Board during the war, she had said, 'He may be all that, Hugh, but, after all, he's still only a tradesman'; and I, hearing this, sat wondering—not without an amazed envy—that she in her little Christian Street boarding house which 'accepted only gentlefolk' could still think of herself as the social superior of any in the famous Pearson family.

I knew that she was now downcast to think that this new young guest of whom she had been boasting came from a family engaged in trade.

Emmeline, in her delivery round, had reached Jane Julia, and her current contribution to the discussion was 'I suppose then this Lord Bartleby must be a millionaire, and I only wish he was my uncle, and I suppose this young Mr Siward and his bride will have all the money they need'; whereupon Willy corrected her, 'You're quite wrong, Emmeline. This young Siward is only the son of the youngest of the Viscount's five brothers, so it's doubtful if he has a penny more than he needs.'

'Still, I s'pose there's a chah'nst he could become a lord,' she argued as she served Perce.

'Only after a general massacre, Emmeline. Five brothers and all their children polished off. All we can do is to wish him luck and hope this'll happen.'

'Willy!' Miryam exclaimed in shock and disapproval.

§

Next evening, at the same hour, the two young people were with us, and Miryam's table was full. It was as I had seen it, or tried to see it, fifty years later, poised on a railing and peering through the blank window of a deserted house, this extremely odd behaviour by a tall black-suited ecclesiastic being screened from passers-by in Christian Street by that tangle of forgotten privets which had grown high as young forest trees.

6

Young Lovers, Fifty Years Ago

It is because of all that was to happen that so vivid a memory remains of this, my first meeting with Siward and Terry. Perhaps Terry was not as 'lovely' as Miryam, with her sentimental enthusiasm, had suggested, but she deserved Miryam's words, a 'radiant young creature'. Her eyes, blue-grey, flashed with her various fervours, and when she spoke fluently about them this first day her hands flew this way and that in, as it were, an inadequate effort to state them fully. I don't know that I have ever seen a girl so ardent, so demonstrative, so completely a picture of slim youth brim-charged with vivacity. The whole essence of her seemed to be 'pressed down and flowing over'—flowing over into these gestures with outspread hands.

For this first appearance before us she had plainly put on one of her best frocks, a gown of old-gold silk with sleeves that broke into cones of flying lace from which the white arms and sensitive hands could emerge to play their part as the instruments of some enthusiasm or excitement. (Did I that night, or do I only now, suspect that within her unresting animation there lurked an instability of which the ardours and the demonstrativeness were symptoms?) A rope of pearls fell over the gown almost to her waist, her shingled hair, a paling chestnut, was brought forward into rich 'buns' over her ears, and long earrings swung from beneath these, as she addressed her fervours to one or another of us. Little doubt that gown and pearls and earrings were the fruits of a wedding three weeks before.

Of Siward little need be said in the presence of so radiant a bride; we speak of little else when female beauty is commanding our interest and holding our eyes. Even Emmeline, for once in a way, contributed nothing to the table talk, rendered speechless by the need to consider Terry while serving us. Of Siward it's enough to say that he was not very tall, inches shorter than me, but tall enough, and that he had the charm of his youth, his gaiety, and a manifestly high intelligence.

I have one memory which shows the interest which the coming of two newly-weds had stirred in Miryam. As I went up to my top-floor room that night after all the others had gone to bed I walked softly so as to disturb none of them, but to my surprise as I approached the second-floor landing and the door of the young people's room I saw Miryam standing very still there in the attitude of a listener, though her own bedroom was on the floor below. When I appeared unexpectedly on the stairs she was clearly at a loss to explain her business up here. After one bewildered moment she went to the landing's window and pretended to be making sure that it was shut. To save her from embarrassment I passed quickly on to the next flight, pretending to be untouched by surprise. But, dear Miryam, I guessed why you were there. Ever able to associate with your warm religiousness, in a way that surprised me, all sorts of dubious indulgences, you were indulging a natural prurience by listening for any murmuring or gasps, or perhaps ecstatic cries, from the two young lovers in the almost bridal bed you had prepared for them. But who was I to condemn you? I had plenty of prurience myself.

§

Siward, and Terry too, soon chose me for their favourite among the guests. Firstly because, as Siward put it, there was no one else under ninety-nine (a most unfair description because Hetty and Miryam were only pushing sixty, and Jane Julia only passing it; and, besides, there was the simple Perce); secondly because I had been a brother-in-arms serving in the P.B.I. ('Poor Bloody Infantry' for those born too late to appreciate this compassionate title); and thirdly, because I agreed with him that Britain had been two nations when she was fighting the Germans, one nation at the Front who knew that most German soldiers were just poor bloody loyalists like themselves, usually decent blokes longing to be done with it all; and the other nation who still believed that the whole German people had best be taught their lesson by an extreme of punishment. Miryam and Jane Julia were still vocal citizens of this second nation; Miryam, said Siward, and Pemberton (as he sometimes called Jane Julia) were of the type that wouldn't stroke a dachshund pup because of its German antecedents. 'Quite so,' I said—though it wasn't really 'quite so'—and I recommended Siward and Terry to 'play' Miryam carefully

43

on this hot subject, if they didn't want to be 'blacked' by her. 'I've played her ever so carefully for three long years now, and so far she still loves me,' I explained.

Then, fourthly, Siward said that he'd never seen so many books in a room and therefore I must be worth talking to; and lastly, that he would enjoy discussing religion, and his total inability to feel any religion in himself, with one whom he called 'Our Resident Padre'. A padre who had withdrawn for a while from active ministry because of some doubts was, he said, 'just the right padre for him. And for Terry too, more shame to her. We believe nothing, your Eminence, and we'd like to believe a little something, wouldn't we, Terry?'

Terry nodded and declared with her customary wide-arm gestures, 'Gosh, I only wish I could believe one single thing that Daddy believes. Poor Daddy, he knows I don't, and he's an archdeacon. I must be a terrible mortification for him. And he's so touchingly sweet about it. He just smiles and says it's natural for me to think he belongs to the day before yesterday.'

'But I hope you realise,' I interrupted, 'that *he* doesn't think he belongs to any day before yesterday. If, as I suppose, he has all the faith that I long to find again, he knows that it has no date. It doesn't belong to any time. It's outside time.'

'There you are, Terry, pet: he's put you properly in your place. You see: you know nothing about these things, my beloved imbecile. Just you listen to the good father. Set her feet in the right path, padre. Mine too, if you can. But I doubt it. Here you have a couple of out-and-out atheists.'

'And in me you have only a half-and-half agnostic.'

'Yes, but you know all about it. And you believe quite a lot of it. Put us on the right path.'

'I don't know that I know a right path. Not yet. I'm only a little way ahead of you. I'm looking for the path.'

They were both in my room when they said these things: Siward in my one elaborate and luscious easy-chair; Terry on my divan-bed with her legs curled up beside her; and myself in my revolving chair swung round from my desk.

'Auntie Miryam—' Siward had cheerfully accepted this title from me—'calls this your Prophet's Chamber. So prophesy. We're all ears. Come along, Rev.'

I could only prophesy by telling them that they were both too intelligent to style themselves 'atheists'. Atheism was utterly un-intelligent because it was a dogmatic assertion inevitably and for ever unsupported by one iota of evidence. It was as much a matter of mere faith as was Auntie Miryam's Christianity down-stairs. 'You may call yourselves "agnostics". I will allow you no more than that. Agnostic meaning "I don't know because no one can ever know" is an intelligent and acceptable creed.'

He turned to Terry. 'There. You see, Babe? You've been a horribly unintelligent little atheist all this time, and now you've got to show a little sense and be an agnostic.'

'But I always thought atheists and agnostics were the same.'

'Well, now you know they're not, sweetheart. You can write and tell your dad so. Tell him we've got a padre here who's train-ing us up in the way we should go.'

'I can't get you very far,' I said. 'But I'd like to get you a little farther than the pure agnosticism of "I know nothing, and I never will". You can get a little way beyond that. Surely it's easier to believe in a Creator with a Design rather than that anyone so intelligent as Siward could have come about by a series of blind chemical accidents—or, for that matter, anyone so beautiful and utterly charming as Terry.'

'D'you hear that, Terry?—'

'Did I *not*? Isn't he angelic?'

'There. You see, padre. She loves you a lot. She told me so the other day. She thinks you're rather wonderful.'

Terry's cheek had flushed with pleasure but she quickly left my praise to return to her father. 'Poor Daddy. He called me Theresa because he so loved Soeur Thérèse of Lisieux. And look what's happened. If there's an exact opposite of Soeur Thérèse of Lisieux it's Sister Theresa o' Bartleby.'

'How different, Terry dear?' I had soon arrived at the fami-liarity of calling her 'dear'.

'Well, Daddy made me read her book, *The Story of a Soul*—'

Nodding, I gave the book its French title, *Histoire d'une âme*—for no other reason, I fear, than to display my knowledge of the book and my knowledge of French.

'Yes, *Histoire d'une âme,* in which she sets forth what she calls her "Little Way" of achieving goodness, and I decided that everything she thought splendid for herself would be quite impos-sible for me. She said that she welcomed every kind of trouble and humiliation and irritation and even insult as something sent from God to help her train her soul, so she never allowed herself to protest or complain or even defend herself if she was wrongfully accused—and that she'd disciplined herself into never showing by a glance or a word or a gesture that she was feeling anything but forgiveness——'

'Well, if there's anything totally different from you,' Siward interrupted, 'it's that——' but I waved him down and maintained that I'd learned at least one thing from Thérèse's 'Little Way'. 'You remember she tells how another nun's rattling of her beads exasperated her but she decided that, in love, she must regard the beastly noise as a welcome thing—well, I can't stand Perce's ceaseless chewing of gum and the strong scent of peppermint that goes before him wherever he goes, but I decided like Soeur Thérèse that I must try to accept it as a joyful fragrance——'

Terry interrupted, 'Oh, I find no difficulty with Perce. I love Perce. He's a lamb. I think he's sweet. And I adore the smell of peppermint. Besides, I think he's rather beautiful.'

Beautiful? Good God! So different a woman's eyes from a man's, when they were assessing a man. For myself, looking only at the mind behind the face, which I found rather silly and pretentious, I had never thought of Perce Bywater as a well-featured and attractive young man. But now I saw him with feminine eyes and granted the good looks; while Siward exclaimed, 'There! She'll be falling in love with our Perce before we know where we are.'

'Oh no, I shan't,' she promised, 'I don't feel like that about him at all.'

'Really?' Siward demanded, as if relieved, but still unsure; while I enjoined her, 'All right, Terry. Forget about Perce, and go on about Soeur Thérèse.'

'Of course Soeur Thérèse was totally different from me. Why, she seemed always to have a longing for martyrdom. Apparently nothing would have pleased her better than to be scourged or crucified or flung into boiling oil—for none of which I have any desire at all—and since none of these delights were granted her, she had to content herself with never refraining from any self-sacrifice, however small—whereas my whole desire is to avoid, if possible, every self-sacrifice, however small. She actually rejoiced that her bed in her cell was no more than a board on trestles whereas I want a bed with the most comfortable mattress and down pillows and—what's more—with Siward in it. Well, you must admit that this is the opposite of darling Soeur Thérèse.'

'In fact,' Siward submitted, 'you're not really a nice type at all.'

'No, horrid. And then I couldn't swallow the ghastly sweetness and pretty-pretty piety of the whole book. Why, the very first words are pretty awful, when she subtitles it something like, "The Story of a Little White Flower"—' again, alas, simply to display my French, I gave her the exact words, *'Histoire printanière d'une petite fleur blanche'*—and she went on, 'Yes, and oh lord, heaven help us, fancy calling oneself a little white flower. Daddy agreed that this was difficult to take and rather too sugary, but he declared that, beneath the sugar, there was a wonderful dish for simple souls. He said that in the war, when he was in France, whole regiments had put themselves under the little sister's protection, and whole batteries too—which seems slightly out of harmony with her "Little Way" of Love and Forgiveness and No Hitting Back—and all this was before she was even beatified. She was only beatified about two years ago but Daddy says she'll be made a full saint of the Church any moment now. *I* shall never be beatified in St Peter's before hundreds of bishops and cardinals and half the population of Rome. And the whole *corps diplomatique*. Though I must say I should rather like it.'

'No, darling and beloved,' Siward agreed, 'you'll never be beatified, because if anyone believes in hitting back, it's you. You wouldn't believe it, padre, what I've had to put up with sometimes, when I've said the wrong thing or done the wrong thing. She just abuses me like a Billingsgate fish-wife when she feels like it, shouting and yelling at me.'

'I don't believe it,' I said.

'Well, just you wait till you've properly displeased her. Though perhaps it's only husbands who have to put up with the whole treatment. Don't know where she gets it from. My old man was a horsy type who could swear like a trooper, but Terry was delicately brought up in, of all places, an archdeaconry. I think the Archdeacon was quite right in saying that this Soeur Thérèse ought to be Terry's patron saint. If she's the patron saint of French batteries, especially if they were seventy-fives, then she's just the girl for Terry, who belches fire at me often enough. She can let loose a whole string of oaths. It shocks me.'

'You're letting loose a whole string of lies,' said Terry.

'Now then, children!' I began to rebuke, but Siward promptly allowed, 'Well, I may have exaggerated a little but it's all fairly true. Anyhow, let us just say that my beloved Theresa's no easy child to live with. And don't you imagine she is! She doesn't take anything lying down.'

'Of course I don't. Why should I? But I can't imagine Mr Fields saying anything that would displease me.'

'There you are, padre. She loves you better than me.'

'If that were so, I couldn't imagine anything more delightful. But unfortunately it isn't so. And, anyway, "Mr Fields" be damned; my name is Hugh.'

'Oh I should have a terrible job to call you "Hugh",' she said.

'Then stick to calling him "padre",' Siward advised. 'Or what's wrong with "Father"? No, I know! "Monsignor"; "Monsignor Fields".'

'No, I shall get around to calling him "Hugh", if you'll give me time. I should so love to.'

'Call me anything you like,' I begged, 'so long as it's not "Reverend Fields".'

§

They went from me, and I was left alone, sitting in my swivel chair. I was feeling a love for them because of their youth and gaiety and affection for me; and this love roused in me a strong desire that my words about leading them 'a little way further' from a simple and dead agnosticism should become something more than words; something real and actual. But I saw that I could only lead them from in front; and, as I had said, I was only a little way in front of them, with my present doubts. What *was* my position about the utterly primary, utterly fundamental doctrine of the Incarnation? I got up and began to walk about the empty room. No dogma, even at its best acceptance, could ever be more than a guess, a hope, a trust—with a question mark at its end. To declare that it had been revealed—once and for all to the saints—was itself a dogma with a question mark at the end. Even Blaise Pascal, great Christian soul and passionate believer, dared speak of it in his *Pensées* as a gamble. Every dogma to be fully accepted must be self-authenticating to the seeker, if it was to be accepted. Self-authenticating like the beauty of a rose, or like the beauty of ten million other variegated flowers, bursting into life for us every spring and summer and autumn. How could such infinitely creative fecundity speak of less than an infinitely creative Artist? Or like the dazzling geometrical beauty of crystals : octahedrons and hexahedrons and dodecahedrons; self-authenticating proofs of some beauty and design in the very depths of nature, often beyond the sight of man. To plunge into the depths of nature, how could infinite small cells obey their instructions to divide and procreate without an Instructor? All one could do was to seek one's own self-authenticated kingdom at whatever risk of loss, and then see what would be added unto one. My love for these two young people was self-authenticating, and so was my certainty that their post-war hedonism and proud agnosticism were pathetic things because they could never be enough. I was delighting in my love for 'these two wandering and wondering kids'—almost, so to say, falling in love with this love. And the thought came to me suddenly, 'Well, you've long had a very real love for the *idea* of God becoming incarnate as a man among us. If you could only, as it were, fall properly in love with this idea of Divine Love Incarnate as Man for Man's sake—what then?'

§

I soon discovered that Siward, for all his fine university degree and his years in the Army, and his belief that he was as modern-minded as any young man of his time, was really far simpler and more innocent than he knew, or would like to have been told. He may have called his father, 'a horsy type who could swear like a trooper,' but I detected that, despite this proliferation of paternal oaths, his parents were Victorian in their morals—or conventions—and that Siward, their son, was now full of a simple pride in his liberation from all the old pre-war taboos on any open discussion of sex.

One evening he was alone with me in my room and he began to speak with this unexpectedly simple pride in his elation—'the wonder', he called it with eyes alight—'the incredible wonder', 'the unspeakable joy of it'—his elation in his love-making with Terry. His readiness to speak to me like this, and the almost humble wonderment he sought to express, charmed me. I was turned towards him, I remember, in my swivel chair with my arm at rest along its back; he sat on the brink of my easy chair with his elbows on his knees and the 'unspeakable joy' in his eyes.

'I take her and possess her, padre, and I can't believe it. I just can't believe that anyone could give herself to me quite in the way she does. She just takes me to her with a kind of rapture. Naturally she's not—I'm afraid she's not the first girl, padre, with whom I've had—well, you know what—but generally these affairs have been pretty disappointing and no great joy to look back upon. There's never been anything like Terry. I never knew I should feel any joy so overwhelming as Terry's giving of herself to me and her longing for me in these last few weeks.'

'That's easy to understand, Siward.'

'How do you mean?'

'It's the first time you've really loved. But go on.'

'We knew we were more or less sunk in love with each other before we got married but I didn't like to take advantage of this because of her father. She likes to think herself as modern and free as most of us but I know that, unlike me, she'd have been quite incapable of giving herself to anyone before marriage. Her father's her father, the Archdeacon; and her home's her home, you see; and, anyhow, she's not built that way. I know I'm the only man she's ever known like this—and given herself to, like this— and, quite frankly, padre, sometimes the utter ecstasy of it all is not only something beyond belief but almost beyond bearing.'

He had his pipe in his mouth as he sat in my easy chair but it had long gone out without his knowing it.

'It's good of you to tell me this,' I said, 'and it's rather wonderful to hear it.'

'I can't think of anyone else I'd say it all to—certainly not to Auntie Miryam or Auntie Jane Julia Pemberton who'd bite my head off, but it kind of eases one to say it to someone. D'you know what she told me yesterday? She said that after we've made love and have sort of turned away from each other to sleep, she lies there telling herself over and over again the loving things I've said to her.'

'Such as?' I asked with a smile.

'Oh, you know : ecstatic things like "God, I never knew I could love anyone like this". And "I'm madly in love with you, Theresa. D'you realise it, woman? If not, I'll make you." Or just simply "My wife. My lovely wife".' He paused, perhaps ashamed of these excesses. 'You can understand, can't you?'

'I can understand very well. I'm happy to think she's heard you saying such things, and I can well believe she repeats them over to herself before going to sleep.' Again I covered a question with a smile. 'Do you say these things to her in the quiet sometimes? After the ecstasy is over?'

'Yes, yes.'

'And in the daytime too? When there's no ecstasy about?'

'Yes, when I take her and kiss her. But of course there's the beginning of ecstasy then. And she gets it again, "My lovely wife" and all that caboodle.'

'I think she must be a very happy girl. As happy as you.'

'God, I hope so. D'you really think so?'

'I think I can honestly say I've never seen a girl look happier or sound happier. She's not much good at hiding it, is she? Why, even Auntie Miryam who isn't naturally eloquent surprised me by calling her one day "a radiant creature".'

'And what about me?' he laughed.

'I wouldn't say you looked glum. I'd say you looked pretty happy too.'

'Well, I ought to, because I've never known anything like this, or ever expected to.'

Miryam's 'Lounge' was the front room above the dining-room in that Christian Street house. It looked straight down Elm Tree Walk, a leafy avenue ill-named because, though it had a giant elm at the corner opposite us, it was bordered on one side by a procession of lime trees and on the other by an unordered assortment of sycamores, ashes and thorns, some large, some small. The lime trees marched like a regiment along a broad side-walk but the capricious assortment opposite seemed to loiter in their private gardens carelessly and uninterested in one another.

This Elm Tree Walk was our quickest route to High Street, shops and cinemas; and often in these first days I would see Terry and Siward walking along it, either leaving us or coming home. I found pleasure in watching them because they reproduced unconsciously but so exactly the behaviour of a hundred million new lovers the wide world over, and the centuries through.

Once—it must have been in 'leafing time', late October perhaps, because the yellow leaves were flying from the sycamores, or dancing and racing up the roadway, but the ashes and poplars were still green, with every leaf of the poplars restless in the lively breeze. And from the far distance near the High Street came Siward and Terry: at first his arm was along her shoulder and her arm about his waist while her face looked up into his; but now they had linked their hands and were swinging them vigorously back and forth for the joy of it; and then again, as they drew nearer to us from among the trees they had broken apart and were buffeting one another or wrestling for a moment together, like any two leopard cubs at play. When near the house they merely linked hands again in a discreet sobriety.

Inevitably Siward of the B.B.C. had advanced beyond messing about in his room with a crystal set and earphones and possessed a multi-valved set powered by batteries in a black box and emitting its music or voices (when successful) through a funnel which flowered into a wide trumpet like that of an old-fashioned gramophone. When he had got all this into fair working order he politely asked Miryam, 'May we have it on sometimes? We won't let it get too loud'; and she answered, 'Of course you may, and one day you must let us hear it. You naturally understand all about it. I can't understand how it works at all.'

'Oh, it works,' he said. 'And often we dance to it. Come and see us dance to it.'

'Dance?'

'Yes, we roll back the carpet and push all the furniture back and get quite a nice dance-floor. You don't mind, I hope?'

She laughed. 'Not as long as you put all the furniture back properly.'

'Oh, yes, Terry sees to that beautifully. Look, there's to be a dance-band tonight. Come up and see it all tonight. Everyone who'd like to. We'll do our best for you.'

All the rooms in that house were large, and Miryam had given one of the biggest—the room under mine—to these two, in part sentimentally because of their newly-wedded status, and in part, I suspected, snobbishly because she was proud to have as guests two such undoubted gentlefolk as the nephew of a viscount and the daughter of an archdeacon. So when we all went up to that large second-floor room, we found bed and furniture pushed against the walls, carpet rolled up as Siward had said, and a row of chairs—some purloined from the padre's room above—for the audience. Politely he put us in our places, and there we sat under the windows: Miryam, Willy, Hyacinth, Perce, Jane Julia, Hetty

McGee, myself—and Emmeline who, hearing our discussion at the dinner-table and contributing lengthily to it, had said, 'Oh, I'd love to come up and hear it,' and she told us all again how her sister and her hubby had 'one of them there machines'.

Siward fiddled with the knobs on his set—got undulating whines, prolonged squeals, raucous voices and distant music from all over the world, but at last found his B.B.C. and with expert fingers contrived that it should be liberated, so far as was possible, from interference by other nations and languages.

This achieved, he extended both arms towards Terry and said, 'Come along, darling. The music waits.' She who, as usual, had been sitting on the bed with legs curled beside her rushed into his embrace.

Terry's dress, it seemed to me, was marvellously ambivalent (a new word just becoming frequent among earnest readers of the new psychologies, of whom I was one). In its front her breasts and waist were hardly allowed to exist, so strong the current fashion for the 'boyish figure', but the back of the blouse (or whatever it was called) was scooped almost as low as her waist to give a full display of her fresh young flawless skin, while the skirt was knee-high allowing a full display of beautiful legs clad in some artificial silk whose colour was that of the same youthful flesh—'nude', I think it was called. And, to be sure, it looked nude.

I noticed Jane Julia's underlip pressing upward in disapproval of this dress, and although Terry's only make-up was a bright lipstick, I'm sure Jane Julia included this in the sum of her reprobations. Not so Hetty McGee : as an old actress I divined that she was much interested in this new manner of dressing by the young girls and possibly regretting that at sixty her own dress had to be so much more seemly.

At first, I saw no disapproval on Miryam's face, but it began to appear like a picture taking faint shape on a screen, when the two young things, with delight but not guiltless of 'showing off' and perhaps shocking, were really giving a performance of all the latest dances, cheek to cheek, breast to breast, loins to loins, their bodies as tightly together as any two clothed bodies could be. Not till this evening in their room had I known any of these dances, I being no dance-goer and becoming more and more of a hermit in my spacious cell upstairs, with my theological books, my writing desk and my dreams. It was they who introduced them to me,

53

Siward giving me some of their names with impish fun when later I suggested that the ladies' approval had been less than complete. 'What? Mean they don't like the Bunny Hug, the Shimmy Shake, and the Black Bottom?'

Soon my sidelong glances at Miryam, who sat next to me, showed that the faint picture of distaste was getting more and more precision, and once, as she caught me looking at her, she said, 'I don't think it's nice. It's no good pretending I do. You can't really say that you like it, Hugh. It's so—so *suggestive.*'

It was all so new to me that I'm afraid I thought much the same, but I didn't want to say so for the two children's sake, and merely shrugged.

'And I wish she didn't put on that lip-stick,' Miryam went on. 'She really doesn't need it when she's already so pretty.'

To please her I said, 'I agree. It's painting the lily'; but Hyacinth, as ever, echoed her mother (actual or adopted), as a good and conventional daughter, and an earnest churchgoer, should do. She said, 'I think it's rather disgusting.'

This was too much for me, and I said impatiently, 'Oh no, I wouldn't go as far as that. I don't see why she shouldn't put it on if she wants to. I'm all for people doing whatever they like.'

But the truth was that I too, still unaware of the new ways in the world, wished she hadn't put it on. I agreed with Miryam that she was pretty enough without it.

Either innocently unaware of this disapproval troubling their audience, or naughtily basking in it, the two dancers, though their cheeks still lay pressed together, were accompanying a vigorous, jazzy, leggy dance with the idiotic words of the dance band's song :

> 'Yes, we have no bananas,
> We have no bananas today.'

When it all had to stop because the dance-band's half-hour was over and gave place to a talk, Siward, leading his partner towards the only place where wearily they could sit down, which was the brink of the bed, asked us all, 'Well, did you like it? But I'm afraid neither of us are as good as some dancers. Some are absolutely marvellous. You should see the real experts doing the "Vampire" and the "Twinkle" and the "Missouri Walk".'

I was glad he had the compassion—or merely the sense—not to mention the 'Black Bottom'.

Miryam contented herself with saying, 'It's all very different from the dances in my day. I suppose it's all right but I can't pretend I altogether approve of it in some ways.' Hyacinth, inevitably, said sourly, 'I quite agree with Mother.' And Jane Julia, beginning, 'I'm afraid I'm one who likes to say exactly what she thinks', thereby assured me that I would be hostile to whatever she was going to say, because I have a native antagonism to all who open their disparagements with this lump of self-congratulation. She said, 'I quite definitely didn't like any of it. I don't know what the world's coming to. In my day there were such things as decency and courtesy and gallantry between couples dancing. At least that was the way our partners treated *us*.' I wasn't putting up with this, so I said, 'I saw no discourtesy in their dancing; only joy and great affection—' but she interrupted with a grumble, 'Oh, I suppose it's just permissible between young married people, but are you telling me that mere unmarried boys and girls dance like that today? If so . . .' and she left her opprobrium in its fullness to our imaginations.

'Certainly they do,' said Siward, now a little hurt and angered.

And Willy, perhaps for the help of all, but probably just speaking the truth, for he never minded what he said, especially in front of Jane Julia, declaimed cheerfully, 'I thought it was all delightful. I was thinking all the time that I only wished dancing had been like that when I was young, but, lord help us, we had to keep about a yard of daylight between us as we waltzed, and we missed all the fun.'

7

Hetty McGee and her Past

To go into Hetty McGee's bed-sitting-room was to go into her past. Her past in the theatre was all around her. On the walls hung framed pictures of herself, thirty, forty years younger—and forty years prettier—in minor Shakespearian or other roles. There were also framed theatrical posters with her name at least among the leading ladies, but I was quick to notice that they belonged to suburban theatres now defunct, some of which I could remember as existing in my childhood: the Kennington, the Balham Hippodrome, the Brixton, and the Wandsworth Scala. On her bookshelves (there were only two) lay albums of press-cuttings, their cheap news-print yellowing or even perishing round the edges. Some of the oldest cuttings were beginning to flush yellow too. These cuttings she strewed willingly before me: all of them spoke highly of her performance, but so perpetual was their praise that I decided she must have omitted to paste in the rude ones. Some of the cuttings included press-portraits of her, and again I thought with surprise how pretty she had been in her stage costumes—and again was suspecting that only the flattering ones had been admitted to her galleries.

Hetty did not come to church like Miryam and Hyacinth but she knew that I helped the Vicar in the Communion services and sometimes with baptisms (I was still in Orders and, anyhow, baptism by a layman is valid); and she was quite incapable of perceiving that I was now something less than a normal curate. Had I expounded to her that I had deliberately lapsed for a time from a teaching priest into a learning layman, she wouldn't have known what I was talking about.

Now, just about this time our church was organising a campaign to raise many hundreds of pounds for some necessary restorations and a total redecoration of the church's spacious auditorium. The campaign was prospering: there was to be a great bazaar and an organ recital by no less a name than Gustav Holst with two vocalists (through Holst's mediation) who were no less persons than Dame Clara Butt, the contralto, and her husband, Kennerley Rumford, the baritone. For this the church, seating some fifteen hundred, would certainly be packed, but since a church must be open and free to the world, all would be admitted free if they had already bought a programme at a cost of five shillings.

There was also to be a performance by the ladies and gentlemen of the Choral Society of Haydn's oratorio, *The Creation*. I attended an early rehearsal of this and must confess that it seemed less like a rendering of Creation than of Chaos, but doubtless, under the enthusiastic conducting of our organist, the whole thing in time would cease to be without form and void, and darkness would have departed from the face of the deep.

Miryam, of course, was full of all this hubbub (she was actually singing in *The Creation*) and she spoke much about it at her dinner-table; so much so that Hetty, having heard about Holst and Clara Butt and Kennerley Rumford, was uplifted by an idea which one evening, when we were alone in the Lounge, she proposed to me as a normal curate and therefore a natural avenue to the Vicar. She hesitated before starting to speak, but at last she spoke. She would like to help, she said; and could she not perhaps give in our parish hall a whole performance—a one-woman performance—of some of Shakespeare's heroines. A kind of *diseuse* performance, she called it. She would willingly do it free for the sake of charity.

I was appalled. Alas, the kindly old lady didn't realise that no one knew of her in these days, and I had a horrid vision of our large parish hall with perhaps three people in the audience—one of them myself. Living among those framed posters and pictures and press-cutting albums she probably liked to think that she must be nearly as well-known, in her way, as Holst and the Rumfords.

'It's most kind of you to suggest such a thing,' I said with a disordered heart. 'And I will certainly put it before the Vicar.'

'You have a large parish hall, haven't you?'

'Oh yes, we have a large parish hall.'

'With a stage?'

'Yes, with quite a good stage.'

'And curtains?'

'And curtains . . .'

'With battens and footlights?'

'There's a row of footlights, yes.'

'Then it could be easily done, and perhaps you could charge five shillings for the front rows and half-a-crown for those behind. I would want nothing, and you might get quite a lot of money.'

'It's all most kind of you. But what heroines would you do?'

'Well, there's obviously Cleopatra and Charmian and Iras. I do the other people with differing voices. Even with men's voices. You have to imagine *them*.'

(Cleopatra? Oh *no*! Oh, *please*.)

'And there's Perdita and her flowers and Viola with Olivia, and Portia with Brutus—obviously Juliet with her nurse or Lady Capulet.'

(Juliet! Oh, God. . . .)

'And Lady Macbeth. . . .'

'Do you really know all these parts?' I asked in admiration. 'Have you acted in them?'

'Done them or understudied them. And I'm a quick study.'

'But what dress would you wear for them all?'

'Oh, I've got the dress; it's there in my old property basket: a Tudor costume with a cambric ruff and a verdingale with black redingote over it.'

'Verdingale?'

'A hooped farthingale.'

'Oh, I see. Yes. Thank you. A hooped farthingale.'

'It's thoroughly Shakespearian; and I would only have to change the head-dress for the differing characters—if that. It's a quite beautiful dress.'

'I'm sure it is. This is a wonderful idea of yours,' I said; and this was not, in all senses, a lie: the Vicar would certainly wonder.

I told the Vicar, and he said, '*What?* Who on earth is she? I for one have never heard of her in all my days. And I'm nearly a hundred——' he was sixty-four. 'And a pretty good theatre-goer at that. Had *you* heard of her before you met her?'

'I'm afraid not,' I said apologetically.

'But, good lord, Hugh, must we do it? Couldn't you steer her away into some other parish? After all, she's *your* friend and protégée. Or perhaps we could set the parish hall on fire. I don't know where you're leading us, Hugh. I thought better of you than this. How old is this lady?'

'About sixty.'

'Well, I suppose she's by no means the first person of sixty to play Juliet. But it's always rather painful to everybody but the actress. Couldn't you kind of . . . discourage her?'

'I don't want to hurt the old thing's feelings. I daresay she was quite good in her time.'

'Yes, but this is our time. Heavens, as if I hadn't enough trouble on my hands without this.' He sighed. 'I don't know what to do. We can't have a fiasco.'

I shook my head in agreement, and he shook his in imitation, and we parted, neither of us having any clear idea as to how we could respond to so disturbing a proposal.

I told Uncle Willy, who said promptly, 'I'll be engaged elsewhere on that evening. I'm no good at suffering. That old bag as Juliet? Hugh, what are you talking about?'

I told Siward and Terry; I said, 'Listen, children,' and told them about Cleopatra and Juliet and Perdita; and I'm afraid Siward exclaimed, 'Oh, Christ, *no!* Oh, but *no!* Not Cleopatra.'

Nevertheless he was the only person who contrived some plans to meet a desperate occasion. 'We simply mustn't let the old girl down,' he said. 'We must simply rustle up a few people to come in. *You* can make some of the congregation come. They love you, Auntie Miryam says, and they'll do what you ask. Tell 'em she was a howling success in her day. I'm sure your God will forgive a good honest lie if it's to help someone in distress. I mean your Vicar, of course; I don't think *she's* in any distress. Then I'll induce a few sportsmen to come, and Terry can do something in the same line. Can't you, ducks? You can dig out some willing martyrs.'

'Yes. *Rather!*' said Terry. 'Of course we must do everything we can for the old pet. She's so touching.' And with her archidiaconal background, knowing her Bible, she quoted something about 'going into the highways and hedges and compelling them to come in'.

'Then,' said Siward, 'I will lead a claque. A well-managed claque can keep the people applauding long after they've wanted to stop, and can even start them up again, when they thought they'd finished. Don't worry, Monsignor. We'll see the old cow through.'

And Terry declared, 'I'll be one of the claque. I'll clap till my hands are sore.'

'If you know how to clap properly,' Siward explained, 'you can make the filthiest row.' And he demonstrated to both of us how, if you make each of your clapping hands into a hollow, you can produce a series of explosions like a series of pistol shots. It was true enough. Sometimes his blasts were like those produced by the bursting of a blown-up paper bag or like the backfiring of a car. We practised under his instruction and were soon discharging a remarkable fusillade—which must have bewildered the people downstairs if they could hear what was going on in this second-floor room. Siward and I were soon conspicuously (or resoundingly) successful at it; Terry with her small hands less so, though she did contribute one or two praiseworthy detonations.

Thanks to these children's activities, and mine, the performance on the day itself was not the fiasco which the Vicar and I had dreaded. There were, of course, far too few people in our large hall despite our efforts. Some four rows of the five-shilling seats were more or less occupied, and there was an assortment of people dispersed all over the half-crown seats. But I couldn't think there were more than fifteen pounds in the house. All of Miryam's household were present somewhere or other, Miryam herself, Jane Julia, Uncle Willy (after all he'd said) and Perce Bywater in the front rows; Emmeline and the cook in the two-and-six-pennies. All had come partly in compassion, partly in curiosity; Uncle Willy 'just to see how the old baggage fared'. Siward and Terry with their claque had deliberately put themselves at intervals among the half-crowners, since, as Siward explained, 'you must control the applause from behind. We know a lot about synthetic applause in the B.B.C.' I, for very shame as the instigator of the feast, had to be seated in front, but I kept myself away from Miryam's row because, in Siward's words, I was 'an outside and honorary member of his claque, supporting it from in front'.

And, between us, we certainly led a magnificent fusillade when the curtains first parted and Hetty entered in her Tudor costume, with its peaked velvet cap, wired ruff, and hooped farthingale. It deserved applause (if not quite as much as Siward provided). And so, to our surprise, did much of Hetty's performance. She might be sixty, but she was a real old trouper who had not only spent a judicious afternoon with her treasured old grease-paints, but really knew how to act; and even if she did 'ham up' some of her roles, the applause was often able to be sincere rather than sympathetic.

When it was all over and a bouquet had been presented to her (my idea) and she had curtsied once and again to the ample Siwardian applause; after the Vicar had made a speech in which I could detect a genuine gratitude mingled with even more genuine relief, and in which, moreover, he managed to suggest that he'd long known and admired Hetty McGee, though in fact he had only heard of her yesterday—a speech which drew from the Siwardian lobby another round of excessively prolonged applause, delivered perhaps on the principle that if this was to be their last performance that night, let it be a real smasher; after the Vicar had looked at me with a knowing, questioning but gratified smile—we were all walking homeward and Terry said to me, taking my arm affectionately, 'Well, to tell the truth, I quite enjoyed that, though my hands are as sore as hell. The old biddy really does know how to do her stuff.' 'Yes, a grand old trouper,' I said, while Terry hastened on. 'Oh, I do hope she feels happy about it all. It was rather sweet of her to want to help, you must say. You do think she's happy, don't you? I mean, I've always heard that the audience looks bigger than it is from behind the footlights, which rather dazzle you. And after all, the applause at times was terrific. Oh, I'm sure the old pet must've been pleased.'

8

The Religions of Perce Bywater

Siward was not the only guest in that house who was proud of
atheism and felt driven to parade it before me, a clergyman.
Perce Bywater was another of them, though he hadn't the intelligence or the gaiety of Siward—and certainly none of Siward's
occasional humility which was proof of the intelligence. I could
see that it was anything but humility which urged Perce to come
and asperge me, a representative of the Church, with liberal
sprinklings of his atheism. In part, I surmised, it was a compensation for feelings of social inferiority. This resolute atheism and
feigned intellectualism were like the round rubber heels under
his shoes: they were worn to make him a little taller.

He would speak of 'all those simple and uncritical women who
make up the most of your congregation, you must admit, You'.

'Yes, but——' I began.

But he had to pursue, 'Which of them has ever been troubled
by the intellectual doubts or difficulties? They just believe because
their fathers believed before them. Look at Miryam and Hyacinth
and poor old Mrs Pemberton. She still says, "I'm a Conservative
because my father was a Conservative, and Church of England
because my father and husband were loyal churchmen—" thereby
admitting that, for all her bossiness and cockiness she still thinks
of any woman as somebody who inevitably follows behind a man.'

'Yes, but,' I persisted, 'have you not noticed that, even if there
are more women than men in our congregations, there are men
all over the country who are devoted churchmen, and some of
them men of the highest scholarship?'

'Yes, that's something I can never understand,' said this
intellectual.

It was not difficult to see that both the atheism and the intellectualism were insecure adornments. He was uncomfortable in
them. He wriggled and fidgeted a little in garments not really
made to measure. Usually it was in the Lounge that he came up
to me like a pack-man with a new little parcel of sceptical lines

to unload before me, but sometimes he brought the stuff along with him when we were walking the streets. We had frequent walks together because, if I did not feel the same pleasure in his company as I did in that of the high-spirited and effervescent Siward and Terry, I liked him just as Terry liked him (though not to the extent of thinking him a lamb and perfectly sweet).

I remember once when we were sitting in the Lounge, no others present, the familiar argument slid from my 'faith in God' to his humanist 'ethics independent of any God'.

'One just knows what is right and wrong without any Bible or Ten Commandments or Christian dogmas. The knowledge is simply planted deep in us.'

I avoided the too simple answer, 'Who planted it?' and tried to make things easier for him by suggesting, 'Don't you think it got itself planted there by two thousand years of Christian beliefs? I wonder what our ethical system would be if Christianity disappeared completely for a few hundred years and became a forgotten religion like, say, Mithraism.'

'Like say what?'

He had never heard of the god Mithras who so nearly conquered the western world during the Roman centuries. I told him to his amazement that there had been temples to Mithras in Britain long before Christianity arrived.

'I confess I've never heard of Mithras,' he said, abashed.

'You can already see a change in human ethics,' I went on, 'among those who, like you, have no further use for old-fashioned Christianity. Look at the question of homosexuality. Lots of those who think like you no longer think it wrong at all.'

'*What?*' he exclaimed, and his immediate surprise at this statement taught me, as never before, that homosexuality hardly existed in the working classes from which he had sprung. Its larger field was among the public school and university classes where the sexes had been segregated in their academies through their years of adolescence. 'You mean to say that they don't think it *wrong?*' He had used for 'it' the rugged but, as it chanced, strictly legal word for this 'abominable crime' (*vide* the *Offences against the Person Act 1861* : 'Buggery').

'No, they certainly don't,' I said, exaggerating a little for the sake of his intellectual health. 'For most of them that nonsense belongs to the world before the war. They now consider many people like Oscar Wilde more sinned against than sinning; victims of old-fashioned and stuffy views.' And I bewildered him further by telling him how, before St Paul had anathematised paederasty, the Greeks in their most brilliant years had admired it and honoured it. I told him how Plato in his dialogues gave high honour to love affairs between men and how Sappho indulged her female version of it in her island of Lesbos. I reminded him that, curiously enough, lesbianism was legitimate in England, so long as it was not openly admitted, whereas homosexuality among men, private or public, could get punishment for life or not less than ten years. 'Shows how far man-made Law has been fair to the girls who haven't the same chance of getting married as the boys.'

His astounded comment was singularly inapt, but I'm afraid I must record it. It was, 'Well, I'm buggered.'

§

It must have been months after this discourse, because it was now early summer, when Terry came stamping up the stairs, in her irrepressible fashion, to my room. It was a Sunday morning and I was sitting at my desk before a tormented manuscript, struggling to find the thoughts and the words that might achieve my still dominant purpose, a reconciliation between the Higher Biblical Criticism and the Anglo-Catholic High Churchmanship which my heart still loved, however far behind it my head stayed lagging. And the door burst open.

Terry stood there, emptied of breath and panting. 'Hugh darling,' she gasped.

'Now what, Theresa darling?'

These 'darlings' may appear strange and excessive, but they had been caught like an infection from Hetty McGee, who in the manner of most theatrical folk called everybody 'darling', even though the endearment might be no more than a substitute for 'my dear'. Terry had heard Hetty say something like, 'Pass the pepper, please, Hugh darling' and instantly after the meal had said she was going to call me 'Hugh darling'. 'After all,' she submitted, 'I love you a lot more than old Hetty does. And you love me a lot . . . I hope . . . Hugh darling?'

I was happy to reply to her in the same idiom.

This morning she said, 'Oh, I know I should have knocked.

You're at work on your marvellous book. I'm sorry. But it's all so exciting. It's such fun.'

'Never mind the knocking and the apologies. You are always welcome.'

'Angel,' she exclaimed, stretching an arm full-length to lay a grateful hand on my shoulder.

'There are no angels in this household, Terry. At least, not so far as I've noticed.'

'Oh yes, there are. You are—now and then.'

'Very much a fallen angel, I'm afraid. Now sit down and cool down. What is exciting?'

'Perce has been changed.'

'Perce has been changed. Terry, dear, would you care to be more explicit?'

She sat down to explain. 'He's been changed by a whole heap of graduates and undergraduates from Oxford at a big meeting.'

'Changed into what?'

'Into something holy and religious. Like you.'

'But he's a ramping atheist.'

'Not now. Perce has found God.'

'Perce has found God. Where?'

'In the Queen's Hall, Langham Place, Upper Regent Street.'

'In the Queen's Hall, Langham Place, Upper Regent Street. And how?'

'I've told you. At a huge meeting conducted by a lot of Oxford boys—and girls too, I believe. He's just told Siward all about it. In fact, he can talk of nothing else, and, if you'll believe it, he's just gone off to your church instead of sitting and working on the Sabbath like you. He's been trying to convert Siward with conspicuous unsuccess, poor lamb. I know he's always argued with you that there is no God. But now there *is* one. And I thought you'd be pleased.'

'I think I am.'

'Yes. Siward takes a very poor view of it all. You'll probably be more sympathetic. You'll get it all, soon.' She looked at my scribbled manuscript. 'But I see you're still at work on the wonderful book. What it is to be clever like Siward and you. Fellows or M.A.s of your colleges and everything. I've never been a fellow of anything. Have I interfered with your work by bashing in like this?'

'A bash-in by Terry, as I've told you, could never be anything but a pleasure.'

'How sweet of you. And what a lie.'

Terry was right enough in her judgment that Perce would be spilling all his new beatitude over me at the first opportunity. That same evening in the Lounge after dinner our usual attitudes were reversed. Perce was now converting *me*.

He approached me where I was sitting, and he, still standing, explained that he'd been 'guided to come to me'.

'Guided?' I repeated, frowning a little.

'Yes, I felt most surely guided to come to take back all I'd said to you about there being no God. After a Q.T. this morning. I felt it was a sin on my conscience—I *saw* it was—and I knew I must come and share my experience with you.'

The words embarrassed me, but I did not let a happy man see this. Rather, smiling, I said, 'Do tell me all. It sounds very interesting. Has something wonderful happened?'

'The most wonderful thing that's ever happened to me in my life. It's changed me completely.'

'Did you say something about a Q.T.? Was that it? A Q.T.?'

'Yes. A Quiet Time. We are told to have a Q.T. early every morning, when, if we listen to God, he will tell us what he wants us to do in the coming day.'

'I see. And does he?'

'Oh, yes, we call it his guidance, and I felt guided at once to talk to Siward and Terry first. I hope I made some impression.' I thought as he spoke, 'My dear fellow, you should hear Terry on the subject,' but he hastened on, 'They were interested but rather inclined to make fun of it. You know what Siward is. Still, I may perhaps have sown some seeds that will develop in the future. This is the first moment I've been able to see you and to speak privately with you.'

Not wanting to spoil his hour of glory, I said only, 'Do sit down, and tell me all.'

I was sitting on a wide settee and he could well have taken a comfortable place beside me. Instead he pulled up a hard chair and perched himself on its edge, far from comfortably. Perhaps this was because the remarkable experience of which I was to be told had thrust behind him overnight (as with many saints) all the old desires to seek his own comfort. Leaning forward with earnest eyes fixed on me, he told his story. One of his colleagues at Groves the Chemists, Charlie Brooker—a pharmacist, a dispenser, he was careful to add, as if this enhanced his value as an authority—had told him during a luncheon-break all about the work of these Oxford lads and begged him to come to 'one of their biggest meetings ever'. Charlie, he said, had been guided to come to him with this invitation, just as he himself now felt guided to bring a similar invitation to me. Never, I sometimes fancy, can there have been anyone whose mental processes were easier to penetrate than Perce Bywater's; and as he talked I was thinking that he, ever fascinated by 'Oxford men' like his landlady's old husband and two of her guests, and wistfully wishing he'd been one himself, had willingly gone along to the great meeting with his dispensing colleague. There he had been overwhelmed, it seemed, by the fervour of these young Oxford boys, and by a conviction that they had found and were experiencing a quality of life far above anything he had known. They seemed alight with a new buoyant life.

Neither of us knew it that evening but, sitting together and talking, we were in touch with the beginnings of what, a few years later, the press, in its perpetual search for headline brevities, was to dub 'the Oxford Group', because these new evangelists had their headquarters in Oxford. This name evoked the wrath of Siward, late of Wadham, and Uncle Willy, late of Jesus. It raised some irritation in me too, for whom any words like 'Oxford Movement' could mean only Keble, Pusey, Newman, Froude and the other great Tractarians.

'You should not only go to one of their big meetings,' said Perce, 'but to one of their House Parties——'

'House Parties?'

'Yes, held in some of the biggest and poshest hotels all over the place. They gather together in hundreds and share their experiences of God and his guidance. You could afford to go to one. I can't. Look, here's an invitation to one. At the Royal Seaview Hotel, Easthaven. A truly posh place.' From a bunch of pamphlets on his lap he fetched with trembling, excited fingers an invitation card and offered it to me.

I took it and read it. It described a 'House Party organised under the guidance of the Holy Spirit'.

I blinked. This enormous statement seemed to be loaded with

67

a confidence that unfriendly persons might define as arrogance.
I couldn't begin to tell Perce, in his present state of grace, that
such language left me, not only doubtful and wondering, but, alas,
amused. Apparently this House Party arranged at a posh hotel
by the Holy Spirit was to be a minor Pentecost.

I remained silent, and Perce, a-splutter with his enthusiasm,
spoke about one 'Frank', who was the founder and leader of the
movement. 'Frank goes absolootly all over the world, You,
organising teams and groups of people who will teach his
message——'

'And the message is?'

'It's perfectly simple. As Frank put it, you listen to God in your
Q.T.'s; he speaks to you, and you are a changed person. You see,
only changed men can change the world, and there's no getting
changed without the strictest standards. So we are sworn to the
four Absoloots.'

'*Four* Absolutes? I thought there was only one Absolute. Surely
the essence of the Absolute is infinite unity and aloneness.' I
couldn't forbear from these flippant remarks. But Perce, neither
heeding me, nor understanding me, was not hurt. 'Yes, the four
Absoloots; absoloot unselfishness, absoloot purity, absoloot
honesty, absoloot love.'

'Golly!' I muttered, as one seeing horizons of unselfishness far
beyond him.

'Look, You,' he begged again and drew from the literature on
his lap, a pamphlet. He licked his second finger to turn its pages
(a dirty habit that always irritated me). 'Here are some of the
places Frank has visited in the last dozen years. Turkey, Greece,
Egypt, India, Korea.' He licked the finger again to turn another
page and read some more. 'Japan, China, the Philippines. . .
There's been nothing like it ever.'

Still silent, I thought there had been many things very like it.
There had been Wesley riding round the world and preaching in
Britain, Canada and America. There had been George Fox,
founder of the Quakers, preaching the 'Inner Light' in the West
Indies, America, Germany, Holland. And there had been General
William Booth of the Salvation Army sending his battalions and
companies, under colonels and majors and captains, all over the
world. . . . There had even once been a St Paul.

With none of this did I hurt Perce; I merely declined to go to a House Party organised by the Holy Spirit but consented readily and humbly enough to go to the next meeting organised by these Oxford lads. In them I was indeed interested. I wanted to see something of new young evangelists and their new methods which had worked a miracle in Perce and, according to him, in hundreds of others. Had I not, for years past now, been striving by much reading and more meditation to re-establish for myself the old Christian God in his fullness, and here were people working this miracle of faith overnight. At least one should go and hear them, and see if they could work some miracle in oneself. Happy with this consent, Perce went smiling away, after laying on my lap the pamphlets he'd been guided to bring to me.

§

The next meeting, so Perce told me excitedly, would be in the Grand Union Hall, Westminster. 'You simply must come. It'll be your great chance. Frank himself is going to be there.'

What that famous hall can hold with its steeply raked galleries and its steeply tiered seats behind the platform I cannot tell, but when I entered it, no more than two minutes late, it was packed from its spacious floor to its high gallery walls. I entered with Perce and, surprisingly, Uncle Willy. Uncle Willy had not come, I was confident, with any idea of being 'changed' or of having Quiet Times with God, but because of the large controversy which had started in the press, and the plentiful propaganda about Frank emanating from Perce. He had come merely to see Frank.

When we entered we had to stand at the back, where there were others behind us pushing to get in. So great a multitude at a religious weekday meeting, with numbers of them young men and girls, impressed me more than I wanted to be, because, since Perce's proselytising assault on me, I had spoken to many people about this 'Oxford Group' and in every one of them I had met only disparagement, head-shaking doubts, and even warm hostility. They had argued that its noisy success, especially amongst the young, was the fruit of typical American advertising—Frank Daniel Buchman being a Lutheran pastor from New England; that the seemingly unlimited money flowing into its coffers came from Heaven-knew-where; and that the idolised Frank, while undoubtedly sincere, was a simple theologian of the old-fashioned

Bible-thumping school—and where was the difference between all this brazen-throated ballyhoo and the famous revivalist missions of Moody and Sankey, thirty years before, of Torrey and Alexander some years ago, and of the notorious Gipsy Smith only yesterday—Gipsy Smith with his extremely hot gospel or good news of hell-fire. Remember Gipsy Smith with his appeal to a packed Albert Hall before the collection plates went round, 'Hands up, all those who are glad to see me here. All of you? Fine! Now put those hands in your pockets.' Or his appeal at the close of his meeting, 'Stand up, all those who need more of God.' The story went that all the four or five thousand in the hall stood up, except about a dozen. So he turned to this dozen of ungodly men and said, 'So you really think you are good enough as you sit there?' Whereupon the dozen stood up, and he had all his thousands converted for at least a minute or two. All of these high-powered revivalists had arrived to a fanfare of trumpets in the press; they had come, and they had gone, and London seemed much the same, neither better nor worse, for their ringing and resounding visitation. Some of those to whom I had spoken had been parsons—my Vicar, for instance—and none of them had any plaudits for Frank, this Lutheran protestant. I suspected some *odium theologicum* here, but as a quondam Anglo-Catholic I had a struggle to suppress in myself some of this traditional *odium* and was unlikely to love with any ease a 'Prot' from New England, U.S.A.

In such a mood was it that I walked into that hall.

In the centre of the platform, behind a small table with a carafe of water, sat a rather plump little man in his late forties, with a round, clean face, crowned by a high round dome and lit by piercing eyes behind large round, steel spectacles. This was a face as much like that of a benevolent and blithe—and wise—old owl as human face could be.

I turned to Perce at my side. 'Is that Dr Buchman?' I asked.

'That's Frank,' he said, as if Frank were a younger brother.

'Lor' love us!' said Uncle Willy; and what that exclamation stood for I don't know.

Since neither of them seemed disposed for further talk, and Perce couldn't take his devoted eyes off the platform and the chairman, I just stood there and watched.

Without rising from his chair Frank began to speak. His manner was easy and colloquial, smiling and gentle, and yet heard in every part of that great hall. I at the far back missed not a word. No barn-storming Gipsy Smith here.

'Brothers and sisters in God, as I hope you are, it's often said by those who don't love us because they know very little about us that our work and our message are directed only to the middle classes and the upper classes—and more especially to those in the money. They call us a class-conscious lot. Well, so we are: we believe in two classes; not in upper, lower, or working classes but in two others: those who are ready to be changed and those who are not ready. Apart from the amazing capacity in human nature to be changed—changed by the Cross of Christ—we believe all humans to be precisely the same in nature, whether they be rich or poor, presidents in their high offices or colliers deep down at the coal-face—all the same in their human nature just as all crows are black and all leopards spotted and all tigers striped. All are built in God's own image and therefore able, if they are ready, to recover in its fullness that image, lost in the Fall—which is all we mean by saying they can be changed. It is also said by our enemies that we are given bags of money by big-business men to fight the communists.' A pause, a smile, and then, 'I sometimes rather wish we were.' (Laughter.) 'But the position is very different: our door is wide open to all—to republicans, democrats, socialists, communists; it is only shut with a bang and bolted against godless materialism, whether this is found among communists in Russia or among big-business men in our own countries. Communists are humans such as you and me; we love them as such and know that they can be changed. To nail these lies so often spoken against us I am happy to call as our first speaker tonight our devoted Tom Bradwell, a miner and in some sense still a communist. Now then, Comrade Tommy, tell us your story.'

While general laughter rewarded the title 'Comrade', a little man of middle but indeterminate age rose from a seat near his chairman. The first thing that struck me about him, apart from his jovial face, was the excellence of his dress. That pin-stripe blue suit so clearly cut to measure, that starched double collar and broad blue cravat tied with a ring below its knot, the starched white shirt cuff emerging from his sleeve when he extended a pointing hand—all this sartorial perfection seemed the last imaginable wear for a miner and a communist. To Perce at my

71

side I murmured, 'That's the best dressed miner *I've* ever seen.'

Proudly he replied, 'It's simple. Surgison Brothers of Piccadilly are among Frank's supporters and as Tommy's one of the best speakers we've got, they've equipped him with all the clothes he requires as he goes about the country—and he's been abroad too—telling everybody about us.'

Uncle Willy said, 'That outfit didn't leave much change out of twenty quid. I can't afford a suit like that, but I'm only one of the ungodly.'

Comrade Tommy was certainly a natural as a platform orator. Much practice in demagogy at Marxist or Trade Union demonstrations had made him, I supposed, what he now was. With a rich northern dialect, patently exaggerated for its comedy effect on a southern audience, he soon had them rocking in their seats. They laughed easily, this audience so largely composed of Frank's youthful followers.

'Aye, Ah wor a miner, Ah wor, as tha's heard from Comrade Frank.' (Mild laughter.) 'And mi feyther and mi gron-feyther wor the same before me, tha knows. Aye, and Ah wor chairman of mi Union branch for sometime. Ah doan't knaw as hah Ah ever had much religion, though mi mother used t'tak' me to t'chapel, where t'minister wor religious, or raather so.' (Loud laughter.) 'Aye, he wor that. Ah mind how once he wor walkin' up an' dahn while we wor prayin' and he saw me kinda' lollin' abaht instead of kneelin' proper, and he fetched me a real clout across mi lugs that shot mi knees on t'hassock an' mi head to t'pew afore Ah knew what had happened; and there he wor, sayin' Cah'nst tha pray in a proper attitude, laddy? He tried the same sort'a thing on another of us lads but that time he onny got a streightleft on his boko fer his trouble.' (Rich, prolonged laughter, which was repeated when he explained the situation, 'Tha sees as hah yon laddie'd heard nowt abaht Absolute luv.')

From here he went on merrily enough about his conversion from godless materialism to Buchmanism, though often forgetting, as he grew more serious, to maintain the Northern dialect in its first full flowering. He had really found religion but not all at once, he said; and he reminded us of the blind man whom Jesus healed; how he touched the man once and asked what he saw, and the man answered, 'I see men as trees walking.' So Jesus touched him a second time, this time on his eyes, and he saw all things clearly.

This was the point at which this one-time ringleader began 'sharing'; that is to say he published before the thousands in the hall his sins before he was changed. He had been a slave to drink and many times unfaithful to his wife; he had bullied her and often lied to her, telling her that he was going to a meeting of his Union when really he was going to spend an evening drinking with friends. He spoke of impure habits, overweening ambitions, nasty little dishonesties, and a gross failure of love for any other than himself, Tom Bradwell.

From all this I recoiled with distaste, though I had learned from Perce that Frank strongly advocated 'sharing' as a means whereby his followers could come closer to one another, all barriers down.

For the close of his oration Comrade Bradwell reverted to the full Nordic speech. 'Ah fair tell mi mates as hah this new move-ment has solved t'problems in mi hoam. At let 'em knaw as hah Comrade Bradwell has pledged hissen to Frank's four absolutes, like it or not. For me it's absolute unselfishness, absolute luv, absolute purity an' absolute honesty. That's me nah, Ah tells 'em. Ah says to mi Union and t'Party, "That's me, an' tha can kick me owt, or keep me on, or just do nowt about it, choose hah." '

He sat down to an uproar of applause and cheers from this audience, mainly young and committed. But I stood there sus-pecting that he was a show-piece in the window to suggest larger supplies of success among workers and trade unions than could be found on the shelves of the shop behind.

A Conservative M.P., a Right Honourable, followed the Com-rade and now I suspected (so compulsive my desire to disapprove) that he was another show-piece, one of the highly placed and influential 'key-men' whom Frank (according to Siward and other hostile critics) went out to catch like big and impressive salmon whom he could display abroad. Where was there a greater con-trast than Comrade Tom from the coal-pit and this distinguished, silver-haired, right-honourable M.P.? How better demonstrate the width of Buchman's appeal?

'Still, be fair,' I told myself. 'What's a platform for if not to display your show-pieces?'

There was no room for disapproval in this good man's speech.

F

It was as unpretentious and quiet as the Comrade's had been jocose and self-assertive and loud. He knew, he said, that Christ could enter a man's life and make it new. And he doubted no longer that Christ was at the heart of Frank Buchman's work, remaking men. No longer could he believe that the changes he had seen wrought in men by this new movement could have happened if Christ was not at the heart and centre of it in all his risen power. Why, at times, they looked like miraculous changes. He himself was all too familiar with big party meetings and inter-national conferences, but in few, if in any, had he felt the extra-ordinary glow, like the brightness and warmth of a new fire, which invariably he found in these gatherings of Dr. Buchman's young followers. As a friend, equally impressed, had said to him : 'Put that man, Buchman, in a forest, and he'll change the trees.' This new movement was bringing the Spirit of Christ to the board-rooms of industry, the benches of Parliament, and, as they had just heard, the homes of politically-minded workers who all too often had pursued hostility rather than harmony. 'As a politician myself, surveying the problems of the world, I am persuaded that there is one basic issue that underlies all else; and it is, as Dr Buchman has just told us, "Shall a godless materialism of a god-guided spirituality govern the world of our children?" Make no mistake about it, this is a fight between two ideologies, but, unlike all other fights, it should leave neither victors nor vanquished but only the common knowledge that all are banded together in the effort to build a new world. One cannot expect impossible perfec-tions, but at least one can keep a vision of perfected humanity towards which one must forever strive. I am not much good at quoting the Bible, but here am I, much older than most of you, and I like to recall that somewhere it says, "I will pour out my spirit upon you all, and your old men shall dream dreams and your young men shall see visions." My old man's dream, and your young vision, is (as I think Dr Buchman puts it) of a hate-free, fear-free, greed-free world.'

This quiet speech was not such as to raise cheers but he sat down to a long round of applause.

There was no burst of adulatory applause when Frank himself opened the speech of the evening because, once again, he had not risen from his chair. Was this because he sought to appear informal rather than important? I thrust away from me the unworthy thought, which had peeped above ground, that this instruction and exhortation from a hard chair might have some small kinship with the *ex cathedra* pronouncements of a sovereign pontiff who, though seated on a throne, was happy to be called 'the servant of the servants of God'. Rather let me think that his sitting position and his quiet voice had no other purpose than that he desired always to be least among the greatest.

Indeed his first words suggested that this thought was in his mind.

Quiet and humble or not, seated or standing, and however narrow, in some eyes, his range of Biblical Christianity, I soon learned that I was listening to an orator inspired.

'This is a magnificent gathering, and my neighbour has just said to me, "You ought to be proud." But, God bless him, I ought to be nothing of the sort. I have nothing to be proud of. Nothing. I have been but an instrument offered to God's hand, and it is he who has worked all. Using me, and using hundreds of you dear young people who are crowded around us tonight. Perhaps not all of you, but whether you are with us or against us, have no doubt of it, Humanity stands at a cross-roads. We are not just standing in the happy and peaceful years after a terrible, unspeakable war; on the contrary, we are facing the start of what may be the breakdown of a centuries-old civilisation; a breakdown when all the faith and the morals that the Bible taught us are being doubted, disputed, denied, and cast overboard. Be sure of this : democracy without God is bound to disintegrate. Slowly perhaps, but surely. Therefore there lie but two choices open before us; either to stay inert and leave the world to the militant materialism that is everywhere on the march, or to meet it with a faith, no less militant, in the way of Jesus Christ. To meet one revolution with the fire of a great Christian revolution. It takes a passion to beat a passion. The Communists have always said that their revolution can never succeed till the myth of God is removed from the mind of man. We agree. And we say, Let us only hold fast to God, and we've got them beat. So there you are : shall it be a new Dark Age for the world, or shall it be a world-wide recovery of moral and spiritual forces everywhere, bursting into life and bringing a miracle to mankind? I repeat, these are *not* easy-going, peaceful, post-war days. This is an hour for Choice. The world stands poised on a brink.'

By now, from that hard seat behind a table, he had enforced a silence everywhere; not a cough, not a movement, not the creak of a chair, no eyes anywhere but were directed upon him.

'Many of you here may have come because you've heard a lot about us—much of it disparaging—and you want to know who and what we are. Let me tell you then. We are no new sect, no new denomination, no new organisation. We long for you to remain happily in the Church or the Chapel of your upbringing. Let us say that we aspire only to make bad churchmen good, and good churchmen better; or bad chapel-goers good, and good chapel-goers better. We seek only to share with you, whosoever you are, Catholics, Anglicans, Dissenters, our vivid and vital certainty, which is that, if you listen to God—perhaps in the quiet of the early morning—and await his guidance, you will get it every day, and your whole nature will be changed; you will find yourselves primed with new powers of which you never believed yourselves capable. God can only act through men. Show me who else there is for him to use. He can only remake the world through men and women like each individual one of you in this great audience. *You* can decide to be one of those who are remaking the world for him. You simply don't know the creative forces that lie latent within you. And you simply don't know the ache of hunger that lies hidden in all men, even the worst, for a world of real peace and goodness. You doubt, perhaps, its presence in the very worst, but I say that it may be crushed down in them, and buried and seemingly forever lost, but it is there and capable of resuscitation. A hundred thousand conversions, in all ages and nations, of sinners into saints proves this. They have learned to long, as my dear friend here has said, for a hate-free world. But there is no other foundation for such a world than men and women like you, new-made.

'May I tell you how I, more than a dozen years ago, learned to listen to God, day by day, and discovered that he had a guiding plan for my life. I was so busy in those days that I had to have two telephones in my room. But my busy life so dissatisfied and disillusioned me—it might be busy but it seemed somehow empty —that I decided on a remarkable procedure—to give the hour between five and six in the morning, when the phones wouldn't ring, to waiting and listening for the still, small voice. And always —sooner or later—I knew what God wanted me to do. I wrote it down. Now there is no virtue about writing it down, but I have an abominable memory. It's like a rusty old sieve; everything goes through it and disappears, so I write it down. If you have a memory as adhesive as a fly-paper, you are lucky, but I am a stupid man, so I write down every thought that comes to me. The Chinese tell us that the strongest memory is weaker than the palest ink.'

At this point he paused in his speech and looked down upon somes notes on his table. The pause was so long that I suspected he was re-reading and meditating upon some thoughts he had written down that morning between five and six. While he paused, the same silence dominated every corner of the great hall. Whether his words were pleasing me or not, I could see that there could be no greater proof of his hold upon his people than this waiting, expectant silence.

When at last he spoke again he said many things that I did not like—though I continued to be mistrustful of my dislikes. He said that theirs was a battle for the soul of Britain and other nations and that he believed their crusade to be a force which was indeed the Body of Christ indwelt by the Holy Spirit—and at once I was angered that he should make for himself and his followers a claim which, in my view—or in my old view—could belong only to the Holy Catholic and Universal Church. As I remember that speech now, all of fifty years afterwards, I feel much sympathy with it, and no small pity for it. Pity because of the brilliant hope aglow within it. It was conceivable, he said, that if they all listened every day and obeyed what they heard, they might, even now, even today, usher in the greatest revolution of all time whereby the Cross of Christ would transform the world; conceivable that the world's statesmen might be 'changed' and the fear of war lifted from mankind; that mankind could abandon the old lie that human nature was unchangeable and learn that God was there to change it and the world's history; that he dared sometimes to believe that already the new era of peace was dawning before their eyes. . . .

But even as he spoke a leader of a German Worker's Party had completed in prison his testament, *Mein Kampf*, and, released from prison with it in his hand, was putting into action the terrible clauses in its Creed, while, further east, a 'Man of Steel' (Joseph Stalin), was battling for control of nine million square miles of the earth's surface under a reign of murdering terror.

§

The close of that long speech was something of an anti-climax. In tones no different from those in which he had declaimed his splendid hopes, and with no pause between the sublime and the humdrum, and no change in his position on that chair, he said, 'We will now have a collection in support of our work and I ask that in each and all of you it should be a matter of God-guided giving.' This was better than Gipsy Smith's, 'Now put your hands in your pockets' and I estimated that, whether or not it was a God-guided remark, it was subtler and would be more successful. Why, even I, though in some doubt about all I'd heard, felt guided to put a ten-shilling note in the bag . . . in case Frank should be right.

9

The Morning After

I have to admit that I came away from this God-guided meeting somewhat shaken in my doubts and dislikes of this new movement, and gravely wondering. Before we left the hall Perce insisted on introducing me, proudly, to some of the youths and girls who, like him, had been changed and were now Frank's most fervent supporters. Some of these were Oxford graduates or undergraduates, and I could see that Perce was proud to have them as friends. I could see too that they all believed they had found something real and true; that their lives were now different from what they had been perhaps only months or weeks before. Their lives were now enlarged, inspired, eager for action, exultant. And to be as exultant as this was to be radio-active; they shook me and left me wondering.

In the morning, alone with my thoughts, I walked up and down my room, between the desk and the divan, sometimes seated for a minute on the divan's brink, and then rising to wander again. I might be walking between desk and divan, but I was also walking between approbation and disapprobation. I had to resolve a conflict between the impression these exultant young people had made upon me and the doubts and the dissentience that still worried my head. As I walked the room or sat to meditate my head shook over these doubts. You might call it the morning's hangover after the spiritual carouse of the night before.

My prime criticism was that the good Dr Buchman's faith and methods were too facile and simple; they took no account of the great tidal waves of Biblical and historical criticism which had washed over the Christian world, coming so largely from Germany through Harnack and Bauer and the Tübingen school, whereas these vast tide-waters were the scene of my labours for the book I was striving to write. The Buchman attitude to the Bible seemed to be purely fundamentalist. Fundamentalist, or literally and uncritically accepting as inspired every word of the Scriptures; which was the very obverse of all I was thinking and writing. For me, it could not fit within the compass of any truly profound thought. In Dr Buchman's speech and the pamphlets which published his doctrine I could detect no heavy burden of study or of learning that would temper their easy revivalism.

Yet this was no final condemnation. If the supreme doctrine of Christianity was true, that Man's redemption was achieved by the passion of an Incarnate God, then those were fortunate indeed who could believe it as little children.

But I was no longer one of them, and could never again be one of them. Only after long research, much study and deep pondering could I accept and believe it all again.

Deep pondering. Pondering on this pondering, I saw and freely admitted that this Buchman propaganda had at least the roots of true religion in it. I had made fun of Perce's 'Q.T.'s' and his 'being changed', but what were these 'Quiet Times' but the old 'meditation' of the greatest saints; and what was this 'being changed' but their 'mortification' of an ego-centric life till it became Christocentric?

Yes; so far, so good; but this discipline of the 'Four Absolutes'? It was too easy—not too easy to obey—good God, no—but too easy to satisfy one's deeper thoughts. I had argued with Perce and his young friends that nothing was one-hundred-per-cent in this life; that there were no dead whites and dead blacks; and that accordingly there could be no 'absolutes' in the eyes of a philosopher. To this they had replied so promptly and unanimously that I guessed it to be the prescribed answer, 'If the standards are not absolute, sir, they are not standards', but I could only shake my head and say that this was no answer to the philosopher's problem; it just left it where it stood.

And here in my room this morning I was asking myself how was it possible to define 'absolute unselfishness'? One must believe in a large unselfishness—but 'absolute unselfishness'; what was it? Even Christ seemed to have allowed some element of self-love —'thou shalt love thy neighbour as thyself'—and if this was his summary how could you define 'absolute love'? And St Paul, who could be pretty vigorous in his demands, had written only, 'I say, through the grace given unto me, to every man that is among you, not to think of himself more highly than he ought to think, but to think soberly, according as God has dealt to every man the measure of faith.' Only so far could I go with the best of my intelligence—or was I evading something relentless but true?

And 'absolute purity'; where and when and how had it ever

been described, delimited and rendered possible? In Victorian times there had been many who said you should only play your full part in the matrimonial bed if you wanted to beget a child. Did many say that now? Or bawdry? The Victorians had condemned all bawdry but the Greeks had delighted in it without shame, and so had Shakespeare and most of the world's comedians, and so did I in their wake. A robust laughter over Man's problem in dealing with this powerful hunger implanted by God seemed to throw open a window and let in happy and health-giving breezes, with ever and anon a burst of gay sunshine.

This 'absolute purity', where was it to be located, since, throughout the ages, and among all races and religions, the norms of purity and chastity had so widely varied? I could see this new fundamentalist puritanism leading to a new puritan censorship (by a conventional, timid, and usually self-righteous minority) such as those which had hampered or persecuted Blake, Shelley, Tom Paine, Rousseau, Darwin, Hardy, and in this present time, Joyce and Lawrence and Shaw. Here was a real fear. For me 'the right of the writer to write' even the most unorthodox and disturbing thoughts was the foremost freedom of all, since by it alone could we defend all other freedoms.

No, these four 'absolutes' were extravagant expressions of splendid ideals, but they did not probe deep enough. Life was more difficult, more complex, and more mysterious than this.

So, in the end of that morning's long meditation, the scale went down—but not too easily—against the good doctor and his ardent disciples. Yet, even as it sank slowly and finally down, I recalled the violent hostility which Wesley with his Methodism had at first aroused—the Reverend and witty Sidney Smith, Canon of St Paul's, calling it 'this venom of Methodism'; and I reflected how so many new movements had aroused hate as well as love, the hate, as a rule, being greater than the love. And how, on the whole, the truer and more necessary the new calls, the more raging the abuse against them.

So things went that morning; and even today, more than fifty years after that first encounter with the so-called Oxford Group, fifty years during which I have stayed aside from its activities, I can wonder if my relief and pleasure, as I pronounced against it, had not, for their small half-brothers, a prejudice, a jealousy, and a fear of those absolute standards.

10

Before the Brightness Fell

Our two 'Bright Young Things', Siward and Terry, pursuing the transient brightness of these years, sought some of it now in Siward's new motor bicycle. This he bought second-hand from an ex-War Department store. It was a Sunbeam touring model, and he adapted the carrier and tool-bag at its rear into a pillion for Terry, whom he now called his pillionaire. He would kick this complicated structure (which he called 'Daphne') into a panting life and streak off along Elm Tree Road, between the towering and the tilting trees, with Terry astride on the pillion, her hands on his waist, her scarf flying like a flag, and her skirt in danger of flying over her knees. I saw them once racing down the High Street at a speed which set me wondering if they would return home alive. No one had yet thought of traffic lights, red, green and amber, to slow down or halt the cravers after speed. Nor had anyone thought of two winking orange lamps at zebra crossings to give pedestrians their chance to cross a highway and live. Siward was bending low over his handlebars like a racing driver and gazing, I thought, less into a safe traffic lane than into the bright eyes of danger. Terry's face, so far as I could see, was blithe and ready to smile, but perhaps touched with fear, as if she found it rather more difficult than Siward to gaze into those bewitching eyes.

And yet she seemed half-happy to be impetuously hurling herself towards their invitation.

When they reappeared, alive and happy in Christian Street, I chanced to be returning home too and I asked the overblown and dishevelled Terry, as she dismounted from the pillion, 'Isn't that a thoroughly uncomfortable and rather alarming means of locomotion?' She replied, 'No, it's heavenly. Why don't you get Siward to take you for a nice drive around London? I'll cheerfully give up my seat to you. All you'll have to do is to hold on tight to him.'

'No, thank you, my dear,' I said. 'I've an instinct for survival.'

'You'll survive all right. Siward's a terrific driver.'

'You've said it,' I told her; ' "Terrific's" the word.'

If Siward in his hours of freedom was not on this machine he was, as likely as not, crouching on the pavement beside it with rags, pail and polishes, making it as resplendent as possible. Almost always he consecrated Sunday mornings to these secular devotions, and we would come out of the gates, one after another, and tell him he ought to be in church.

'Surely,' I offered one day, coming out for church, 'it would be better to polish up your soul a bit instead of that far less worthy object.'

'Sure it would,' he retorted promptly, 'if only you can find me a suitable polish. There ain't any. Not for me. So I'm limited to beautifying Daphne. And anyhow she's a most worthy and lovely object.'

But Daphne's day as Siward's mistress was soon ended. She was jilted for a later love whom he called Deirdre.

A little before this time, Lt-Col Sir Herbert Austin, Chairman of Austin Motor Company, Ltd, had been vouchsafed a vision. In it he had seen, dimly at first, and then more clearly, a car: a car so small that it could yet hold four passengers; a car so cheap that it would be within the means of the less pecunious or of young married couples. He designed and produced it in large numbers, and so popular was it that his output could hardly keep pace with the demand. It was known everywhere as the 'Baby Austin', the smallest and cheapest car in the world.

Little wonder that Daphne was betrayed, sold to the first easy buyer; and Siward's love, and Terry's too, was for the new Baby Austin usually standing against the kerb in front of our windows or being burnished there by both Siward and Terry on Sunday mornings. One of their habits now was to set off with other young people on midnight treasure-hunts. The hunters were given a catalogue of foolish objects, that lay hidden here and there in the neighbourhood, which they must find between midnight and two in the morning; and of clues, planted here and there, which would direct them from point to point towards the place of final assembly. In the exercise of this sport they would roar through the night, disturbing the sleep of the more sensible with raised voices and the banging of car doors. Siward and Terry played their part in many of these hunts till Miryam, instructed

83

by Jane Julia, complained of their 2 a.m. noises within and without her house. They promised 'to be creepy-crawly' in the future, but she would have none of it. 'No, go to bed at a reasonable hour like good children,' she said; and they with sorrow, but with sympathy and understanding, abandoned the delightful pastime.

This pursuit of gaiety by the well-to-do young was but a superficial gloss on these post-war years; beneath the glossy surface lay ugly things smouldering for an explosion. In the industrial north grey slum-dwellings still overspread a once beautiful land, acres and acres of drear terraced homes, with back-to-back walls, low slate roofs, and an endless procession of stunted chimneystacks; four-roomed homes with perhaps a proliferating family in each room. And half of these families, or more than half, unemployed. The country's Prime Minister, a fortnight after the war's end, had delivered himself of his historic remark, 'What is our task? It is to make Britain a fit country for heroes to live in'; but seven years had passed and what had been done, Siward would ask me, for the heroes returning from the war? 'Nothing. Less than nothing.' The old methods of greed and getting and Devil take the hindmost had been allowed to take over the country's economy again, and the heroes were left to make the best of it, the stronger, such as Siward, finding what work they could, the weaker going to the wall and slouching there with the unemployed. It was a world of inhuman factories and workshops where only a labourer's home struggled to be human.

The coal mines were running at a loss of many millions, and the coal-owners were insisting that the only feasible plan was to reduce the miners' wages and increase their hours of work. But the miners had a leader, a Mr Cook, who understood the magic of words, and he answered this demand with a simple sentence, 'Not a penny off the pay, not a minute on the day.' So the owners gave notice that the current agreements would end in a month's time, and if by that time, the miners were still unhelpful, their lesson would be a lock-out.

The Government, after declining at first to help either owners or miners, panicked on the vigil of the lock-out and promised a subsidy that would hold wages at their present level for nine months during which a Royal Commission would parley on the matter. The nine months elapsed, the Royal Commission proposed various plans for the future but accepted for the meantime, 'since disaster was impending over the coalfields', a reduction of wages.

Only to be met by Mr Cook's, 'Not a penny off the pay, not a minute on the day' and by an even simpler and briefer answer from the miners' president who, when asked what his men would do to help the owners, replied, 'Nowt.'

Siward, passionately on the side of the miners, came rushing to me, as the only person in the house likely to sympathise, and he read to me Mr Cook's more detailed exposition : 'Our case is simple. We ask for safety and economic security. Today up and down our coalfields the miner and his family are faced by sheer starvation. He is desperate. He will not, he cannot, stand present conditions much longer. He would be a traitor to his wife and children if he did. Until he is given safety in the mines, adequate compensation, hours of labour that do not make him a mere coal-getting medium, and decent living conditions, there can be no peace in the British coalfields.'

'Nowt.' The owners used, of course, a more gentlemanly language, which amounted, however, to the same. The miners were locked out. But all their brothers in other unions came to their support, and at a midnight in May all the smouldering stuff beneath the gaiety of the Twenties blazed into the General Strike.

And in the morning a strange quiet brooded over the whole country. The mines, the factories, the railways, the buses, the docks, the mills, the great machines, the power-stations, the news-presses—all were silent and still.

§

Our little company round Miryam's board was, I imagine, a fair microcosm of the whole country in its attitudes to the Strike. Miryam, Jane Julia, and Uncle Willy had nothing but condemnation for the strikers; Hyacinth was their faithful echo; and Hetty McGee fluttered between two opinions as one or another of us argued. So did Perce Bywater. And Emmeline with our plates. I too was in some state of conflict, believing that the miners had an overwhelming right to our pity and support, and that there was something magnificent in the rallying to their help of all their brothers in other industries, but believing also that a strike on such a scale came close to being a revolution against the

State, and that it would have to be quelled by the State. Siward was on the side of all the strikers—or wanting to be—and Terry was just silent, pleading inability to understand. 'I only know that my heart bleeds for the miners . . . poor darlings. But it doesn't bleed in the same way for some of the others. At least, I don't think it does.'

I remember especially one evening round the board when the battle between State and strikers was about three days old. Uncle Willy was carving a sirloin on the side-board. Resolving to be jolly in spite of strikes and the threat of revolution, he made his usual and too often repeated joke, giving an accolade to the joint by touching it with his carving knife and saying, 'Rise, Sir Loin'— while Emmeline waited for the portions to carry around.

Jane Julia was in no mood for jollity. Indignant with Siward (whom she called to others 'a socialist puppy') she was obviously aching to provoke him. She opened fire with, 'I hope, Mr Bartleby, that like everyone else you're going to use your precious new car to help people to get to their offices—those who are still kind enough to work.'

Terry looked up, alarmed. I could see that she was afraid some uncomfortable rudeness would develop between her husband and Jane Julia. But Siward, to my surprise, was tactful and courteous. He retorted with no similar provocation. He didn't tell her he was using his little car in the evenings to help the Trades Union Council get their messengers around, with a sticker on its wind-screen 'T.U.C.' for its protection. He said only, and quietly, 'No, Mrs Pemberton, I'll do nothing to break the Strike.'

Jane Julia went silent, but it was a silence loaded to cracking point with antagonism. Uncle Willy was not silent. Leaving the joint and Emmeline and his carving knife on one side, he turned toward Siward and said, 'The Strike has just *got* to be broken, Siward, old boy. It's nothing less than a declaration of war against the Government. If the question is, Shall our country be governed by Parliament with all its faults or by the T.U.C. Congress in Eccleston Square, or wherever it is they live, I know what my answer is.'

'*Hear, hear*,' cried Jane Julia, in italics; and Emmeline, still waiting, offered, 'Yes, I reckon the Master's just about right, I do, reely. We don't want no revolutions. I mean to say!'

'Of course I'm right,' said Willy, returning to the sirloin. 'This strike is nothing less than a pistol at the head of our whole constitution.'

Siward, still temperate and quiet, replied only, 'It's at least arguable that it was the Government who declared war on the T.U.C. It was they who broke off all negotiations because a few compositors, without the authority of their union, refused to print anything hostile to the Strike.'

'And quite right too,' said Willy, while we still waited for our beef. 'It was necessary to teach the whole of Fleet Street a sharp lesson. It's an editor's responsibility to decide what goes into a paper, not his compositors.'

'True enough.' Siward remained studiously amiable. 'I don't support what the compositors tried to do, but it's a small matter compared with the piteous state of the miners and the refusal of the Government to stop the owners from reducing their wages that are low enough already——'

'They can't run their mines at a loss,' Willy put in, carving away at the joint, while Emmeline served us with our slices.

'Of course they can't,' came from the smouldering Jane Julia, who was plainly restless to flame into words but could not think of the right ones.

'No,' Siward agreed. 'They can't run their mines at a loss, nor can they run them by making underpaid and overworked men pay them a subsidy and work harder.'

'There's something in that,' Emmeline accepted as she served me. 'Yurse, I see what you mean. I see something in that.'

And Siward, encouraged, ran on, 'Do any of us really think what the miner's job is—digging deep down under the earth or the sea at a coal-face and accepting the danger of death down there, so that we can sit comfortably round a fire? Even my old man used to say—and he was a red-hot Tory—"There's blood on our coal." '

'And that was pretty sentimental twaddle, if you'll forgive me, Siward, old boy,' Willy objected. 'What about soldiers and sailors? Isn't there blood on their uniforms?'

'Just so,' from Jane Julia, fervently. Willy was providing her with words.

'Yes, what about soldiers and sailors?' Siward seized on the point triumphantly, though I couldn't see how he would use it. 'But firstly,' he began, 'don't you think it's wonderful the way the other great unions, to a man, have come out in support of their brothers in the mines? There's nothing in this strike for them; only loss. They're asking nothing for themselves, and I'm sure they're not the least interested in overthrowing the State; they are only seeking a fair deal for the miners. To me it's a staggering example of universal brotherhood, perhaps the most wonderful the world——'

But Jane Julia had found some words for herself. 'A staggering example of rebellious behaviour by wicked men who care only for themselves——'

'All right . . . let me finish . . . "wicked men".' Siward's request to be allowed to finish was as polite as before. 'You say they are bad men. But yesterday they were fighting for you as soldiers and sailors, and then, as now, they were asking nothing for themselves, unless it was death. Only something for us all. You called them good men then. You——'

'Leave it, Siward,' Terry murmured, fearing a quarrel.

But Siward persisted, maintaining the same unangered and friendly tones. 'You called them heroes and said the country must try to be worthy of them—and, incidentally, nobody did anything about *that*. These are the same men; they were good then; and they are good chaps now.'

His voice had broken as he spoke these last words, and I saw that he had nearly moved himself to tears. He had to repeat them. 'They are still good chaps.' And to add, 'Not wicked.'

Though I could not fully agree with his attitude to this frightening strike and inclined—not too willingly—to the attitude of all the others that it had *got* to be defeated, I yet preferred Siward's manner and deportment to any of theirs—unless it was Emmeline's. It was possible, of course, that his polite and temperate speech might be partly determined by a desire not to offend his hostess and lose a home that suited him well; but nonetheless I could see a deep sincerity behind his words mixed with the strong desire of an intelligent young man not to lose self-control and, as he would have put it, 'let fly'. He felt driven to repeat quietly, 'They stood by their country then, and they're standing by their brothers now.'

Jane Julia had no intention of appreciating the sincerity or of approving the self-control. 'Brothers!' she exclaimed. 'A lot of loafers who won't work are no brothers to me.'

This brought Siward to the edge of rancour, but he still covered his words with a smile so that they might not hurt. His words were, 'And don't you think, Mrs Pemberton, it's just possible this may be because you won't be a sister to them unless they're fighting for you or for what you believe in?'

'Siward,' Terry begged. 'Please.'

But before I could stop myself, I had applauded his question with, 'Bravo, Siward. Excellent'; and so lost the goodwill of Jane Julia for three or four weeks.

§

As a servant of the British Broadcasting Company Siward was quickly able to recover the goodwill of Miryam, Willy, and, in their wake, Hyacinth (though not so quickly Jane Julia's) because all the daily newspapers were temporarily dead and, apart from an official news-sheet, *The British Gazette,* published by the Government under the editorship of Mr Winston Churchill, Siward's Broadcasting Company was the one full and strongly flowing, ever mounting, stream of information about the Strike. And of all in that house he alone possessed a wireless set. He told us proudly, 'We've been permitted to broadcast news, not just in the evening, but in the middle of the morning and at lunch time and tea time, as well as twice in the evening. We reckon we have already about two million listeners and that over this little business we shall soon have ten million. And we'll be a good deal more impartial than old Churchill's *Gazette*—' not his most conciliatory remark. 'Old Churchill glories in being completely partial. He says, "It's impossible to be impartial as between fire-brigade and fire".'

'Quite right too,' grumbled Jane Julia. 'A typically wise and witty remark.'

'Yes, but equally you might say it's impossible to be impartial between the hose-water and the fire.'

'And pray what would that mean?'

'It means, according to our Chief, that the only hose-water that'll deal with the fire is the truth. That's why he's quite determined we'll be as independent of the Government as any newspaper is, and tell you all that's happening and not only what the Government thinks it's good for you to know.'

'Splendid,' said I.

'Yes, and he says that if people aren't told everything frankly, they'll believe every horrible rumour that's going the rounds; and rumour, he says, can be far more dangerous than the truth. They must trust us to have told all, and then they'll stay steady.'

'And he's perfectly right,' I said, partly to make clear my opposition to Jane Julia, with whom my relations were still wanting in mutual acclaim.

'So if you desire to hear the truth, any of you,' continued Siward, 'come up to our room whenever you like. If I'm not there, Terry'll turn it on for you. No, I think I'll instruct Hugh how to do it. It's man's work. Terry usually gets only a lot of frightful noises instead of London. And, by the way, bring any neighbours you like.'

So we would go often into their room and hear how Hyde Park was closed so that it could act as a dump for milk and food stocks brought there by lorries with an escort of armoured cars; how troops were standing by to help the police deal with any rioting; how trains were being driven by willing amateurs who'd always wanted to be engine drivers; how buses were crewed by amateurs with perhaps a copper or a soldier at the conductor's side after some of them had been overturned in the angry dockland area; and how an army of special constables had been enlisted, mostly foot constables, but some of them mounted on their own horses with long menacing staves in holsters or their hands, instead of hidden truncheons.

Nine days, only nine days, and the Strike was over. It faded out as quickly at it had bloomed. The T.U.C. surrendered unconditionally as *The British Gazette* had been barking and baying for it to do. Those who all along had been hostile to Strike and strikers warmly maintained that it had collapsed only because of a speech in Parliament affirming that a strike of this magnitude was illegal and therefore its leaders could be sued for condign damages and even perhaps arrested.

But Siward would have none of this. He declared that the leaders had been doubtful from the first about its success; the forces which the Government could mount being far too great. The Strike was over and the miners stayed locked out. Locked out for another six months till they too were driven by starvation into unconditional surrender. 'Yes,' said Siward, 'the coal-owners have won this battle, but they've lost their war at the same time. Labour is bound to come to power one day, and the whole

T.U.C. will see to it that the mines are taken over by the Government as a nationalised industry. Then Jane Julia's beloved and supremely innocent coal-owners will be no more. They've sentenced themselves to death.'

§

Another advantage which Siward enjoyed as one employed and rising fast in the B.B.C.'s 'Programme Output' was his knowledge of news which at present was of too small import to be suited to the news-room or the talks department. But it was now the year 1927, and among these unpublished items were the early symptoms of the Great Depression which would hit the world like a pandemic in the last year of the Twenties and the first years of the Thirties. Great American corporations, already hit, were importing less of Britain's products and making less use of British ships. The markets of the world were beginning to shrink. As yet little of this had invaded the minds of the general public. Wages remained steady and, since the prices of imports were falling, those in work were better off than before and believed that the bright prosperities of the post-war years were still around them.

Not so Siward. He would come often to my room and talk to me about the likely depression, quoting more than once a favourite line of poetry, 'Brightness falls from the air'. He was a routine quoter of favourite lines, and this was another reason why he liked to come and talk with me. He knew it would be difficult to quote any verse which I couldn't continue with him, because I loved it as much as he. And who else in the house, he would say, could do this? Could you imagine Miryam or Perce or Pemberton—or Hetty McGee, unless it was traditional Shakespeare—who would know these lines or rise to them as I would? 'Uncle Willy ought to know them, but can you imagine him caring a damn about them now? He may have got a good degree, but I don't think he reads now anything but Beatrix Potter.' Siward even sometimes could be—not impatient, but surprised and disappointed—with Terry if she'd never heard them, but of course her education, as a girl, had been less prolonged and complete than his. And at any rate she rose to them with proper, and even perhaps a characteristically extravagant fervour.

One evening I was in their room listening to a programme of dance music. Siward had insisted that I must come. 'If you want to make this old book of yours an up-to-date affair instead of antediluvian Victorian stuff,' he had said, 'you should get in touch with youth.' So there we were : I on their one easy chair; Terry, as so often, sitting on the carpet before the mild gas-fire with her legs tucked under her; and Siward, supposed to be sitting on the bed, but frequently getting up to retune his set and standing beside it to make sure it was tuned aright. Strange to remember that this was the first time I'd ever listened to the bewailing of a saxophone against a background of rhythmic noises from other instruments which I could not identify, apart from a piano bang-ing and a drum or drums beating, rolling, chattering. A vocalist broke in at intervals with the words of the ditty. His voice was a fine baritone, and could have been put to better use, for he kept it sad, drawling, and usually loitering half a breath behind the notes of the band. To shock and amuse me, Siward used the language of the dance bands. 'That's Sam MacCreary. He takes care of the vocals.'

'Good God !' I said, dismayed by such terms and providing Siward with the reaction he desired.

Of Sam's vocals that evening I recall amongst others, 'Bye, bye, blackbird', 'When the red, red robin comes bob, bob bobbing along', 'My heart stood still', and 'I ask you very confidentially, "Ain't she sweet?"'.

It was when Sam was taking care of one appalling vocal that Siward, worked up by my uncertain approval, turned to Terry and exclaimed as if inspired, 'Terry, my heart's delight, we must get him to a night-club. He just sits upstairs there—' here he pointed through the ceiling— 'and creates a huge theological book that I'm sure is much too heavy. He'd write it better if he saw more of life.'

Terry said, 'Oh, yes, *yes*. Of course he must come. And dance with me. I'd love to dance with Hugh.'

'Almost thou persuadest me to come, Siward,' I said, quoting in my turn; 'if Terry'll dance with me.'

'Hurray,' Siward cried. 'And I'll certainly lend you Terry for a dance or two. Usually we dance only with the partner we've brought, but you shall have Terry once or twice. Or—better still—tell you what—I'll get you a girl of your own. You're sup-posed to bring a partner. A few dances with Terry, and all the rest with your own girl.'

'Oh, no,' I objected. 'No, children, please, *please*. I can't do your horrible dances. I don't know them.'

'That doesn't matter. All you've got to do is to hold her tight and slither around to the music. That's all a fox-trot is. She'll be quite satisfied if you talk nicely to her as you slither, and swing her violently about once or twice. I know, Terry: it's Dorothy; we'll get Dorothy for him.'

'Who's Dorothy?' I asked, becoming ever more apprehensive.

'Dorothy Cotteril. Exactly right for you. She's dazzlingly brilliant; the most brilliant product of her day at Roedean and Somerville. An M.A. and a Fellow of Somerville and God-knows-what-else. Fellow of her college just like you. Why, you'll be like two love-birds. You can talk classics or Sanskrit or Old English Literature or God-know-what-all as you swing her about, and she'll know as much as you on any subject and enjoy it all as much as you.'

'You're only terrifying me more and more, Siward.'

'You won't be terrified when you see her. Besides being brilliant, she's the easiest thing on the eye you'll have encountered for many a long day. Isn't she, Terry?'

Terry, that vessel of urgent ecstasies, went even further in her superlatives. 'She's absolutely lovely, Hugh. The loveliest thing I've ever seen. The last word in red-heads. I could sit and stare at her for ever. Mostly in envy.'

'*You've* no occasion to be envious of anyone.' The words gave me as much pleasure in the speaking of them as she in the hearing of them. She rewarded me with, 'Isn't Hugh an absolute peach sometimes, Siward? But you haven't seen her yet, Hugh darling. Wait till you do.'

'I can hardly wait.'

Meanwhile Siward was saying, 'Yes, it's extraordinary to have such brains and such beauty too. She's only twenty-three and she's already an Assistant Principal at the Home Office——'

'And I'm twenty-three too,' Terry lamented, 'and nobody'd think of making me an Assistant Principal—whatever that is. But then I've no brains worth speaking of. And I'm not as beautiful as she is.'

'Then, Terry,' I said, 'she must be beyond imagination beautiful.'

'Darling Hugh! He always finds the perfect answer. Siward,

93

why don't you say lovely things like that more often?'

But Siward wasn't listening to her. Inspired again, he said, 'Tell you what, Terry beloved. . . . Of course, of course! He shall come to Mother Meyrick's. To the Forty-Three.'

'The Forty-Three?' I begged elucidation.

'Yes. The Forty-Three Club. At 43 Gerrard Street, Soho. Mother Meyrick's most famous night-club of all. Used to be Dryden's home.'

'And who's Mother Meyrick?'

'You don't know Mother Meyrick? Thought all the world knew Kate Meyrick. She has several night-clubs but the Forty-Three's her pride and joy. Surely you've read about her? She's been up before the beaks again and again. And she's just done her half-stretch in Holloway.'

'Please, what's a half-stretch?'

'God save us, Theresa, honey-sweet, he knows nothing. And sits there writing books. A half-stretch is six-months' bird.'

'Bird?'

'Quod. Clink. Cooler. Jug. Sometimes called Stir. By the best people.'

'And Holloway's a prison for women, isn't it?'

'Got it right first time. A House of Correction for the girls. Ladies only.'

'But isn't a sentence to prison damaging to her club?'

'Not a bit. Good publicity. Brings the people in. You'll see heaps of famous people there : artists, actors, authors, prize-fighters. You might even see royalty. The Prince of Wales has been seen at one of her clubs. And you may well see Prince Nicholas of Rumania, with his girl. Katie quite likes having her clubs raided by the cops. Maybe the old Forty-Three'll be raided when you come. That'd suit her fine : having a parson arrested.'

'Well, it may be good publicity for her, but it wouldn't help the book I'm writing. Not the slightest.'

'Oh, I don't see that. It might make people think you're human.'

'Siward, this is a serious theological work. It will not be addressed to frivolous children like you. My arrest at some notorious night-club wouldn't help it at all.'

'But your Eminence won't be arrested. We'd get you out through a window. There are windows and doors conveniently behind the stage through which people escape into a back-yard. While the band goes on playing.'

'I'm not going through any window. I should leave all hope for my book on the stage behind me. With the band.'

Comfort came from Terry, seated on the floor. 'You're not going through any window, Hugh darling. He's only trying to be funny. You must come. You've promised to dance with me.'

'Well, I'll come, if only to see a home that was Dryden's. Not that I think his fame as one of our greatest poets can be sustained, but as a satiric verse writer he's unsurpassed, and I see him as the first great prose-writer in modern idioms.'

'Listen to him, Terry. That's just the sort of stuff he can unload on to Dorothy as he swings her around. She'll love it. She'll eat it.'

'But he mustn't be more interested in his old Dryden than in dancing with me.'

'No fear of that,' I answered. 'That'll be tops.'

And Siward exclaimed, 'God save us! He's coming on. He's getting the language right. "Tops", look you! The Forty-Three it shall be. With Dorothy Cotteril. Between you and me, friends, unless I'm much mistaken, things in a year or two aren't going to be as bright as they have been in this country or anywhere else. So let us be jolly while we can. Trouble's brewing fast'; and he began to quote : ' "Brightness falls from the air. . . ." '

The Forty-Three

We went from Christian Street to 43 Gerrard Street in the Baby
Austin, Siward putting me in the front seat with the assertion,
'There'll be room for your long legs there,' a too sanguine assess-
ment. On our way there through the early night, at some illegal
speed, we fetched Dorothy Cotteril from a Ladies' Residential
Club in Queen Anne's Gate. I was curious to see her after Terry's
rhapsodies, but what with the half-dark and the scarf around her
head, it was not easy to see if her beauty was really remarkable.
It was curious also to see Gerrard Street in the first of the dark,
because it might be in the City of Westminster but I knew that
its pavements, together with the pavements of its neighbouring
streets, Wardour Street, Lisle Street, Newport Place, and the
Soho streets across Shaftesbury Avenue were favourite hunting
grounds of London's prostitutes, with Gerrard Street perhaps
the best favoured pavement of all. Now we were in the street,
and I looked at the odd grey mixture of eighteenth-century,
Regency, and early Victorian houses, once the homes of the
wealthy and the highly respected but now, as I knew, many of
them were seedy brothels. Some had cards or stickers in their
windows, advertising 'Tall Show Girl seeks Part Time Employ-
ment', 'Fair Girl gives French Tuition', 'Beautiful Art Student
seeks interesting work'; and other such covert parables of the
underworld. On the roofs, the cornices and the chimney-stacks
of these dubious houses, the starlings were addressing the first of
the dark with a medley of noises : chucklings, chatterings, hiss-
ings and other mimicries. Beneath their gregarious gabble a man
entered, now and then, somewhat secretively and ashamed,
through the narrow open door of one of these old-time houses.
Or the narrow door was opened by a woman to the uneasy ring
of a bell by a man glancing to left or right over his shoulder. Evil,
unashamed, welcoming furtive lust. But it was a fine evening and
several of the 'ladies of the town' were walking up and down
the pavement or loitering in the doorways of blinded shops or

standing in a good tactical position at the two corners of Wardour Street. It surprised me that, here and there, they pursued their calling in pairs. Evidently they, for the most part, knew and perhaps helped each other. Appropriately or not, round the corner of Wardour Street, a piano organ was jangling a tune for these haunts of stealthy pleasure.

All this I was able to see because our Baby Austin was halted by a huge articulated lorry twelve times its size. Whether my rapt interest in it all could have been condemned as prurient I remain unsure; it still seems natural and inevitable. Anyway, there it was.

And now our car was halted before 43, Dryden's old home. It seemed a large mansion for a poet and writer who had to struggle against indigence during the later years of his life. Looking up at the plaque, 'John Dryden, poet, lived here. B. 1631, D. 1700,' I remembered how he must have once returned to this house battered and bleeding, after being cudgelled in Rose Alley by a gang of roughs engaged, so it was rumoured, by the Earl of Rochester who imagined Dryden had libelled him in a satirical poem. He must have staggered to this door at about this time of night because he'd been returning home from his favourite recreation of an evening in Will's Coffee House in Covent Garden. As I dwelt on this old memory Siward was locking and leaving the Baby Austin by the kerb, so small it was and untroublesome in those easier days. Then there was talk between Siward and the door-keeper, and two other men who had to be fetched from somewhere. Cash passed between them, and Siward told me directly we were within doors, 'I had to sign on Dorothy and you as members of the Forty-Three and get those blokes who'd never seen or heard of you to act as witnesses. Sponsors to your excellent characters, I suppose. So don't think you're getting this night's entertainment for nothing. The place is a den of thieves.'

While this legal, or semi-legal, business had been transacted I had been staring at the large ground-floor room before me. Had it perhaps been the old poet's writing room? I could imagine him seated at a desk beating on its top as he struggled to dredge up words from the richest language in the world. Perhaps in his struggle he sometimes got up and wandered around the room as I so often did in my upper chamber, casting and casting my line into this vast Mississippi of words.

We had to go down a steep stairway to come upon the dancing-floor of the Forty-Three. This basement area was nearly as spacious as our parish hall. Many people sat on chairs aligned against the walls while others were dancing on a shining floor to the turbulent music of a band on a stage at the room's far end; an orchestra of piano, clarinet, banjoes, drums and, of course, the saxophone, master of all with its whining melancholy. Through an aperture behind the stage, I could see what looked like glass conservatory windows, and Siward, following my gaze, said, 'That's the escape route. The cops have to get through the doors and down those steep stairs, and then past the orchestra on the stage, which takes time—for the band's still playing heartily—so you can generally get away.'

'I see,' I said. 'Thank you.'

'Don't mention it,' he begged modestly and helpfully.

I went to a chair but he would not allow this. 'Oh, no,' he expostulated. 'Take your Dorothy around. She's come here to dance, or, rather, you've brought her here to dance as your partner. I mean, go and see the book upstairs.'

'But I'm terrified of her,' I submitted.

'Terrified? Why?'

'I don't know, but I'm sure she's as tough as hell. Look, lend me your Terry first so that she can teach me a few steps.'

'You don't need any steps, as I told you. You've only to go skating around, and whisking her about, more or less in any way you like. The wilder the better.'

'All the same, I'd rather start with Terry. I'm not afraid of her.'

'Okay. Go on, Terry sweet. Start him really going. Work him up.'

Till this hour in 43 Gerrard Street, I, a bachelor student and writer, becoming ever more something of a happy hermit (to say nothing of my investment in Holy Orders) had long been without interest in dancing, and so without experience of these post-war dances, save those I'd seen performed by Siward and Terry in their room for our instruction; and I must confess to a surprise and some pleasure when Terry in my arms hugged me tighter than ever girl had held me before, her breast close against mine, her head at rest on my shoulder, and her face often looking up affectionately into mine, for I was much taller than she. I could not doubt the affection; there was a little more than mere custom in this tight embrace; she was holding me as possessively as I had seen her hold Siward in their room that evening, years ago. To such affection I could only feel a tender response and, Holy Orders or not, I could not deny the physical pleasure. She was an excellent dancer, and I soon found myself dancing easily too. I learned then how all expert dancers, male or female, can flatter the dancing of their partners. No difficult waltzing here; this fox-trot or jog-trot or one-step or shimmy or whatever it might be that she was teaching me, she made as easy as our mutual laughter.

'Why, you're dancing beautifully,' she said. 'But hold me tight. Don't be worried about holding me tight.'

'Worried. I haven't enjoyed anything so much for ages.'

Whereat she squeezed me yet tighter in gratitude and dimly I remembered Miryam and Jane Julia, with Hyacinth for their dutiful echo, commenting, 'I don't think it's quite nice. I can't pretend to think it's nice.'

Whether or not it was nice to watchers of an older day, I couldn't pretend that I wasn't finding it very nice indeed. The ex-curate in me was in some doubt about this pleasure.

When Terry, as mistress of the situation, led me by the hand back to Siward and Dorothy on their chairs, she said, 'But he's magnificent. I strongly suspect, if the truth's known, that he's been doing it all his life. Or else he's a born dancer. Dorothy ducks, I envy you your partner for tonight.'

'Don't trust her, Miss Cotteril, she's a——' I began, but Terry intervened, 'For the Lord's sake don't call her "Miss Cotteril". What world is he living in? She's our Dorothy.'

'Don't trust her, Dorothy. She's a horrible little liar. I did no more than copy her in everything she did.'

'But one can be an *inspired* copier,' Terry argued. 'You were, Hugh darling. Go on. Take Dorothy. I want to see you dancing with her. She's a better dancer than I am. But then, she's better than me in everything. I'm absolutely nothing.'

Extending my hands towards Dorothy, I asked her in the old fashion of my schooldays, 'May I have the pleasure . . .'

And it promised to be a pleasure. Here in the bright lights I was seeing this Dorothy Cotteril properly, and she was beautiful. Tall and beautiful. Siward and Terry might have exaggerated her beauty, but it was not possible greatly to exaggerate it. Terry had called her 'The last word in red-heads', but I would have called her hair the colour of an autumn leaf. She must have abandoned the bob and the shingle if ever she had followed these fashions; now she was allowing the burnished hair, wavy and full, to be parted in the middle and grow down to her shoulders—in a fashion almost universal forty years later. In the same way she had abandoned the knee-length dresses and was wearing a long full evening gown of a red-gold tint, manifestly designed to carry all eyes to the fox-red amber of her hair. I doubt if one man in a hundred notices the colour of a woman's eyes; and I could not state the colour of hers to this day; I only know that they were large, wide-spaced, long-lashed and often glittering. If I cannot tell you the colour of her eyes, I can affirm that, as I was admiring the shape of her small hands, I saw with amazement that their nails, studiously pointed, were varnished a bright red. This was something I had never seen before on girl or woman; and indeed it was only just becoming a fashion among the sophisticated. I had heard it mentioned once at our dining-table, when Jane Julia said it was disgusting, and Uncle Willy promptly countered that it had been a habit for a few thousand years among the ladies of Ancient Egypt. Nevertheless, as I had never lived in the times of the Pharaohs, it was not less new to me; and it was the one thing I didn't admire about Dorothy. I would even say it worried me.

I had not danced with her twice round the room before accepting that Terry had been no liar on this occasion : Dorothy was an even better dancer than she. And because she was even better than Terry, so was I better than ever; the inspired copier was yet more inspired. I began to be pleased with and proud of my dancing.

'Terry's right,' said Dorothy. 'You're a natural dancer.'

'Nothing of the kind. But I've learned tonight that it's impossible to dance badly with a perfect partner.'

She smiled up into my face. 'Yes, Terry told me you were a gifted flatterer.'

'I'm no flatterer at all. Merely one who tries to deal in truths.'

At that point the lights dimmed and we were dancing in a darkness that wanted only a few more degrees to become complete. There appeared to be no lights in the hall except a few coloured lamps on the ceiling and the illuminations among the bandsmen on the stage, who seized upon this sentimental moony darkness to play more excitedly and tumultuously than before.

Soon my eyes became used to the dark and I was seeing like a cat.
I have always remembered that it was while the band was thus
assaulting the dark with its bangings and drummings and dron-
ings, and the saxophone was bellowing forth its latest despon-
dency—its *tedium vitae,* as I suggested to my partner, swinging
her round and round or varying our dance with a walking step—
that it was then, of all moments, that we found ourselves deep in
a theological and ecclesiastical debate, our feet at lively and
ludicrous issue with the words from our lips. Not for this had
Mrs Kate Meyrick created her dancing clubs. Not for this had
the electrician dimmed the lights. Not for this was the riotous
band playing an accompaniment. Not to disturb this did police
come sometimes raiding.

Dorothy began it. 'It fascinates me, Hugh—may I call you
that?—how anyone can swallow all the stuff that Terry tells me
you still believe in.'

'Such stuff as?'

'Well, belief in a God who's all benevolence.'

'I certainly believe in that.'

'And you're still a parson?'

'Of sorts.'

'But I can't understand it. You with your fine degree and a
Fellow of All Souls.'

'No, only a fellow of my college. Like you.'

'Forgive me, but to me it seems extraordinary for someone of
your age and intelligence to be still worrying about this sort of
thing. I settled it all for myself before I was nineteen.'

'Then I'm sorry for you.'

'And why?'

'These things are not solved by children. Unless you accept
them on authority, which I'm very sure *you* don't.'

'I certainly don't.'

'Have you met Perce Bywater?'

'No. Who on earth is he?'

'One of our guests at Auntie Miryam's. He said to me much
what you're saying, and I tried to show him how unintelligent it
was and how sorry I was for him. And, by the way, he was then
an out-and-out atheist and he is now a white-hot gospeller in the
tracks of Dr Buchman. I was sorry for him, and I'm sorry for you,
and now I'm sorry for myself, because I'm no longer lost in admira-

tion for you. Which is a pity because I was enjoying it.'

'Marvellous your gift for making really rude things sound flattering.'

'One's never rude to highly intelligent people who can take truth.'

'There you are! Done it again. Thank you very much.'

'Not at all. Merely truth.'

For this I received, not a rebuke, but a grateful squeeze. 'But, Hugh, is it un-intellectual to look upon your kind of faith as a purely emotional need?'

'Certainly. Of course. Because for me, while it may meet an emotional need, it's far more surely an intellectual need.'

'*Intellectual?*'

'Yes. And I'm not the first fellow of his college, Dorothy dear —if I may call you that—who has believed in all I believe in— and, indeed, in rather more than I fully believe at present. I am more likely the nine-hundred-and-ninety-ninth.'

'Yes, that's what beats me. I thought that all that sort of thing was more or less dead in this day when civilised man has really grown up.'

'Dead for many now, certainly.'

'But not for you?' She looked up with a mischievous smile.

'Only in parts. In a few parts maybe. But I strongly suspect and hope that these parts may not be dead but only sleeping.'

'It still beats me. Do go on and tell me how you manage to believe it all.'

'Oh, *sorry*!' Lost in this fascinating discussion, and in the dim-lit dark, I had bumped her into another revolving couple, to whom I apologised, receiving the answer, 'Don't mention it. Nothing to worry about,' as they swung away.

'You were going to explain. Never mind a bump or two.'

'Very well. Consider: you're extremely beautiful and intelligent—' rewarded by a squeeze—'and I can find no sense in thinking you were created by a series of blind, unpurposed accidents. I need an intellectual base for your intelligence. And, indeed, for your beauty.'

'Thank you.' A second squeeze. It could only be defined as a sexual hug, but we went on with our theology. 'So it needed the creator of all the stars in heaven to create me?'

'Nothing less.'

'And that goes for Siward and Terry?'

'As I have told them. And even for me and my thoughts. And still more—far more—for those who are very different from us.'

'Who?'

'All the truly——' I began. But now Siward and Terry, dancing brilliantly together, came swivelling towards us, and Terry was able to call, 'But you're doing superbly, Hugh,' and I replied, 'How could I do other with such a partner as mine?' which won me this time an amorous, even a continuing hug.

When they had whirled away from us, Dorothy resumed, 'All the truly who?'

'All the truly selfless people in the world. There have been thousands—millions—of them. Those who have allowed themselves to be possessed by self-sacrificing love. You may say what you like but we all—all—whether atheists or agnostics or humanists (as I suppose you'd call yourself) we all fall down and worship self-sacrificing love. Now, please, I'd like you to explain its existence and where it came from. Nothing can rise higher than its source. Utter goodness can't.'

'But that argument would go for the utterly evil too.'

'No, not as I see it. Goodness is the positive thing; evil only a negative thing, a denial——'

Here she interrupted, 'But if evil is a denial of good, surely it is a positive thing?'

'Yes, it's positive but it's also, by its very definition, negative too. Whereas goodness is positive, and nothing else.'

'Well, go on,' she encouraged, as if only half satisfied.

'Evil is the lack of something. I see goodness as the destined end of man, and evil as his failure to attain it. All the greatest spirits among us have seen this for twenty-five centuries, from the days of Gautama the Buddha in Nepal, Lao-tse in China and the Second Isaiah in Babylon. One day we shall accept, perhaps, all that they saw then. They all said the same : that just as violence is the natural law of the brutes, so to rise above violence is the inevitable law for our species.'

'I can't understand why you gave up preaching. You must have been a wonderful preacher.'

'I gave it up because it is not enough to believe in what I have just said. There is more—more to believe in.'

'Shall you ever go back again?'

I didn't answer this, because I didn't know the answer.

Instead I asked, 'Do you know what I've been thinking as the band's been sending this foul din through the ceiling to the room above?'

'No.'

'It was somewhere in those rooms above that Dryden wrote his Song for St Cecilia's Day, and I've been wondering what he'd think of this ungodly row.' Then, not only to parade my knowledge but because the words so exactly fitted what he had been talking about, I quoted, after my fashion, ' "From harmony, from heavenly harmony This universal frame began; From harmony to harmony Through all the compass of the notes it ran, The diapason closing full in Man." Well, Man as a species has a long way to go before the diapason ends.'

She laughed as we danced. 'Yes, Terry warned me to polish up my Dryden as you'd almost certainly start discussing him;' and since Siward and Terry, whirling around together now bumped us a second time, not undeliberately, she, no less ready to parade her knowledge than I, found some of Dryden's words to apply to them, ' "Pains of love be sweeter far Than all other pleasures are." That's Dryden, if you please,' as she watched them whirling away.

At this moment the lights went up, dispelling the darkness; the band closed its tune with a crashing chord and a roll of drums; the people applauded and strolled back to their seats; and Dorothy and I, hand in hand, went to join Siward and Terry, who suggested that we should go to the buffet-bar and drink, while midnight was still some distance away, and drinking was still within its legal hours. Not that the Forty-Three was scrupulous about honouring the Law in its absence.

12

The Last of Perce Bywater

I cannot remember the exact date of our famous visit to the Forty-Three Club, but I know that it was a year or two later, in the spring of 1928, that Perce Bywater disappeared from among us in clouds of mystery. All he told us was that he was going to live and work in the country with a friend. 'What part of the country?' we asked. 'We don't know yet,' he said; and the clouds remained. They were penetrated a little way by me when he came to my room to say good-bye.

'Now, Perce,' I chided. 'What are you up to, and where are you really going? Sit down in that chair, and come clean.'

He sat down and said, 'I'll let you know a little, You.' The aspirate was still liable to play truant. 'You're the one person who might understand.'

'Me? Why?'

He paused and asked, 'D'you know the works of Edward Carpenter, the author of *Towards Democracy and Civilisation: its Cause and Cure*?'

'Do I know Edward Carpenter?' The words were a rebuke. 'Good lord, who doesn't?'

How strange this retort seems now. Who ever hears now the once great name of Edward Carpenter, poet and prophet of a new way of life, which was an amalgam of socialism with a gospel of the Simple Life lived afar from the disabling and frustrating horrors of an Industrial, Mechanical, Materialist civilisation. Perhaps his gospel in its briefest might be acclaimed as 'Back to the soil, back to Man's proper toil along with the labouring poor, back to the living earth instead of our dead and deathly pavements.' His was a famous name in the studies and Common Rooms of our youth; but it is faded now and forgotten. The Socialists of his pleasant dreams took the opposite road from his and rushed towards all the material profits that technology could win for them, leaving far behind them his Simple Life with a spade and a cow.

Faded and forgotten now. But I'm not sure that he may not
return as an apostle for all the Hippies, the Drop-outs, the Beautiful People and the Flower Children, who reject with some justice
our civilisation of today.

He was still alive and among us on that day when Perce came
into my room. He died a year later amid paeans of praise from
the greatest in the land.

'I thought that you must know about him,' said Perce. 'I mean
he was once a curate like you and after a few years abandoned
his Orders.'

'I haven't abandoned my Orders. Anything but. And whether
I was a mere layman like you or an out-and-out heathen like
Willy, I'd still have known the books and poems of Car-
penter.'

'Oliver is a great disciple of his.'

'Oliver?'

'Oliver Grayston, the friend I'm going to live and work with.
I met him amongst those Oxford Group boys. He's Eton and
Oxford. St John's, Oxford.'

Here was the old spell cast over him by the idea of university
graduates, especially if they carried around them the shining
aura of Oxford.

'Carpenter has many philosophies,' I pointed out. 'Which is to
be Oliver's and yours?'

'Like him we're going to build ourselves a cottage, or find one
in some remote village and live off our own bit of land. We're going to get shot for ever of all the unrealities of this mechanical
age and have the courage to live our own life regardless of the
conventions of the world.' Here were no natural words of Perce's.
They were fresh from the lips of Oliver, or from the pages of
Carpenter. He gave me more of them. 'We want to be done for
ever with all the insufferably stifling and destructive superstitions of so-called Society. We're going to be done with all the
old class barriers. They're down for us. Down for ever.'

'Where is this paradisal cottage to be?'

'Oliver is searching for it now. Somewhere in the Slowcombe
Valley of Sussex. If he can't find it, he's going to buy the land
and build it.'

'The lad has plenty of money, then.'

'Oh, yes. His father's a Lord of the Manor in Sussex, with a huge Hall and a park; and besides that, Oliver has an income of his own.'

'That should come in useful for those who are trying to lead the simple life of the poor.'

It was never possible to withhold banter from Perce, but whether or not he accepted this as chaff I don't know, for he evaded my suggestion instantly. 'Oh, naturally it'll cost something to get started, but once we're started, we intend to live as Edward Carpenter did, by our own work on our own land.'

'Still, it's nice to have private means to fall back upon.' Aware that Perce had no means of his own, I was led to remark, 'This Oliver must be very fond of you.'

Quite simply and naturally Perce answered, 'He is. That's what we believe in. Have you read Carpenter on Comradeship?'

I had; and as Perce said this, the clouds began to part.

§

'So the ardent religion of Perce's Oxford Group friend, and of Perce himself, has advanced from Frank Buchman to Edward Carpenter.'

I was thinking this as I sat at my desk and watched Perce Bywater close my door before he left Miryam's house for ever. It closed.

'You've read Carpenter on Comradeship?' Oh yes, I knew that Carpenter's all-possessing belief, though he had forsworn his Christianity, was that the only mortar which could ever bind Society in a happiness together was Love. From his works it was not difficult to discern that, like the Greeks, he conceived the love between male and male to be the noblest, 'passing the love of women'. No one had exceeded him in his fearless calls for recognition of, and fair dealing for, what he called Homogenic Love. Leaving my desk, I went to the bookshelf that held *Towards Democracy* and others of his works, such as *The Intermediate Sex* and *Intermediate Types among Primitive Folk.* Browsing among these, I read how he believed that 'intermediate types', so far from being banned and despised, should be valued as people who had much of value to give the world. I took down *Towards Democracy* and, leafing the pages, read :

> The love of men for each other—so tender, heroic, constant;
> That has come down all the ages, in every clime, in every nation,
> Always so true, so well assured of itself, over-leaping barriers of
>   age, of rank, of distance,
> Flag of the camp of freedom.

Flag of the camp of freedom? How far Carpenter's Homogenic Love included the physical coupling by members of the same sex I found it difficult to determine; nowhere did I read a word that did not lift this love to the highest and purest Platonic levels. I even found in his *Anthology of Friendship* that fine old Caroline medico, Sir Thomas Browne, quoted in support of Carpenter's philosophy. Here from the *Religio Medici* came : 'I never yet cast a true affection on a woman; but I have loved my friend as I do my virtue, my soul, my God.'

In Carpenter's last work of all, *The Psychology of the Poet Shelley*, I found the young poet, whom one would have supposed to be as heterosexual as young man could be, praised for his contention that what the world needed for its salvation was a new human type that would blend the female with the male. Shelley, it was obvious, had always been a potent influence on Carpenter : Shelley who as a poet and therefore an 'unacknowledged legislator for the world' foresaw and attacked the exploitation, enslavement or deprivations of men by the monstrous onrush, in a masculine world, of machines, profiteering and hungry mergers in a whole dark technological culture.

By the side of my Carpenter books there were a few others associated with his work and in one, *The New Chivalry and Other Poems,* published but ten years before, I read these lines on Greek love in an English clime :

> Far off across the seas
>   The warm desire of Southern men may be:
> But passion freshened by a northern breeze
>   Gains in male vigour and in purity.
> Our yearning tenderness for boys like these
>   Has more in it of Christ than Socrates.

And in another, published just after the Oscar Wilde scandal by a Homogenic enthusiast, there was an attack on Wilde for having sunk so low as to seek physical expression for a love which should be above sensuality.

So I decided that there was nothing in this new chivalric friend-ship of Perce Bywater for Oliver (I had already forgotten his surname) that need distress me. Surely there was something far too innocent in Perce, far too ordinary and unoriginal, for so rare a deviation. To decide that there was little of intermediate sex in him I had only to remember his bewilderment and coarse comment when I had once mentioned to him the prospect of toleration for homosexuality in our new age.

Of Oliver I knew nothing. He could well be an intermediate type, and as such have seen in Perce, as Terry had seen, but not I, much that was attractive about him. 'Rather beautiful,' she had called him. Mercy on us! Or was it 'sweet'? Certainly it was a 'lamb'. Or—no—was it a 'pet'? I also remembered someone expounding to me the odd phenomenon that many wealthy or aristocratic 'Greek lovers' liked to have for their beloved, because it ministered both to their benevolence and to a desirable sense of superiority, someone of a social grade lower than their own. This could fit the relationship between Oliver, a wealthy squire's son, and Perce, the late counter-boy. I came away from my book-shelves contenting myself with the belief that this relationship was in no way displeasing but merely, in Samuel Butler's phrase, 'more Greek than English'.

§

In May of the following year, '29, by which time I had almost forgotten Perce, I received a letter from him. 'We've been properly set in for some time now. Can't you come and see us one day? I remember you were so interested in what Oliver and me had in mind. Well, come and see the home we have found and us at our work. The country all round is absolutely beautiful.'

I accepted willingly since my interest was astir to know how these two disciples of Edward Carpenter might be putting his social philosophies into practice; and one afternoon I took a slow, stopping train that eventually stopped at the wayside station nearest their home. Perce was on the platform and, if you will believe it, wearing the corduroys of his peers in the labouring classes. And, just as there had been honourable battlefield mud on my uniform when I first returned from the war, so there was honourable Sussex mud caked on his corduroys now. I guessed that he was pleased I should see him in this wear, and that he had

only a wagon with a shaggy horse between the shafts to carry me
to his humble home. We had to drive two miles in this vehicle,
with Perce, late of Groves the Chemists, making a show of his
skill with the reins, though I was convinced the old horse would
have gone the right way home with ease, knowledge and dis-
cretion, fulfilling all the laws of the road, if the reins had been
just tossed on to its back.

Deeper and deeper into the country we went till at last the
horse stopped, patently of its own free and unhurried will, before
a wide gateway in a lofty quickset hedge.

'I'll leave Thompson here,' said Perce of the horse. 'He'll graze
quite happily off the footpath while I show you the estate.'

'Estate? I thought we were at one with the toiling poor?'

Never quick to return one's ball in this game of raillery, Perce
said only, 'Oh, you know what I mean. We've got a nice bit of
land with a patch of woodland and some apple orchards. The
garden's worth a study.'

It was. I had not gone two yards from the gate before I stopped
and stood still. The beds on either side of the driveway were
resplendent with gillyflowers of colours uncountable; and as
I walked on I saw that among the gillyflowers were tulips and
narcissi with clusters of primroses, polyanthuses, periwinkles and
saxifrage. Behind this flower-show was a low rock-wall brilliant
with clumps of purple aubretia alternating with yellow alyssum.
And springing from among these handsome gentry was the common hedgerow plant which lesser men called cow-parsley but I
loved as Queen Anne's Lace.

Nor was this all to admire. Tall shrubs of lilac, white and mauve;
of guelder rose, red japonica and red maple bent down over the
flowers as if to enjoy their scent.

'How on earth,' I gasped, 'do you come to possess a garden like
this when you've only been here for a year?'

'It was pretty good when we came. The old gentleman who
had the cottage, before Oliver found it, was no end of a gardener,
and Oliver's spent a packet on it since.'

'But how about the simple life of the poor?'

'Oh, as I told you, Oliver's idea was to start well, and then get
going.'

'I see. Exactly.'

Behind the young May green of the tall shrubs was a splendid background of copper beeches, and the fragrance from the lilac bushes brooded over the driveway as we rounded a curve in it and saw the house. So far from being a cottage, it was a small farmhouse of two storeys with a deeply eaved roof of rough Horsham slabs which, in their happy manner, had caught and collected over the years, with the help of the southerly breezes, lichens and mosses of varied colours: buff, sage-green, and rusty gold. No other man-built roof could merge so gently into the country around than one with coarse Horsham slabs like these. And no other timbering than this stout Sussex oak could bear such a weight of local stone.

'With the deepest respect,' I submitted, 'that's hardly a cottage.'

'No,' he agreed apologetically, 'but it's not large and we only use three rooms of it, the living room and our two bedrooms. The upper rooms we use mainly as apple lofts and store rooms. But now you must see our little bit of woodland.'

'I'm eager to see it. But I must repeat that your Oliver has spent a goodly amount in the course of embracing poverty.'

'He had to start by degrees. You must remember that he was used to a luxurious garden in Auldridge Park where his father was Lord of the Manor. He knows a lot about gardening. I've never known anything about it myself.'

'Nor I,' I admitted, so as to be at one with him. 'We poor urban types know nothing.'

Somehow I found it enjoyable to be led through his little wood by Perce in corduroys; Perce whose life hitherto had been nothing but London pavements, shop counters, and Miryam's dining-board. The wood was a little congregation of tall cypresses, standing like sentinels on parade, fine old yews, junipers, hornbeams, and Scots pines. Everywhere among the trees were rhododendrons in their first flowering.

When Perce had stabled Thompson, the hairy old horse, we went into the house and its living room, and there I met Oliver. Unlike the garden and woodland the room was austere enough for these two Sons of Poverty: a table for each and a few tired easy-chairs. Oliver was a tall, broad, massive figure. Whatever might exist in his soul, there was nothing in his fine masculine frame, and that 'afternoon shadow' over his lips and chin, to suggest intermediate sex. He too was in labouring kit: heavy, hob-nailed boots and pale corduroys strapped below the knee.

I began by congratulating him on his garden but, in the way of devoted gardeners, he apologised for its present state. 'Oh, but you're not seeing it at its best. We call May the awkward month, before the roses, the annuals, and the bedding plants are really out and after the tulips are really over.'

'Well,' I laughed, 'if your garden is below par now, I'd like to see it at its best.'

'Soon,' he explained, 'we shall have masses of irises, purple and yellow and white. And some annuals that I sowed in the autumn—they'll only bloom if autumn-sown and here in the south of England.'

'Such as?'

'Love-in-the-mist, Jerusalem cowslip, Californian poppy. . . .'

But our talk was soon done with garden flowers, and he and Perce were telling me about their labours in kitchen gardens and apple orchards and how they carried their produce to a market miles away. And about the single cow, Susan, which they had bought and with whom they were now on the happiest terms. And then, of a sudden, we were dealing with something else. Something that had nothing to do with common everyday men.

It was this, and not the flowers or the simple life, that, for me, made this visit to two young disciples of a chosen prophet a day memorable and outstanding. It was this too that helped me again to believe there was nothing in their life that need distress me, because their aim was to drive towards all that was best in their Master's teaching. And somewhere he had written of his Homogenic Love that, 'if prone to sentimentality, it was not so given to sensuality. With its genius for affection and comradeship it exercised a penetrating influence into Society, acting as a reconciler and interpreter of the two sexes to each other.'

I had begun to treat of something that deeply interested me, Carpenter's loss of his religion and churchmanship, when Perce interrupted to teach me the truth. 'How can you say he had no religion, when he had the greatest religion of all?' Perce, as ever, teaching me, but through the lips of a wiser man. 'What about his "Universal Consciousness"?'

'And what, please, may that be?'

Perce turned to Oliver. 'Come on, Oliver. Explain it all to Hugh.' The aspirate had become securer in Oliver's company.

'Oliver'll explain it all better than me. He's had an Oxford education.'

I encouraged Oliver to explain. He shrugged. 'The trouble is there's no defining it in ordinary language. It's supra-rational. You may say there are three forms of consciousness : mere awareness of the things around you such as the animals have; then self-consciousness which Man has, and which enables him to know himself as an object and to reason about things; and then Universal or Cosmic Consciousness to which only a few men have attained throughout the centuries : Buddha, and Plotinus, and Dante, and Boehme and Blake and Whitman—and, of course, Carpenter himself. He expressed it best in his *Civilisation: its Cause and Cure.*'

'That was a book in which I soon found myself far out of my depth and speedily swam back to shore. I still don't know what Cosmic Consciousness is.'

'Go on. Tell him,' Perce urged.

'It seems to be a consciousness so huge in its difference from our normal self-consciousness as that was from the limited consciousness of the animals. It's a revelation that all things are one and all are eternal and that our Time and Space are temporary illusions, adapted to our present limited and more or less embryonic state. Just as Eternity can be seen as one still Now, so Space by the very fact that it is illimitable can be apprehended as no more than a speck of dust that can be fiddled between finger and thumb. Like Blake's "Hold Infinity in the palm of your hand And Eternity in an hour".'

I shook an uncomprehending head. 'I can never understand Blake.'

So Oliver continued. 'It's a consciousness, as Carpenter says, that is in no way related to the body of here and now but apprehends in a flash all time and all space and knows that it is all good and a matter of unimaginable joy.'

'Sounds pretty incredible to me.'

'Of course it does. And so must the first experience of normal sight seem incredible and overwhelming to a man born blind. And beyond imagination joyous.'

'Have *you* experienced this sight and this joy?'

'God, no. Only a few have ever known it. But all those who have known it say that just as what is known by our ordinary consciousness is known for ever and cannot be denied, so it is with these brief flashes of Cosmic Consciousness. Once experienced they can never be denied.'

He quoted some of these statements from Carpenter, and even Perce supported him with an excerpt or two. Perce contributed, 'Under the eye of my beloved Spirit I glide. Oh joy : for ever, ever joy. I am not hurried—the whole of Eternity is mine'; but Oliver who had a real gift for speaking verse (and knew it) was far more impressive with :

> 'Soon shall the song
> That rolls down all the ages blend its voice
> With our weak utterance and make us strong;
> That we, borne forward still, may still rejoice,
> Fronting the wave of change. Thou who alone
> Changeless remainest, O most mighty Soul
> Hear us before we vanish. O make known
> Thyself in us—us in Thy Living Whole.'

I thought I detected a meaning somewhere in this. 'Are both of you trying to attain this wonderful consciousness?'

Oliver smiled. 'It's no good sweating after it. It may come to you or it may not. Don't you remember your *Towards Democracy*?'

'I remember mainly that I agreed with much of it and didn't understand the rest.'

'Well, look at it again and you'll find that he tells you that if it's to be yours it may come at any moment.' And Oliver, in his singularly beautiful way of rendering verse, even blank Whitmanesque lines, spoke slowly and softly :

> 'That day shall come to you in what place you know not; it shall
>   come but you know not the time.
> In the pulpit when you are preaching, behold !
>   Suddenly the ties and bands shall drop off;
> In the prison, One shall come, and the chains which are stronger
>   than iron shall dissolve. . . .
> In the field with the plow and the chain-harrow; by the side of
>   your horse in the stall. . . .
> It shall duly, at the appointed hour come.'

13

The Odeon

When I came back from the war to the Prophet's Chamber awaiting me, there was only one cinema within walking distance of Christian Street; and this, calling itself The Plaza, was little more than a long rectangular hall with a stage and curtained screen at one end. There were no dress-circles above the floor and I can't recall that the floor with its red-plush tip-up seats was even raked. There'd been some attempt to embellish the sea-green walls with coloured festoons and arabesques, and the uninspired flat ceiling with some coloured lights. There was no orchestra pit because the only approximation to an orchestra was one energetic pianist and one serious, excited or soulful fiddler, both these musicians modulating their art to fit the drama, the pathos, or the love on the screen. The beam from the projection room stretched over our heads to the screen, and occasionally disappeared while one reel was extracted from the projector and another affixed. Sub-titles told us what the actors were saying, unless a straight-left from the hero or a drawn revolver from the villain needed no explanation. Nearly every film ended with a 'close up' (in at least three senses of that phrase) of hero and heroine embracing, after ninety minutes of odds against them.

But now had come the day of the huge cinema-palaces built to hold in stalls and circles an audience of thousands, with an orchestra pit before the stage accommodating a real orchestra, and on either side of the proscenium the lavishly decorated pipes of a huge Wurlitzer organ. When it was time for the organist to play us his solo piece and display his gifts flamboyantly, his console would ascend from the depths of the orchestra pit with him seated before his keys and his stops, and opening his contribution to a great welcome from the audience. His tune finished, he usually turned and bowed to an applauding audience; then, resuming his seat at the console, he accompanied with a 'voluntary' his descent from the sight of men.

And such was the almost celestial Odeon they had now built

at the bottom of King George Street in our neighbourhood. One day in '29 saw Terry, Siward, Dorothy and me seated in the middle of the front row of its Great Circle. We always liked these seats, if we could afford them and get them, because nobody could crush past our knees and no usherette could bedazzle our eyes with her torch. From my front seat the whole gilded auditorium spread in a picture before me; and I often think now that the builders of these enormous palaces, costing Heaven-knew-how-many thousands, must have foreseen long years of enlarging prosperity—but the maggot was already in the apple.

1929 when we four sat there, and the maggot was a little man who, five years earlier, had been messing about in a small room above a shop with lenses, cylinders, metal discs and bright lamps. He produced fluctuating shadows on a receiver by means of a wire, but the daemonic desire possessing him was to produce the same, not with a length of wire, but by wireless through the air; or, to state his aim more picturesquely, through the wall into the next room over the shop. If you could broadcast sounds by wireless why not sights? Months and months of messing about, and at last, on an autumn day in '25 he did manage to shoot the shadow of a face from one room into the next through the brick wall. Television was born. And the autumn, if not the winter, of the great cinemas may be said to have begun. So soon! It was not that these Gloriana palaces would have to die in Siward's favourite lines like 'queens young and fair', and dust to close Helen's eye, but that their sovereignty would be taken from them more quickly than their founding fathers had imagined, their lives restricted, and their activities lamed.

The little man's name was John Logie Baird, and even as we sat that day in our Odeon, the B.B.C. had started a brief programme of television to the handful of people—some thirty, according to Baird—who had sets to receive it.

In the end the B.B.C., now the British Broadcasting Corporation, cast Baird and all his gadgets aside in favour of a rival apparatus developed by later hands. His years of experimenting, and at last his brief view from an exceeding high mountain of all the kingdoms of the world, had culminated in a sorrowing descent from the mountain top on to undistinguished plains; but at least the common people of the world have always crowned him as the pioneer of television.

Remembering that day in the Odeon's Great Circle when, thanks to the League of Nations established nine years before, and to the loudly acclaimed Locarno Pact, guaranteeing the inviolability of all present frontiers, we chose to believe that great wars were now things of the past and a European peace would go on for ever, and we could give ourselves to the pursuit of happiness, it is not of John Logie Baird messing about with metal oddments and strong lights that I think. Rather of a rough and sinister figure in a soiled raincoat, with a drooping forelock and a toothbrush moustache, who had come out of a German prison with a written testament in his hands, *Mein Kampf,* 'My Struggle', which was the very Bible of Antichrist. 'The heaviest blow that ever struck humanity was the coming of Christianity.' We sat there, Terry, Siward, Dorothy, and I, and not one of us had so much as heard the names of John Logie Baird, or of one who was the son of an Alois Schicklgruber, but was now known as Adolf Hitler. A name barely known in England then, and certainly to none of us; one year later it was a thundercloud in the West. It foreshadowed the end, in no distant time, of our blithe, hearty, carefree peace, and the opening of the Second War.

We were enjoying a French film which Dorothy had insisted we must see and hear because the acting, she said, was marvellous and its theme song haunted her. Together with this French film there was a new animated cartoon of *Felix the Cat,* who walked and walked across the screen to the accompaniment of his own theme song 'Felix kept on walking'. After this cartoon the screen disappeared, to leave the stage free for a variety act, the 'Sesame Sisters', which showed that the Kings of the Screen supposed the real menace to their world-conquest to lie with the 'live' acting in variety theatres and not with any nonsense of the B.B.C. transmitting blurry pictures to less than a hundred people.

We had watched and listened to *Sous les Toits de Paris* in an admiring silence, but so far as was possible—after all we were in a circle's front row almost alone, and with a vast area of decorative emptiness in front of us—we whispered and talked while Felix the Cat walked and the Sesame Sisters sang. Terry sat on the far left, then Siward and Dorothy and I. The curtains ruffled quietly across the screen and then parted again to disclose a grand concert piano and the Sesame Sisters, two blonde and broadly built women dressed to look like twins ten years younger than they were. One sister sat at the piano and began pounding it seldom less than *fortissimo*, while the other leaned against its bay as they sang their first duet with their faces turned to each other. After this item the standing sister sat herself somewhat archly on the lid of the unopened piano and sang from there, swinging her legs. Their opening songs were those of a young Master, still in his twenties, who had broken into an almost cosmic fame by seeming the very voice of this young age with its gay irreverences, its impish laughter, its pursuit of happiness, but, at the same time, its faint, incipient doubts.

> Cocktails and laughter
> But what comes after
> Nobody knows.

The opening of this song was greeted with applause from all parts of the house, for it was then a top favourite in restaurants, night-clubs and vaudeville shows.

> Poor little rich girl,
> You're a bewitched girl
> Better beware. . . .

It was while Felix the Cat had been walking, sometimes with his paws linked behind his back as if he were a soul in deep meditation, that Dorothy turned her face from the other two and asked me, 'Do you find this funny?'

'Now and then.'

'I'm afraid I find it sublimely unfunny. How's the great book going?'

'My book?'

'Of course. What else?'

'I'm not sure it hasn't gone for good.'

'Oh, nonsense! We can't have that. You've been sweating over it for years, haven't you?'

'Seven. No eight.' Some braggartism here.

'Eight years over a book! What some earnest people will do! Eight years of whole-time labour?'

'No, far from whole-time. But it's required an immense amount of study.'

'Study of what?'

'My dear girl: of all the Biblical Criticism, historical and textual, that's been pouring out of Germany and England for fifty years and all the modernist writers in the Roman Church whom the Holy Father is busy excommunicating.'

'And you want to prove the modernists wrong?'

'Not at all. Rather the opposite. My ambition is to show that they may be right, but that the ancient worship and ceremonies are right too; that Modernism and Catholicism can and ought to live perfectly happily together.'

'*Roman* Catholicism?'

'No, no, no. *Anglo*— Anglo— for me always. I could never swallow Rome in its entirety, and I'm sure they could never digest me. Furthermore I quite simply believe that Anglicanism with its ill-defined unity and its tolerant diversities is a profoundly beautiful thing; the one Communion most likely to appeal to the modern world if we ever set out to reunify the Churches.'

'And you've stayed all the time in Miryam's comic guest house?'

'Not all the time. But I happen to be a bachelor and a lazy one, and I don't want to go looking for a housekeeper—or a wife —till I've done with the book. Miryam understands all my wants.'

'I wish this cat'd walk off the screen for good. Some people are too easily amused. I often wonder why Siward and Terry go on staying there. *Why?* Surely by now they could have found themselves a home.'

'*I* sometimes wonder too.'

'How many words have you written?'

'Probably three hundred thousand words. But they're only the rough block of stone from which the angel has to be hewn.'

'Angel? Please, what are you talking about?'

'Didn't Michelangelo stare at a block of marble and say, "I see an angel in it"? And didn't Aristotle quite a few years before say "Every block of marble contains a statue"?'

'They did, did they? And you can't quite see your angel? Is that it?'

'It exactly. That's why I wonder if the book can ever be done, and if all my work'll go for nothing because I can't see the angel's head.'

'Sorry. I'm lost.'

'I can't see that I can bring the book to the climax I wanted. It needs more faith than I can achieve. I don't know that I shall ever achieve it now.'

'Religious faith?'

'Naturally. Isn't that what the book's about?'

'Well, explain. And damn this idiot cat.'

'What *are* those two talking about?' asked Terry from the far end of our row.

'God, I think,' said Siward.

'Good lord!' muttered Terry. 'But what does our Dorothy say about God? She isn't interested in him.'

'She seems interested enough now,' said Siward. 'She's giving poor Felix her cold shoulder.'

Dorothy, unheeding them, persisted, 'Never mind those two children. They're probably amused by this animal. I'm interested in *you*. Go on. Explain.'

So we left Felix walking. Hardly aware of his adventures before our eyes, I explained that unless I could finally believe that Christ was God Incarnate, and that he died and rose again, there could be no sacraments, none of the old offices and, indeed, no Catholic Church at all, with its beautiful historic ceremonies—nothing for me except a blind Unitarianism, empty and dull.

'There's one other solution,' she said. 'To believe only in Man and in nothing supernatural; and to remain quite happy with that for your faith like Siward and Terry and me.'

'That's impossible,' I said. 'Because I believe in God.'

And Felix kept on walking.

When Felix had walked finally out of sight, and the Sesame Sisters had sung their last, the curtains, after veiling their smiles and curtsies, parted to give us the screen again and the new and beautiful documentary, *Drifters*, with its sea-scapes and its North Sea herring fleet, their corked nets drifting across the flow of the tide just below the surface instead of trawling the sea's bed. The film plunged us into silence because everything in it captivated us with its quiet loveliness. Not a word did Dorothy speak. Nor I. I was hardly conscious of the companions at my side, except for one moment when I leant forward to rest my arms on the circle's parapet and relieved my eyes for a moment by turning them towards an ornate wall on my left. Then, to my surprise and with a shiver of distress, I glimpsed across Dorothy's lap that her hand was grasped secretly and tightly by Siward in the dark little breach between their seats. I swung my eyes away that they might not know I had detected this. Surely it could be no more than flirting—oh, yes, no more—but a little later, curious and wondering, I contrived a side-long glance again. He was now, I could see, pressing her hand lovingly. Her face, I thought, was alight with happiness—with a sensual joy that had little to do with the film.

Terry was looking straight ahead at the film, rapt by its beauties, amused by its comedies, and her lips slightly parting in a peaceful smile.

14

In that Chamber on the Wall

By now Siward and Terry had been married five years, and their love, so passionate at first, had matured into the customary mutual devotion, stilled and tranquillised, but full of laughter and lively adventures shared together. Or so I thought. So I thought, even after that surprising—and troubling—glimpse in the darkness of a cinema. And it was not till some weeks later that I observed and was saddened by a dark change which had descended upon our Terry—Terry of the high spirits and the eager—perhaps over-eager—emphases. Where was the old ardent gaiety; where the old demonstrative enthusiasms? I had dubbed her the most demonstrative girl I'd ever met, and inevitably her behaviour in this new mood retained some of the old excitability and insistences. But now, when Siward was away, having sped in his Baby Austin to some Midland B.B.C. station, her silences in the Lounge could be prolonged and at times there would come an abrupt exit from the room which gained emphasis from a closing of the door that was younger brother to a slam. And the door of her room above would shut with an even sharper bang. So too, when she went from the house for a lonely walk, she could vent some of her unhappiness on the hall door. And strangely, in seeming dishar-mony with some hidden choler but really, I think, wholly con-sistent with it, her behaviour towards us all was emphatically gentler, kindlier, and more selfless. So much so that, in these new striking moods of quietude and gentleness I was thinking that she was becoming a little like the gentle Soeur Thérèse of Lisieux after whom she had been named, but of whom she had pronounced herself the extreme opposite. This was a joke I should have loved to share with her, but not a word could I bring myself to say to her about her manifest unhappiness. Nor did I allow her to see I was detecting it.

It was she who spoke first.

As we all left the dining-room table one evening she touched

my hand, and there was affection in the touch. 'Hugh,' she said.
Very softly.

'Yes, my dear?'

'Can I come and talk to you one evening? Only when you've
nothing else to do. Only when you're not busy with your book.
I don't want to be a nuisance to you. But there are heaps of things
I want to ask you. Any old day would do.' She tried a smile.
'That's what you're for, isn't it? Didn't Siward—' I noticed a
hesitation before she spoke his name—'didn't Siward call you our
Resident Padre?'

'But, Terry darling, I'm only a very poor sort of spiritual direc-
tor now.'

'Gosh, there's nothing spiritual about it. It's not about religion.
I guess you've had enough bullying about that from Dorothy.' A
flavour of hostility rather than of fun in these words. 'Anyhow,
you're just trying to be modest because you know you're easily
the most understanding person in the world. It's just that I want
to talk to somebody . . . rather badly.'

'Then you mustn't be kept waiting. Come at once. What's
wrong with coming tonight?'

'No, no, you're busy. I mustn't disturb you. Some other day. . . .'

'Terry, you're to be at my chamber door in exactly fifteen
minutes' time.'

'Oh, you *are* good!'

'What's good about getting someone you love to come and be
with you?'

'You are beyond question the nicest person in the world.'

'Only nice to those I love, I'm afraid.'

'Well, here's one who loves you.'

'Then don't dare to keep me waiting. I give you fifteen minutes.'

Upstairs in my room I made some attempt at tidying desk and
divan and chairs, and I set the gas-fire aglow as a welcome for
her. The evening was cold, and while I waited for her I went to
a window and looked out. Rain drops speckled its panes as an in-
coming tide of grey cloud threw shreds and spindrift before
it till, in less than a minute, the whole sky was like one grey
lampshade over the world. A high wind rose, whistling and moan-
ing at first and then dimming into a low roar like the sound of
continuous traffic in distant streets. This low roar switched my
eyes, over the back-garden trees, to the pavements of my pseudo-

nymous 'Linden Highway', now grey and glistening beneath the rain.

And as I write this, I remember that I was then standing at one of the twin windows of that 'chamber on the wall' at which, as I have told you, I was to stand gazing from the Highway fifty years later, when the house was deserted and looked haunted, and all its windows were vacant and blind.

More than the fifteen minutes passed and she did not come. I left the window and paced the room wondering. Was she recoiling from all that she'd wanted to say? Was she deciding that perhaps she'd been unwise in asking my help and had better leave me untroubled, apologising humbly in the morning?

Then I heard her step, and the handle of my door turned—but only to stay still. Her hand must be resting on it.

'Come on! Come on!' I encouraged. 'Nothing to be afraid of.'

The door opened and she took a step or two into the room, without releasing that handle. 'I've no business to disturb you like this. It's wicked.'

'You've every business to. As you said downstairs, that's what I'm for.'

'No, I think I'll go away again. Yes, I'm sure I will.'

'Theresa.' I spoke the name with a show of severity, and I went and took her empty hand while I kicked away the door from her other hand's grasp. I led her towards the gas-fire. 'I imagine that, as usual, you'll sit on the floor.'

'If I may.'

'You may, and I hope you will, because there's only one really comfortable chair in the room, and I like to lounge in it myself when I'm really happy with someone.'

She lowered herself to the floor, sitting first on her heels and pretending to warm her hands at the fire, then folding her legs beside her.

I sat in my capacious chair thrusting it backwards so that I could stretch my long legs at full length. Since she remained silent, while the gas-fire purred and chattered in front of her, I said, 'I'm more than ready to hear everything.'

A few more seconds of silence, and, still gazing at the fire with her face averted from me, she said, 'If you love a person enough you know everything they're thinking.'

'I doubt if that's true of everybody.'

'It's true of me. I love Siward, and I know everything he's thinking—always. And . . . I've known for weeks past that he's in love with someone else.'

'*No, Terry*——'

'But yes—yes. He's terribly in love with her. It's Dorothy. Dorothy Cotteril.'

'He loves *you*.'

'He loves me too in a way, but no longer as he used to, and not as he's now loving her. There were other girls before me, I know, I know—he told me all about them—but he used to say there'd never be another after me. He meant it then. He really loved me then. But he's proud of believing in what he calls "free love" and in arguing that no one should be tied in the prime of their youth and during the best of their years, to a lot of old worn-out rules. It's a favourite saying of his that it's taken hundreds of years to set thought really free, and now it's time to set love free. He used to find girls who were ready to believe all this and act on their beliefs, but I'm simply not that sort, Hugh darling. I've pretended to believe in all his theories because I wanted to be one with him, and I daresay I do believe in them a little; but if I do, I simply couldn't act on them.' Now that she'd started she was pouring it all out to me, unable to stop. 'Dorothy can and will, but I've always joked with him that my beloved father put archidiaconal bands all round my head and my heart. Dorothy is quite unhampered by any such fetters. We went to that cinema again, and pretended to be easy and natural and all of us modern and fond of each other, but I knew. I knew. She's beautiful, and she's in love with him—which I can quite understand. And Siward is simply distracted by her brilliance and her love. How can I compete with her? They're on the same intellectual level. I've none of her brilliance to offer him, only my love——'

'And my God, Terry, I'd rather have that than all her brilliance ten times over.'

Hardly hearing this, she rushed on, 'When we got back from the cinema I charged him with it. I said, "She's madly in love with you, and you are with her, aren't you?" He believes in being always frank and honest—he's not *bad*; he's so good in many ways—and he admitted, "Of course I can't help loving her. Love breeds love. But I love you too." I insisted on knowing if she was now his mistress and he said Yes, she was. And, Hugh, as the years have gone by our love has naturally been less of an obsession than it was, but now—since I guessed about Dorothy—my love has swung back to what it was in our very first days. I'm terribly in love with him again, and I know that he loves her more than me, and I can't bear it.' Her face plunged into her hands and lay buried there while she abandoned herself to a paroxysm of sobbing, her shoulders shaking before me. 'Hugh darling, I can't bear it.'

I rose and lifted her to her feet and drew her into my arms, holding her tight and patting her back to comfort her.

When she managed to speak through her tears, she said, 'If only we'd had a child . . . but never now—never—never! Because I won't have him near me . . . unless . . . My whole world is destroyed and I don't want to live. But why do I trouble you with it? Let me go, and I'll leave you alone. What do I matter?'

'You matter to me, darling.' Before I knew what I was saying, her helpless suffering had forced these words past my lips. And I found myself stroking her hair, pressing a kiss on her brow, and calling her 'Theresa', as I often did when I was trying to comfort or please her.

'What am I to do?' she pleaded, her face at rest against me.

'Theresa, dearest——' I had never called her this before, but my language was at the mercy of my pity. 'I think I know what my advice should be, but it'll be asking an awful lot from you.'

'What is it?'

'That the only thing to do at present, the ideal thing, is to accept, to forgive, and to wait. Because you mean more to him than anyone else. That I *know*.'

'I don't. Not now.'

'I believe—everything tells me—that he will come back to you. He has often talked to me of what you mean to him—sometimes as if he was surprised that anyone could mean so much to an ordinary selfish chap like himself.'

'When he was in love with me—yes. But that's all over.'

'It isn't. Because he was more than in love with you. He loved you with the kind of love that I don't believe any man can easily lose. Wait . . . and he'll be surprised again. That'll bring him back to you.'

'I'll never have him near me while this is going on. I won't. I won't. I have to have him in my bed because we've nowhere else to go, but I turn my back to him. I won't let him touch me.'

'I haven't asked you to do that. I only want you to forgive him when he comes. There's nothing to do in this world but forgive.'

'I'm not big enough to do that. I think I'm leaving him. I don't yet know how I can, because I've no money of my own, and I don't want to tell Daddy and Mummy yet.'

'No, not yet. Wait.'

'But I want to punish him. I know you'll say it's wrong, but I want to punish him. And her too. Are you saying that I ought to forgive *her?*'

This was difficult to answer. I could see that, at present, a 'Yes' must seem like asking the impossible. After thought, I could only say, 'My dear, I told you it was something tremendously difficult I was suggesting to you. I can see that in some cases a forgiving must be very like a dying. But then it is always at its best and greatest.'

'Well, here's one who's not dying for him or for her. As I've told you there's nothing in me like your Sister Theresa of Lisieux.'

'I think there's much in you very like Sister Theresa.'

'I'm going. I shall leave him. I'll leave him to her.'

'And where would you go?'

'I don't know. I tell you I don't know. Somewhere. Somewhere. Far from him.'

'Don't go, dearest. It would break my heart if you did.'

I kissed her on her cheek, and in that moment, while her body was pressed against mine, and she looking up at me, in pleasure at these words, with all the beauty of her young face marred by tears, I knew that I was in love with her. To use her own word, that I was 'terribly' in love with her. I was in love with her, and my love was not less than Siward's in those first days.

It may seem incredible, but here was I, fifteen years older than she, and in all my young manhood, as a fervid scholar, as a priest, as a chaplain or a kind of reverend ranker during years of war, as a writer engrossed by a book that had most of his love, I had never yet desired a woman, either her love or her body, for more than transient, and not very worrying minutes. Body and mind had become trained to a continence, long appeased by some idle notion that I'd marry, perhaps, one day.

But now in this moment, with this Theresa in my arms, my mind was like a theatre screen on which glowing visions hastened past, melting into one another. She could divorce Siward and come to me. And what a wife! Loved not only as a wife but almost as a daughter. She in my arms—and my bed. She lying there, the source of those ecstasies that Siward had once loved to describe to me. She seated, after her fashion, on the floor before the fire in our home till, in a passion of desire, I took her up into my arms.

This was one of the great moments of my life, both exquisite with love and sick with loss. Because everything in me, my loyalty to my Orders that still held me chained to God, told me I must never have her. I had a sort of love for Siward too, and I knew I must not wean her from him. Unless I was to cast my conscience for ever away, the work before me was to labour at bringing these two young lovers together again. Against myself. Against an impassioned desire. Even against what had become, in a moment, an aching need. My mind adopted her own words to suit my present state, though modifying them as an older person should. 'She loves him far more than me, and it's not easy to bear.'

Yes, it was no small hour in that chamber on the wall when, one evening, I met Love and Loss together, side by side.

She was still holding me tight as if I were some rock to which she must cling, so after laying another kiss on her forehead, I withdrew from her embrace and picked up one of her hands instead, while I assured her, 'I think I can promise he will come back to you. I'll do all I can to bring him back to you.'

Surprisingly, she lifted up my hand that was holding hers and kissed it, saying, 'There's no one like you anywhere in the world'; then turned and ran towards the door. 'I must go. I must go, and leave you in peace.'

Peace? She was gone, leaving me at a helpless wander about the room, while I contemplated all the hurrying visions that must ever be fond imaginings and never be real. And yet it is the truth to state that the knowledge that I loved was a leaping joy in my heart even though its partner was the knowledge that mine was a love that must never know fulfilment.

§

Directly Siward returned from his mission for the B.B.C. (if that was the whole truth about his days of absence) Terry in her rage of love and anger told him all about her visit to me and my words to her. That this produced a rupture in which feminine fury played its part I knew because it was late one evening when he returned, and from their room under mine I could hear their voices—or, rather, Terry's voice, and I learned that in her misery she was not above shouting. Not once did I hear Siward's voice.

Some of Terry's actual words I heard, because I was standing very still to listen—in curiosity, of course, but more, I hope, in distress and love. My failure to hear a sound from Siward led me to guess almost exactly what was happening : he was enraging her by declining to do battle on her terms, maintaining instead an infuriating masculine attitude, dignified, quiet, aloof, sardonic. That he could adopt such an attitude I knew well, because I'd often seen him at play with it, but hitherto only because those whom you love you tease.

All of what happened he told me at a later day.

Terry was undressing for bed as he came in. Instantly she turned her back on him as if he did not exist. She dropped down her underslip, stepped out of it, and reached for her nightdress. For seconds her slim youthful figure was nude before him, and the old desire stirred; then the white chiffon nightdress dropped like a curtain around her—and desire could rest.

All this time she kept her back turned to him, and she was about to get into the large bed when he spoke. Trying to be friendly in spite of all, he said with a laugh, 'What? No greeting?'

She swung round, and they were face to face. Her eyes were red round the rims with weeping, but hard. Never, he told himself, had he seen those beautiful eyes—usually gentle and soft or laughing and alight—so ruthlessly, coldly hard. Her words matched them. 'Do you suppose I'm going to greet you when I know you've come from her? What do you think I am?'

'You know I've come from her.' He merely repeated her words as if to ridicule their injustice.

'Yes, from her to me. And you expect a loving welcome. Thank you. No. Not from me.'

'You don't believe I've been in Bristol as I told you?'

'No !' She shouted it at him. 'I don't believe that your so-called business in Bristol has required three whole days and two nights. I don't believe for a moment that you've been days and nights away without seeing her. I may not be as brilliant as she is, but I'm not quite a fool.'

'Very good then.' He kept voice and manner quiet as he took off his jacket and troubled to hang it neatly over a chair's back. The very neatness of the hanging was probably an offence to her. 'As a matter of fact I haven't been near her these two days and nights—if only because there was no opportunity. But I don't suppose you believe me. You've decided I'm a liar. And that's that.'

'Yes, that's that,' she shouted. 'Of course I think you're a liar. You kept this business with Dorothy dark as long as you could, imagining I was blind. But I wasn't; and let me tell you this : I don't believe you now, and I shan't ever. Nor shall I believe in you in any other way. How can I? Why should I? When you're being the utterly cruel beast you are. Because that's what you are.'

'Oh, I see.' He might be keeping his voice easy, as waistcoat followed jacket and he began to undo his tie, but his temper was rising, and he meant his next quiet words to hurt like a whiplash. 'Well, let me tell *you* something. No one has ever bellowed crude and vulgar abuse at me in the way you do. I can assure you Dorothy doesn't do it. She's at least incapable of that.'

He could hardly have said a crueller thing. The cruelty of it stopped her speech and fixed her eyes on him. Knowing it was unjustifiable, he had to justify it to himself as inevitable by producing more of the same kind. 'As you know, there were other girls before you, and I daresay they were nothing to write home about, but not one of them was low enough to fire fish-market abuse at me like you. They were a bit above that. Frankly, I'm not used to it.'

The cruelty not only fixed her eyes on him but lowered and steadied her voice when at last she spoke. Then she said, 'I never knew you had it in you to be like this. I never knew the time would come when I'd wish I'd never married you.'

'I see. You no longer think I'm the sort a nice, well-brought-up, well-mannered, well-spoken girl ought to have married.'

'That's it exactly. You couldn't have put it better. I don't.'

'I see. Good. It's as well to know where we are.'

'I quite agree. We may know where we are at present, but we may not know it for long.'

'And what precisely does that mean? Words like that are always interesting.'

'I'm going. I'm going. I think I'm going. That's what they mean.' Believing these to be no more than words designed to stab, he answered coldly, 'You're going? Where to?'

'Yes, going, going. And you can go to her. Go to her.' The steady voice was breaking now. 'Go to her. I shall survive.'

'You're going. Where to?'

'That's what Hugh asked me. I don't know where I'll go, but I'll find somewhere.'

'Oh, Hugh's in your confidence, is he? That's interesting.'

'Of course he is. I went and told him all. D'you imagine I can endure this alone? D'you think I don't want help? I do, and he was sweet, as he always is.'

'I suppose he condemned me outright?' His tone suggested an indifference to any opinion I might have offered, but his pose was one thing; and the distress behind it another.

'He didn't say so. In a sense he was on your side. He told me I wasn't to leave you. Or, at any rate, not yet.'

'You mean he suggested you could leave me at some time or other?'

'No. I think he meant I was to wait for ever. In case you might, of your own sweet will, choose to come back to me. And I bloody well told him that I wasn't anything like good enough for that sort of noble patience. And I'm not. I'll go. I'll go! Somewhere. I don't think it'll be home, though my beloved father'd welcome me back tomorrow. But one thing's certain, a little more of this, and you'll have seen the last of me.'

These were words that really did stab to the heart, but he tried for a moment longer to maintain a show of quiet, easy acceptance. 'My dear, as soon as you've decided to go, just tell me. Or, if you like I'll go. Say the word, and *I'll* go.'

In her feminine fashion her next words bore no relation to what he'd just said. 'I've been faithful to you as completely as any wife who's ever lived, and, let me tell you, a good deal more faithful than some wives I know. And all the thanks I've got for being faithful is that you're just killing me.' The very opposite to what she had just said about her sure survival. 'This is killing me.'

The words awoke at last enough compassion in him to arrest the desire to stab back at her. The knife dropped from him, and he said, 'Terry, let us be sensible. I've often told you that I love you as I love no one else.'

'You can't. You can't. Not while you're doing what you're doing now. Talk "sensibly"? God, that's the only sense of it. You can't love me and her.'

'Oh yes, I can. In one sense those words are as true as ever they were, but——' her refusal to come one step towards him in his attempt at appeasement re-awoke his resentment so that he picked up the knife again—'but if you don't want to believe them, don't. There they are. Take them or leave them.'

'And I bloody well leave them.' It was a shouted sneer. 'Who but a fool would do anything else? I leave them for good and all, thank you.'

'All right, then. That's okay by me.' A brutal remark, offered with a shrug, while in his heart, and in his head too, he hated it. And hating it, he was driven to repeat it, so as to defy head and heart. 'Okay by me every time.'

'By me too,' she said. And she leapt into the large bed, drew the clothes over her, and turned her face to the wall.

§

My heart was pouring down a compassion upon both of them, because there was agony in Terry's voice, and though my heart had been aching for days with love of her, this had not diminished my affection for Siward. Strange that though Siward stood between me and the possession for myself of Terry, that incredibly beautiful dream, I loved them both enough to hate their poor muddling of a love that had once seemed as good as young human love could be. Both were children of a bright intelligence, Siward remarkably so, yet neither had attained—and how many people have?—to the ultimate wisdom which will have nothing to do with retribution or chastisement or wounding, and whose names are more like mercy and understanding and forgiveness. Despite their cleverness they were still two sad, silly children. And silent now. What agonies lay speechless in their silence?

§

Late as it was, there came a knock on my door. A diffident knock. Which of them it might be I did not know but I called one or the other to enter. Siward. Siward with jacket and waistcoat still off, and the two ends of his tie lying adrift on his shirt.

'Are you still up, Hugh? Could you——'

'Of course I'm still up. The night is still young.'

'But you're busy.'

'Not at all. You've just caught me at a moment when I was standing by the window idly dreaming.' I didn't tell him about what.

'But you want to get back to your work?'

'Not half so much as I want *not* to. You couldn't be more welcome.'

'It's unpardonable to burst on you at this time of night, but it's your fault really. You've always been so ready to listen to us, and you know what you are to us.'

'Sit down, Siward. And stay just as long as you like.'

He tried for a moment to be amusing. 'I suppose that a parson, like a doctor, ought to be ready to give day-or-night service.'

'That's the idea,' I admitted. 'Sit down and go ahead.'

He declined my heavy fireside chair, saying, 'No, no, that's yours,' and pulled up a hard bedroom chair.

'Have a smoke,' I said, offering him my cigarette case.

He took a cigarette but kept it within his fingers without lighting it. He said 'Thanks' and straightway forgot it.

Thinking it was perhaps best forgotten, I made no attempt to light it, but said only, 'You look tired, old fellow. What about a stiff brandy? I have a cryptic bottle kept for secret drinking on special occasions.'

'No. I don't want to drink anything. I only want to talk to you.'

'Well, let's light the fire and talk.'

'Hugh . . . Terry tells me she's told you all about me and Dorothy. I'm afraid everything she's told you is true. I haven't been able to lie to her because she seems to know everything whether I speak or not.'

'That's what it is to love as she does.'

'I suppose so . . . but, Hugh, I cannot see that I'm wholly wrong. As you know I cannot accept your Christian insistence that there can never be any love-making outside marriage, and she doesn't pretend to be a Christian either, so why——'

'My dear boy, don't be silly. She loves you as a man might well give his soul to be loved, and if she was not by nature monogamous, as I think she is, this would have made her so. She's suffering very terribly.'

'God, I don't want her to suffer. Honestly, I don't. I love her.

I know she's been a wonderful wife to me, but I can't help believing that some allowance must be made for a man if his sexual need is something far stronger than his wife's.'

'Siward, there are several things that I used to preach and teach, about which, alas, I don't feel the same certainty now, but there is one thing in which my faith is unshaken and will stay so for ever.'

'And that is?'

'Simply that there's no final happiness outside Christian marriage. Or you needn't call it Christian. I'm sure the wisest of humanists and heathens can see that this is a truth too. I merely mean a marriage in which husband and wife are resolved at all costs to be faithful to one another. So far from being Christian it might well be an irregular union between a man and his mistress after a marriage has failed, but a faithful union. Anything else gets you nowhere in the end. Except into loneliness. The other will get you somewhere.'

'Where?'

'To somewhere good. Anything less ends only in angers and partings and jealousies. And—as I said—worst of all, into loneliness. I know this, not as a parson, but as a man. It's possible to see that a truth is a truth without one word from the clergy. And I just see it as a blinding truth.'

'You mean one is to be wholly bound to one partner till death?'

'Till death.'

'I can't accept it. It's asking impossibilities.'

'All right. Take the lower road . . . and learn that it leads nowhere. Presumably if you believe in it, you'll persist in it and find only nothingness and emptiness at the end.'

'Your road is too damned steep.' His head shook many times. 'I say again, it asks the impossible.'

'Not the impossible, but much. Sometimes very much. But, my God, what you buy is worth the price.'

He thought awhile and then argued, 'It's all very magnificent, what you're saying, padre, but it takes no account of reality. Look at all the other animals, the males of the species, the rutting stag, the ram with its ewes, the stallion who sires——'

I interrupted. 'Here the old back-sliding parson must speak. He still believes in many things, and one is that God's pattern for men is that they should transcend the brutes. And love perfectly.'

'That hardly goes for the Muslim boys.'

'Their God is not my God.'

'Or for some of the noblest men in the world : say, Cyrus I of Persia. He had plenty of wives and "as many concubines as there were days of the year"—it was said. And he followed one of the noblest religions, Zoroaster's. Which, by the way, taught the Jews to believe in one God only—*your* God.'

'Zoroaster was seven hundred years before Christ and my God.'

'And what about King David and King Solomon?' he persisted.

'A thousand years before Christ.'

'And you have no answer for those who can't believe in your God?'

'Only what I have said. That the Christian doctrine is as true for heathens as for anyone else, and that the best of them know it.'

He dodged this, having, I believed, no answer ready. 'We were married in church, of course, but only because her old man was an archdeacon. I couldn't feel then that the vows demanded of us were justifiable.'

'I'm not talking about vows or contracts or churches or archdeacons or even Christianity itself. I'm talking about happiness and the only road to happiness. There's a hell of a price to pay for it. You're not prepared to pay for it, and that's that. As you please, my dear fellow. Follow your own road. Into emptiness and the desert.'

So, all unknowing, I had given him the two words they'd been hurling at each other : 'That's that.'

'I don't know a single friend of mine who would agree with you,' he said.

'I can well believe it. I'm pretty sure there's a large majority of your generation, and possibly in the whole country, which is against all I'm saying. But that doesn't make it less true for me. I'm sure I don't belong to this present world, and I don't care a damn. As I've told you, the Truth isn't dated. It's outside Time. I am what I am, and I suspect the Church will only begin to be really great when it begins to be despised and rejected : it is then that its saints and martyrs rise. I am quite prepared for it to become, if need be, little more than a voice crying in a wilderness. The ways of God are foolishness to men. Unless and until you perceive that they happen to be very wise.'

Again he shook his head, still refusing persuasion, but still without an answer.

So I attacked again while my opponent's van was in disorder and unready. 'Can you imagine Terry possessed by another man? Could you bear it?'

He shivered. This assault had driven his forces into further disarray, and he could only answer weakly, 'But surely things can be different for a man. Terry is not made my way.'

'And how lucky you are. So this freedom is to be only for you?'

'I suppose it works out like that. With us.'

This stung me into a blunt riposte which I tried to soften. 'Siward, I know you're always willing to take unpleasant words from me. All right. You have a splendid intelligence, and everything you're saying is unworthy of it. It's all a futile attempt to justify what you know is wrong. It's an argument that, if it's produced to the full, reduces a wife to the level of a kept woman in King David's or King Solomon's harem. You set yourself up as a good Socialist, but this is an insult, not only to Terry, but to all women everywhere. And you know it. Is that good Socialism? I don't know. I'm not one.'

His only retort was to counter-attack *my* beliefs. 'I believe in freedom. You are a Christian. Is there no freedom in Christianity?'

'Most certainly there is. Freedom to choose or reject a way of life that's far above mere natural drives to which the beasts are subject, and that acknowledges spiritual standards which are utterly out of their sight.'

He had no answer. So after waiting I went on, 'You do love Terry but you're willing to hurt her beyond bearing. You love Dorothy and you love Terry. Which do you now love the more? Come. The truth.'

'I love them both. . . .' It was a halting answer. 'And love them truly.'

I said, 'Which do you love the more?'

'Dorothy, I suppose.' At least I could admire his honesty and his readiness to leave with me some impression of a haunting doubt. 'Dorothy is being very wonderful to me,' he offered in lame explanation.

'So was Terry. You told me so once—here in this room. Have you forgotten what she was to you then?'

'No, but she's making it very difficult to love her just now.

She's capable of shouting the most violent and atrocious things at me.'

'And do I wonder? Not for a moment. When you stab someone, good lord, why shouldn't they scream?'

'You're on Terry's side wholly?'

'On every side of her.'

'With no feeling for Dorothy and me?'

'With great feeling for Dorothy and you, because I know that whichever way you turn, there's suffering waiting for you. But one way will end in happiness; the other—believing as you both do—in nothing. You don't suppose, I imagine, that you're the first with Dorothy?'

'No. She's told me everything about herself. *Everything.* Dorothy's no liar; she's too proud for that. But I never suspected anything else, and I don't think it's ever worried me : what she may have done. Naturally a girl with her beauty and opportunities has——'

'You needn't go on,' I said. 'With her youth and beauty and beliefs, I can understand.' Indeed I could.

'But she swears her love for me is different from anything that's gone before. And I believe that's the truth. She loves me in such a way—' here at least was something he could speak of with pride—'that I dare to hope I shall be the last.'

'With Terry you would have been the first and the last.'

When I said that I saw in his eyes that I'd won a little corner in his heart, so I sought to drive my advantage home as far as I could. I know that what I said now was not spoken for my own sake or to bring some hope to the idle, entrancing dream I'd been indulging the moment he entered; I know that it was spoken only as an alarming note that would help Terry. And him. 'Just as you've often told me of your inability to believe in anything, so I've often told you of my doubts and difficulties. One of them is that I cannot go along with my church in its pronouncements against divorce. I feel that if a husband is unfaithful to a wife it is fair that he should lose her, and that she should have the chance to find a man who would love her enough to be faithful to her.' And, without mercy, I stressed, 'A man who would be worthy of her.'

The alarm was there in his eyes. 'Have you said this to Terry?'

'No,' and here again with all my heart I spoke against the

desire in my heart. 'And I shall never suggest it because I want you to come together and to be happy together again.'

He spoke in despair. 'I don't know what to do. I love Dorothy and I can't give her up. I can't. And I still love Terry. How could I do anything but love her? I love them both. I don't know where I am.'

'You're where you've put yourself.'

He shrugged at this, and then went into a silence. I began to feel an unprofitable counsellor, empty of further words, and waiting for him to speak again. When he did it was to tell me the staggering, unexpected thing. 'I think you ought to know that this affair with Dorothy has gone on some time, and there may be—there may be a child coming.'

The old brilliant hope, the old unspeakably happy temptation blazed before me. Siward married to Dorothy for the sake of the child. Terry mine. Mine. 'Throw them together now, and take Terry. Terry for your own.'

But again I knew that, by my loyalty to my Orders, by my love for such faith as I still had, by my love for this poor blundering boy, and, above all, for sure, by my very love for Terry, my only honourable task was to strive to bring them together again.

And with this knowledge came the first tiny flash that was to lead me at last to the long-awaited climax for the huge unfinished manuscript on my desk. If to such a self-preoccupied creature as myself could come a love so certainly, for once in a way, self-sacrificing, what limit could be set to Illimitable Love's self sacrifice on behalf of poor muddlers, blunderers and sinners?

This was but a tiny flash of vision that events were to brighten.

But the child? I could hardly believe their conjecture was right. Why did they suspect this, I asked.

'She's missed two months.'

'But that carries no certainty, does it?'

'Not certainty, no. But a probability.'

That two young lovers of such prime intelligence should have made a havoc of their love-making seemed at first unlikely—till I remembered that I'd long come to the decision that nothing is impossible to believe of the wisest in the world.

I thought long and then said, 'If your suspicion is right, I don't really know how to advise you. All I can say with all my heart and soul is that if you still love Terry—as I know you do—and since she is your loving wife, and her whole life is bound up with yours, *I* think your first duty is to her.'

If only I could tell him as he rose to go sadly away, that I was fighting for his sake and Terry's and entirely against my own . . . but this could not be said. Mine was a love that dare not speak its name. When he left me, saying in answer to my apology for advice so purely personal, 'But thanks, thanks all the same,' I knew that we had reached no decisions, but I suspected I had done a little to salve a marriage which had been perfect for a while.

15

Crisis in that Chamber

During the next days it was plain that, if I had plunged my sword a little way into Siward's heart, it had not reached far enough for him to consider a parting with Dorothy or the rescue of Terry from her torments of love and jealousy. I had little doubt that he was worn by the conflict within him; he did not lie when he said that he loved Terry, that he hated the thought of hurting her, but to break with Dorothy and lose the embraces of a girl of such beauty and passion and quality was beyond him; he lacked the will to embrace a martyrdom.

So he could do nothing but argue with himself that in this free, modern world he was entitled to both this new passionate love for Dorothy and the old but now tempered love for Terry. I could understand and feel a pity for him as well as the almost unbearable pity for the girl who had suddenly become a wonder and a strange sweetness in my heart. Old days of long ago, but I can still recall with assurety that this sudden love for Terry was a transporting joy strong enough to carry everywhere the pain of accepting that her love was directed, and now wildly so, elsewhere. And that this stable pain—at times a spasmodic pain—was blent with the poignant happiness of fighting to win for her all that she longed to have again.

How could I do other than pity those two young creatures when I knew they were sharing their bed in the room below mine, each turned unhappily away from the other, the girl sometimes shaken with sobs and the boy, not empty of pity, but unable to speak or argue or justify, and still less to touch and comfort her as he longed to do. He could only lie there with his heart forbidden one single ministering caress.

All this he told me one evening. 'Whenever I wake she seems to be still awake. I know she's awake though she's turned from me. She's not always sobbing but, if she is, she tries to hide it. Oh, God, padre, what am I to do?'

I answered compassionately but uncompromisingly, 'There's

only one thing to do if you want to hold Terry. It may cost you the earth, but, if you'll listen to me, she's worth it.'

I could do nothing in the following days but watch the sufferings of Terry. Few things wounded me more than the courage with which she acted a show of ease and content before all the others around Miryam's table. I don't think one of those eager-eyed and gossiping women—not Miryam nor Jane Julia nor Hetty nor Hyacinth nor Emmeline who could have been lyrical (over her dishes and plates) if she'd known the truth; and certainly not Willy—suspected anything at all about the anguish at work within her. All that this chorus of watchers in our little domestic tragedy might say or sing, if they observed now and then a quietness in her, was something like, 'It's touching the way she misses him. She's wretched when he's away. All her liveliness stops when he's not in the house.' Or another voice : 'Yes, we all used to love like that, I suppose, when we were young.' And another; if Terry had risen and gone rather silently and sadly from the dinner table, 'She never spoke once through the whole meal. What it is to love !'

Only I knew the truth, and I wondered and waited helplessly. But night after night in my bedchamber I put up a prayer that her heart-ache might be eased. Most of my prayers were formal, dutiful, repetitive things, but this one was fire. The easing of her heart-ache could only be achieved by the destruction of all my impossible dreams, and I prayed for it. Over and over again, passionately, before rising from my knees and getting sadly into bed, where I probably repeated the prayer again. If only I could put enough power into it, I told myself, surely it must work something for her. Our world was not a world of stable 'being' but of invisible, restless, wayward 'becoming', and who knew the part that passionate thoughts and prayers might play in it?

Siward, at this time, could be away, for night after night working, so he proclaimed, greatly to the interest of the chorus, in the Midland stations of the B.B.C. No doubt there was truth in this explanation—and an occasional lie. No man has ever led a double life without an occasional lie, and at least it could be argued that such lies as he told to Terry or to us were spoken to save her pain.

She never knew when to believe them. During his absence an invincible restlessness possessed her like some cerebral disease; it could attack her like a seizure, forcing her to get out of the house and into the Baby Austin, and to drive anywhere, anywhere. I might ask her pityingly on her return, 'Well, where have you been today, darling?' and she would answer, 'Oh, anywhere, anywhere.'

I knew, and it tore my heart to know, that one day she dashed from the house, sprang into the Baby Austin waiting on the drive, and drove it fiercely to the Strand and Savoy Hill, that little leafy square where a tall red-brick Victorian building, tall but unassuming, was the headquarters of the B.B.C. Opposite it was the King's Chapel of the Savoy, grey and grim with its stump of a tower and its sooty garden fringed with forgotten tombstones.

I say it rent my heart to think of Terry hiding her little car on the Embankment and returning up Savoy Street to linger spying from its corner to see if Siward really left the B.B.C.'s headquarters and, if so, in what direction he went. Lingering there conscious that it was all a mad business, because how could she know if he was in the Savoy Hill building, or whether he would leave it, or where he would be going if he did appear.

Then came a week when surprisingly her behaviour changed : she seemed steadier and more complacent. At our table, during one of her silences, there could be an enigmatic smile in her eyes and playing about tight determined lips. And after dinner one evening there came again that affectionate touch on my hand and, when we were all leaving the dining room, the murmured but smiling request, 'Can I come and see you this evening, Hugh dear? *Do* let me. *Please*.'

' "*Let*" you"? And "please"?' I repeated. 'Why, you know that there's nothing that ever gives me greater pleasure. "The pleasure is mine", as the polite people say, but in this case it happens to be sincere. Come at once.'

The others had gone ahead so I was able to take her by the hand and lead her up the stairs to my high chamber, giving her hand a strong pressure to show how fully I understood and was with her in all things.

Hand in hand we went into the room where, closing the door, I said, 'Now sit down and tell me anything or everything.'

Tonight she did not sit on the floor with her legs curled under her. Her thoughts, I imagined, were too disordered for so peaceful a pose, and she went and sat herself stiffly on my divan.

'What? Not the floor?' I laughed. 'If you're tired of the floor, you can have my chair and be really comfortable. But come——' and I picked up her hand again. 'The floor, I think. I like you best on the floor.'

'Oh, well,' she said with a sigh. 'Why not?' And she arranged herself on the floor while I lit the fire for her.

She did not speak even when I was comfortable in my chair; she sat gazing at the tall, stilted, regimented flames of the gas-fire, till I encouraged her with a 'Well?'

She began, 'You said it was not in me to do what he's doing. But now I'm ready to do anything he does. At once. Why shouldn't I? If it's all right for him, it's all right for me.'

'You mean?'

'I mean that I should take a lover too. Why shouldn't I?'

'Why?' This was no more than a repeat of her question before I found an answer.

'Yes.' It was her turn to encourage me.

'Why? Because it's not in your nature. You'd be doing violence to yourself just to punish him.'

'Oh, no, I shouldn't. I could love someone else and I'm going to.'

'You mean you'd do it here and now without——' I avoided the heavy word 'adultery' lest I seemed to be just preaching—'without being legally parted from him?'

'Yes. Yes, of course.' She tried to say it with enthusiasm. 'Now. Right away.'

With some sort of sympathetic smile I asked, 'But, Terry, where is the man?'

'I'm sure there are plenty who would have me if I was ready to do as he does.'

'I am very sure of that too. Good gracious, yes. But——' I shook my head—'it's not possible for you. You couldn't do it without loving; and, as you told me, and as I can understand, all your love is now more tremendously his than it has ever been. No, Terry dear, it's not possible.'

'Yes, it is, because I could manage to love one of them. Probably there'd be only one, and I should love him. As far as I know there's only one girl with him now. He swears there is and, if I don't believe him in everything, I believe him in this because he always says it so gently. Only one, but one is enough. I could divorce him tomorrow—or I suppose he could divorce me, but he wouldn't. I know him. With all his faults he'd never let the blame fall on me. He'd accept it all himself. I'd divorce him and then I'd marry the man I loved. But I'm not going to wait months and months for that. I want to give myself to someone else. I'm not going on like this. I can't sleep. I seem to have lost the power to sleep. I suppose, quite simply, I want someone to comfort me. Someone to love.'

'But, dearest—' yes, I said that—'I know you, and you say you know him, and I know you couldn't do this with any happiness because your real love is tied to him.'

'I don't know that it's tied to him any more.' A silence, looking down. 'Sometimes I think it isn't. He's tried me too far. I know there are others I could love.'

'Can you tell me even one of them? Do I know him?'

'Yes.'

'Who is it?'

'You. You, of course. I know I could give all my love to you. You've always been so sweet to me. I love you, Hugh. I do. I love you already. Terribly.'

Impossible to speak. There broke before me a vision that raised an ecstasy of hope. I had to rise from my chair and stand, while I dealt with it, while I fought it. In all my life, before and since, never have desire and duty, longing and a higher love, done such battle in my heart. The vision displayed joys beyond belief. Inevitably the thought of my love for Terry, completing itself with her in my bed and in my arms, inflated my breast and disturbed my breathing. Even Terry's children and mine appeared in the vision, laughing at us gaily. Beautiful children, because they were Terry's; beautiful and almost beyond abandoning. Here was a wild temptation in my heart and body, the greatest I had ever known, but . . . I must win, I must win. It must not be. A spiritual death was on one side, life on the other.

And while I stood there, one part of me entranced by the vision, and another part struggling with it and struggling with an old memory— 'We are not of Alice, nor of thee, nor are we children at all. The children of Alice call Bartrum father. We are nothing; less than nothing, and dreams'—she said the words that were meant to save the vision for me, but destroyed it. 'I love you, Hugh. I do. I know I do.'

That 'I know I do' told me that she was but striving to replace her love for Siward by a love for me, and to believe that she had succeeded, but that she was not sure of it, and it was he whom she still loved.

And so, yet once again the ruthless eyes of duty expressed the truth for me : all my past, and, more than anything else, all my love for her and all my lesser love but real compassion for Siward, made it impossible for me to take her.

I had been assuring her that it was not in her nature to do this thing and now I knew it was not in mine. I must never overthrow, for either of them, what I had once said to Siward about faithfulness in love. This must not, *could* not, be done.

And again my anguished pity for her brought that other flash of vision, of revelation, larger now—brighter than before. If to a poor sinful lover like me there could come this intolerable pity and self-identification with sufferers, was not the same pity and self-identification in its highest conceivable shape the very substance of that Incarnation in which for long years I had been struggling to recover a full belief?

A quick passing thought, but in its brief moment it seemed like Illumination, as if all my difficulties with the living heart of my book might be at an end.

She had risen too, seeing conflict on my face, and she threw her arms around me, the first of us to speak. 'I love you; couldn't *you* love me? You say you no longer believe in all your Church demands. Couldn't we be happy together? I love you so.'

I only kissed her forehead and said with a helpless smile, 'What? Here in this house?'

'Yes, yes. You could have me in secret. As he does with her. Whenever you wanted me I'd come.'

The poor quaking forces of Duty and Truth which I had assembled were near to being shattered as she said this and I looked at her. They had to dig in deep.

Once she had said there were bands around her head and her heart; now I accepted that there were forbidding bands around mine. 'Darling,' I said, 'I love you very dearly, but I love Siward too. I want to see you both happy together again. I believe this is possible and I want to bring it about. I must do nothing to prevent it. If ever I believed it was impossible, and if you were free, then, oh my God, I——'

But she dropped her arms from me sadly . . . since I had refused her offer of herself.

So I hurried on, 'Darling, never believe that when I said I loved you it only just meant that I have a deep affection for you. It meant much more. It meant that I am in love with you. I've known this for some time and you've made me more than ever in love with you tonight. Don't believe that I'm not denying myself and don't want you. I can't imagine anything more perfect than to have you for my wife. But don't you see that I can't ask you to do things that would be wrong for you to do. I love you too much. Do let it be a comfort to you that I'm here truly loving you with all the love that a man can feel for a woman.'

She turned from me and let her eyes fall to the heedlessly purring, orange-flamed fire. 'Yes, yes. I suppose you're right. You always are. And I suppose I know in my heart that you are. It's sweet to know you love me like that——'

'By heaven, I do. And you're the first I've ever loved like that.' Here I tried for her sake to smile and ridicule myself. 'Forty, and enduring all the torments of first love.'

'I'm not worthy of it; I don't begin to be worthy of it, Hugh dearest, but it *is* colossally comforting to have you there. . . . You really won't take me? You won't have me?'

'Darling, I can't. I mustn't. Would to God I could, and could believe it right.'

'No, of course you can't. I see it. I know it too. It was silly of me to think it might be possible—you're too good for that sort of thing—but I did know that I loved you, so I thought it might be all right. Ah well, I must go on somehow; I must go on, but oh—' she added, speaking more to the fire than to me— 'if only I could sleep.'

16

'If only I could Sleep'

For many days the rift between Terry and Siward stayed hope-lessly unresolved. She could not master her misery or accept anything less than his final parting from Dorothy; and he was still unequal to any such heroic resolution. Round our dining-table at breakfast or dinner Terry enacted some sort of normal behaviour, but once the meal was done she absented herself from us all behind the shut door of her room. Within that enclosed pen she would sit upon the bed thinking and thinking or wandering round and round till in despair she dashed aimlessly out into the streets. I knew all this, for ever and again, in the Lounge or on an empty landing, she would tell me all with a brave self-deprecating smile, whereafter I would give her a kiss of consolation and perhaps add, 'He will come back to you, darling. It's you he really loves,' at which she would only shake her head despairingly.

Hitherto she had smoked but seldom, but now she was smoking cigarette after cigarette in trembling procession. When Siward was at home they hardly spoke at all. Nor did they speak in their bed, but lay side by side, turned whenever possible from one another. Sometimes Siward was away for the night, reputedly on programme work for the B.B.C., but which of us two, either Terry or I, could believe that this was certainly the truth?

So passed several days and then one night Siward was away at the Leeds studio of the B.B.C. and would almost certainly not return before morning. Of course she suspected that he would really be spending the night with Dorothy, and she talked wildly to me about ringing up the B.B.C. late in the evening to learn where in fact he was. I saw no reason why she shouldn't do this, justifying the request with some talk of important news. But she didn't do this; I don't know why; perhaps she didn't want to have her suspicions confirmed or enlarged; it might even be that some part of her didn't want them destroyed.

Instead as that evening darkened, she set out on one of her distracted drives in the Baby Austin round and round, 'anywhere,

anywhere'. Among other places she drove speedily towards, and slowly past, the Ladies' Residential Club in Elvaston Place where Dorothy had her home. What she expected to learn from the blank face of that portentous stucco mansion who can say? From it she learned nothing.

Terry had told me much but not all. One thing she told nobody. I suppose she felt some shame about it because at this time, nearly half a century ago, the habit of taking a sleeping drug was not the widespread custom it is today. It was frowned upon and despised. I remember once, when I was torn by new religious doubts from bringing my book to its possible climax, I endured two or three nights of sleeplessness and wrote to my doctor suggesting he gave me some bromide or chloral. His reply was like a gunshot. 'Leave it,' he wrote. 'Let it rip. It will pass. Indulging in hypnotic drugs becomes all too easily an addiction. They may give you a glorious relief at first but you have to be for ever increasing the dosage if they are to have any effect, and in the end the addict may become little more than a drifting hypochondriac.' As I didn't wish to become this, I let it all slide. It passed and soon I was sleeping peacefully again.

But Terry in her craving for sleep, after nights of what she called 'a wooden awakeness', had sought out a local doctor. Her own family doctor was a hundred miles away in Cissborough, and since in all the years she had been with us she had enjoyed the unbroken health of her early twenties, she had to look now for a doctor near-by. She chose a woman doctor, a Dr Marion Lessingham, imagining that if she had to explain the sources of her insomnia, a woman would listen more understandingly to such troubles, and minister to them better than any man. Dr Lessingham, blonde, plump and of comfortable figure, was a good choice, as I could not doubt when later events involved her in telling me all about the interview in her surgery.

Terry, after stuttering apologies, told her all her story, only too relieved to have someone to tell it to fluently. Seated before the doctor's desk, she told it stressing its sadder parts, in her fashion, by out-thrown gestures of one hand or both, and she ended, 'Doctor, I must sleep. Please, please help me to sleep.'

Dr Lessingham, sympathetic, able and compassionate, laid a kindly hand on Terry's where it was now nervously fingering her desk, pressed down on it as if she would still its restlessness by comfort and advice and said, 'My dear, I can understand every-thing but——' and here she tried to dissuade her from the use of any drug, just as my doctor had dissuaded me. 'You so young and healthy can stand up to what seems a prolonged sleeplessness without the use of a drug, however great your trouble, and I understand how great it is. You know, you probably sleep more than you think you do. We nearly all of us do, even with heavy troubles on our minds. We could swear that we haven't slept one wink all through the night but it isn't so. If we looked at our watches we would see that we have slept a whole hour, or an hour and a half between one harassing thought and another. And in any case it's not loss of sleep that makes you feel worn out and drained and empty in the morning; it's the tension itself, the anxiety.'

'Oh, please, doctor, please.'

But the doctor's head still shook. 'And you see, dear, all hypnotics are dangerous weapons; you can't have them without paying their price—I don't mean money, but their final effects. They can depress heart and lungs and perhaps the whole of one's system. Then think of this : the truth is that, if people don't sleep for their expected eight hours or so, the fact is that they simply don't need to. Many people only really need six, five, or even four hours. Some of the most brilliant people in the world have needed only four hours. One can get more and more used to only a little sleep every night. Take my advice and try, anyhow for a little longer, to do without any draught or pills.'

'Oh, *doctor.* . . .' That and no more came from Terry.

And Marion Lessingham saw the deep disappointment on her visitor's face, a kind of sick overthrow behind a blind silence, and she weakened. 'Very well,' she said, 'I'll give you—not a draught— but a very small supply of a new sleep-inducing tablet called Sophronyl, but you're never, never, to take more than two and, if absolutely necessary one more four hours later. Promise me that, please.' Then with a gentle laugh she said, 'You're not very big; if you were twice the size and twice the weight I might let you take more. You see the larger and heavier the patient the more he can absorb safely. I'm not saying that more than two can be lethal, but they wouldn't be good for you and I fear they would only increase your depression. So remember every word I've said.'

Terry said 'Oh thank you, thank you, doctor' and went out of the house carrying the pills in her hand like a prize.

Tonight she would sleep.

§

That night, trying scrupulously to 'remember every word' the doctor had said, she took only one tablet at first; it produced no sleep at all; it did nothing to defeat the tossing misery in heart and brain; so, remembering that Dr Lessingham had said she might take two but no more at first, she took the second. After this she seemed, now and again, to get a few minutes of drowsing sleep but no more; and in the morning, worn and aching and emptied, she told herself with despair that there was nothing any-one would give her which would ensure the healing she hungered for : a long spell of sleep.

In the evening she set forth in the Austin to drive and drive and drive, with some idea that this, in the end, would tire the eyes to the point of somnolence. Surely she must sleep properly soon. Where to drive? Well, anywhere; what did anything or anywhere matter? And, so driving, she found herself once again in Elvaston Place and passing, at a slower speed, that magnetic pole, the Ladies' Residential Club. Why there? Why not? One might see something. And it must have surprised her, and seemed like an answer to prayer when, turning out of Elvaston Place into Queen's Gate, she saw Dorothy returning from the direction of Kensington Gardens.

Probably she could not decide whether to read comfort in this; it seemed more like comfort than anything else; but she stopped the car and ran back to talk with Dorothy.

All the substance of that strange, unnatural talk was given to us later. To me, then in my middle years, and with a life-long background in the Church's shade, it seemed incredible and crazy. There had been no violent quarrel between these two girls : Dorothy chose to believe that 'the civilised thing to do in these modern days' was to accept that promiscuity in love was natural and legitimate; while Terry, in the chaos and tempest of her thoughts, rather than let her supplanter think it was in her power to hurt, pretended to some agreement. Running from her halted car, she said with a brave show of friendliness, 'Hallo, Dorothy, don't pass me by.'

Dorothy, despite her published faith in freedom, could not cover up a slight embarrassment. 'Hallo, Terry, what are you doing round here?'

And so on the pavement these two girls, children of their age and rivals in love, stood talking amicably together.

'Oh, driving around,' said Terry. 'For something to do. Siward is away in his old Leeds. Did you know that? In Leeds, and won't be back tonight.'

'Yes, I think he told me that.'

'It's too unutterably boring at home. There's no one but all those old biddies to talk to. I never want to talk with anyone except Hugh, and I can't be for ever forcing myself on him. What are you doing?'

'Oh, been wandering round the Gardens. Along the Nurses' Walk looking at the flowers, and then along Brick Hill Walk and gazing absently down into the Serpentine from the bridge. I don't know why one always has to stop and stare at water.'

Doubtless Terry thought that here was the lonely musing of a girl in love. In love with *her* Siward. Passionately wanting him. Deep in the sadness and sweetness of love, as she gazed down, like Mélisande, into the water. But Dorothy offered no such picturesque explanation.

'Like you, I'm just bored,' she said, 'and there was nothing else to do.'

'Been to any more cinemas lately?' One must talk easily.

'No, there's nothing worth seeing. You been anywhere?'

'No, no. . . . I haven't felt like it. You've not been back to the old Forty-Three?'

'Gracious, no. I don't even know that it's still in being. Mother Meyrick is safely in prison for bribing the police, or something —there for months yet. Meanwhile the great place is her "Silver Slipper". All the celebrities go there from every known milieu : art and stage and music and literature. And Royals in plenty. Including one, full-blooded King. Poor exiled and harassed Carol of Rumania with his current lady.'

'You've been there obviously?'

'Once. And saw the King and his girl.'

Terry did not ask 'With Siward?' though her heart must have been throbbing, hammering, with the question. Not once did she cry out, 'Why can't you leave him alone? Leave him. Leave him to me. He's mine. He's always been mine.' She said, 'What are you going to do now?'

'I suppose I'm going home to bed.'

'Bed. You're lucky if you can sleep. You can, I suppose?'

'Oh yes, I sleep well enough.'

What must Terry have thought of that? Did Dorothy, friend and supplanter, conscious of Siward's distant love, drop at once into a happy, untroubled, impenitent sleep? But say nothing; say only, 'Lucky you,' half laughingly. 'Dorothy, I haven't slept really properly for ages. I seem to have lost the art. That's rather why I'm driving round and round. To get tired.'

If Dorothy saw a reason for this sleeplessness, which she probably and instantly did, she chose to show no sign of it. 'Can't your doctor give you something?'

'I've got something.' And even to a rival whom in her heart she must hate, Terry poured out the story of her doctor and her Sophronyl, as people always will, about their pains and their doctors. 'But it doesn't work. I wouldn't say it produces nothing, I daresay I doze a little, but it doesn't seem like it. It seems like being awake the whole night through. And tossing and tossing everlastingly. Still, there it is. I daresay everybody has periods like this . . . for no apparent reason.' No apparent reason. Didn't Dorothy even shiver, if ever so slightly, at those words? 'Well, I won't keep you from your happy bed. I'll just go on driving round a bit, and then home to bed. Wish me luck.'

These last three words had a strange tone in them, Dorothy thought. 'Wish me luck.' Why strange? What more could they mean than 'Wish me sleep tonight'?

Terry, with a smile, went back to her little car and, when in it, opened the near-side window, lifted a hand in farewell, and said, 'Good-bye.'

'Good-bye.' But Dorothy's wave was not seen by Terry whose face had swung quickly back into the car.

Dorothy turned home.

§

Surprisingly Siward came home from Leeds very late that night—or, rather, in the small dark hours of the morning. He told me afterwards that it was an increasing anxiety about Terry and an aching pity for her that persuaded him to take a train between nine and ten that travelled through the night. So all our house was asleep when he softly opened the front door at about half-past three in the morning. He tip-toed up the stairs and softly opened the door of his room lest Terry should be asleep. She lay with her face to the wall turned away from the room that had once been the place of her happiness. She did not stir as he crept in but she was breathing slowly so that he hoped that at last she was sleeping peacefully. Carefully he got into the bed beside her, and tonight, in his pity, lay with his face towards her. For some time he just lay there, listening to her slow quiet breathing but then he peeped over her head and saw, to his surprise and distress, that her eyes were open. At once, overcome by remorse, he, though forbidden to touch her, turned her forcefully round towards him, gathered her into his arms, and whispered, 'Terry . . . you do know that I love you as I love no one else?' Her arm lay listless but he folded it around him and repeated, 'I do love you, sweet.'

Was there for a second a response; did that enfolding arm for one brief second try to close on him in a faint, almost reluctant, response? It was only the slightest movement, barely enough to be called an answer, but it had been there, and enough to please him, so that, tired after his six-hour journey he dropped into sleep, while his arms were still about her, and her one arm lying over him. Her eyes when last he saw them in the greying dawn were no more than half open, and he did not know if she was asleep or not.

His was a long sleep from which he did not wake till after eight. Then he came rushing up to my room. 'Hugh, Hugh, Hugh. Terry's unconscious. I can't wake her. But her eyes are half open. Oh, Hugh, what is the matter? Do come.'

I went down to their room and looked at Terry lying there, her eyes half open, half shut, her hair disordered on the pillow and her lips parted to allow a slow, slow, rather sterterous breathing. Her face had little colour unless it was a grey-white colour, and the lips were a little blue. In alarm I touched her on the arm. It seemed unnaturally cold and yet damp to the touch. It was clear that she felt nothing; that she was motionless, senseless, and could not be aroused.

'God, Siward!' I exclaimed. 'Get a doctor. Quick. She's plainly in some sort of coma.' And I tried to comfort him—and myself—

saying, 'I know nothing about this sort of thing, except that a coma isn't necessarily alarming.'

'Oh, Hugh, she'll be all right? Tell me she'll be all right.'

'Yes, yes,' I said, though my heart was sick within me. 'She's so young and strong. Loss of consciousness can be produced in all sorts of ways, and it's only temporary.' So I said, but my heart was saying, 'Oh, my God! My darling, my darling. . . . Oh God, help her. . . . Let it be nothing. . . .'

The hateful word 'stroke' occurred to me, but how could this come to a girl so young and fresh, so charged to the brim, and beyond the brim, with vitality? I remembered too, for my comfort, that a stroke was far more common in men than women. 'No, Siward, this is but a faint of some sort . . . a faint.' But he, beside himself with fears, pale as a mask, was crying out louder than he knew, 'Terry . . . Terry . . . my Terry . . .' and then, 'Oh, it's my fault. I know it is. Oh, tell me, padre, she'll be all right.'

Again I lied amply to strengthen him, though I had just seen on the mantelpiece the bottle of tablets and a glass. 'I'm sure she will. Why, we've never known her ill. Of course she'll recover soon. I'm sure it's only a matter of time.'

When possible, I went back to my room and prayed, for how long I know not. I could not lift myself from my knees. I prayed blindly, indifferent to all my doubts, ransacking every memory for hope and prayers . . . my thoughts wandering, recovering, stumbling on. . . . Oh, Christ who walked in Galilee healing . . . Jairus's daughter. . . . Be not afraid; only believe : the maid is not dead but sleepeth. . . . *Talitha cumi;* which is, being interpreted, Damsel, I say unto thee, arise. . . . Not dead, but sleepeth. . . . Not dead . . . *Talitha cumi.* . . . Oh God, God, if thou wert *he* who walked in Palestine—if thou art there—forgive my imperfect faith and don't let her for whom I pray suffer for it . . . I lay her before thee . . . I leave her with thee . . . Amen, amen. And so on. On . . . and on. . . .

In time a strange doctor came, for as yet we knew nothing about Dr Marion Lessingham; he summoned an ambulance and two gentle, kindly men carried her away with Siward beside her to St Benedict's Hospital near at hand.

I went back to my room and prayed, 'Oh please God, help them both'; and again I found it difficult to rise from my knees. I prayed as if I could believe—what it is impossible to believe—

that God could alter the past and make it that she had *not* taken a dangerous number of those sleeping tablets. 'Oh God, *please, please*....'

But this was Terry's last sleep.

And whenever I remember this, I wonder with a full heart, 'Did she for one moment in that last sleep hear those words from her husband, "I love you as I love no one else"?' Were these the last words she heard in her life? And always, even to this day, I pray that she heard them.

17

The King's Interest

A room like a small Baptist chapel with Gothic windows and a roof soaring upward to a point; a dais at one end where a holy table might have stood but which instead held the Coroner's desk and handsome chair; above this chair, on a blank wall, the Royal Arms, manifesting the duties of a Coroner, which are to watch the interests of the Crown. On the left of the Coroner's seat was the witness box; to its right the long pews for a jury, should a jury be empanelled; and before it a handsome table for counsel, and a less handsome one for the press.

Beyond the windows' Gothic tracery one could see the lawns of a public garden, but the sky was grey and lowering, so that all the lights, pendent from the roof, had been lit to disperse a morning twilight from the room.

Ten in the morning. For the present only two uniformed police officers represented His Majesty's Coroner, one at a door behind the Coroner's desk, the other at the public's door. Among the public seated in the pew-like seats were Siward and Dorothy who would be witnesses, and all of us from Miryam's house.

We sat in a line, Miryam, Willy, Hyacinth, Hetty, Jane Julia and myself. Siward sat beside me. Dorothy sat apart.

At the end of our row sat the most striking figure in the room, another of Miryam's guests, if a temporary one : Archdeacon O'Neale, father of Terry. 'Venerable' is the title of an archdeacon, and in figure and face Terry's father was worthy of it : tall figure, silvering hair, and fine features from which perhaps Terry had inherited some of her looks. In these distant years archdeacons did not shrink from wearing for formal occasions their full formal dress, gaitered and aproned like a bishop, but lacking pectoral cross and ring. This was a very formal occasion, indeed a King's occasion; and Archdeacon O'Neale was dressed for it. Every eye fell upon him, as the people entered. His face was very sad, and I noticed that once or twice he touched a corner of an eye with a finger.

Now another man of fine appearance, with wholly white hair and clipped moustache, entered by the public door carrying a sheaf of notes; and a fussy little know-all, sitting on my other side, whispered, 'Professor Daniel Tullet. The famous pathologist. Professor of Forensic Medicine at the University of London.'

'So?' I said in no great gratitude. And 'Really?'

The Professor sat himself in the front row of the public pews with some documents and a newspaper on his lap, as if he were no more important than any of us.

Suddenly, while I was day-dreaming with my eyes on the lawns and flower-beds without, the policeman on the dais called loudly, 'All rise for His Majesty's Coroner.'

We stood for the Coroner's entry. No wig or gown for a Coroner: he was just an ordinary man in ordinary dark clothes who might have walked in from the street. Tall, slender, hair untouched by grey, his manner as he took his seat was one of quiet, untroubled competence. He might have been a business man arriving at his office, or a doctor in his surgery—and indeed the fussy little informant at my side, eager to impress, whispered, ' 'E's a doctor and barrister both. You have to've bin a practisin' doctor of five years' standin' for this game, but 'e's a barrister too.'

'I see. Thank you.'

The Coroner dealt first with some cases that he'd decided to adjourn, but in which he was prepared to authorise immediate burials. Then after some talk with his police officer he announced in a voice no louder than a voice in a fireside conversation, 'This is an inquest into the case of a young woman, a Mrs Theresa Bartleby, who was discovered in a coma on Thursday of last week and died in hospital the following day without recovering consciousness. The precise cause or causes of her death we have now to establish.'

Instantly the police officer called loudly, 'Mr Siward Bartleby, please.'

Siward left my side and walked with a firm step to the witness box, but I could see that this was no small effort; his face was strained and white, his brows frowning, his lips tight-set, and his fingers trembling or clutching into fists.

'Oh God, help him.' Some fear forced from me this ejaculatory prayer.

In the witness box the officer appeared to be asking him whether he would take the oath on the Bible or prefer, as an unbeliever, to 'affirm', and it surprised me to see—or perhaps it didn't now surprise me—that Siward seemed to have lost all interest in his once strongly declared atheism, and likely enough didn't now know or care what he believed—for he put out his right hand languidly to accept the little black testament from the policeman. And the policeman, holding the same testament, said, 'Say after me' and dictated the oath, clause by clause—whereat there leapt into my mind that this was just what the priest had done when he dictated to Siward the plighting of his troth with Terry : 'Say after me. I, Siward, take thee, Theresa, to my wedded wife . . . to have and to hold. . . .'

Now he was repeating after the policeman, 'I swear by Almighty God that the evidence I shall give shall be the truth, the whole truth . . . and nothing but the truth.'

The policeman took back the testament and for some reason unexplained said in a low voice, 'Just leave your hands on the desk.'

Siward obeyed, laying his trembling fingers on the brink of the desk.

The Coroner turned towards him and spoke gently, sympathy and understanding softening his voice and manner. 'You are Mr Siward Bartleby of 18 Christian Street, an employee of the British Broadcasting Corporation and the husband of the deceased?'

'Yes, sir.'

I noticed that the words, 'British Broadcasting Corporation' had been enough to start the reporters writing on their pads, anything about the B.B.C. being always likely news.

'And you have identified her in the hospital of St Benedict as your wife, Theresa Bartleby, who was born in 1905 and was therefore some twenty-five years of age?'

'Yes, sir.' He only managed this answer by conquering a gulp.

After writing his Notes of Evidence on long pages of foolscap the Coroner proceeded, 'I must come now to the circumstances in which she died. It was you, I understand, who found her lying unconscious in her bed?'

'I didn't know that she was unconscious at first, sir. It was only in the morning at about eight o'clock.'

'I understand.' The Coroner writing, writing. 'But it was you who first found her unconscious and hurried for help. Now would you try to tell me all about her state of mind in the days previous to her death. What do you know of the circumstances that immediately led to her death? Tell me in your own words.'

'She had been terribly unhappy, sir, because she thought that I . . . because she knew that I . . . because we'd been very happy together for a long time, but now—' at last he spoke the words, with head lowered towards the two hands on the desk—'she knew that I was in love with someone else.'

The reporters writing, writing. A human story here.

Seeing his distress, the Coroner, after himself writing a note, encouraged him in still gentler tone, 'Go on.'

A long silence. Silence from Siward with his head still lowered; and silence, a staring silence, from everyone else in the court. Though silent, one apprehended a generous sympathy from most parts of the room. And in the silence the rumour of the world's traffic, heedless, unending, became suddenly audible from across the garden lawns. I caught some easy birdsong from among the trees; a thrush, I thought, and a blackbird. For the first time I heard a church clock far away chiming the quarters.

The Coroner encouraged him again. 'There's no hurry. Only tell us when you feel you can. Try to tell us all.'

Siward lifted his head. 'I came home unexpectedly because I was unhappy about her. I came back by a night train from Leeds and didn't arrive home till about three in the morning. I went to our room and she seemed to be lying asleep, but her face was turned from me so I could not be sure. I got into bed beside her, but I could not sleep because her stillness worried me and I thought her breathing a little strange, so I turned her round towards me and put my arms around her to say something comforting. It was then I believed she was conscious, or had a moment of consciousness, because when I held her tight and . . . said that I loved her, there seemed to be an answering clasp—a sort of grateful clasp—for a moment only and then—I don't know—she may have been unconscious again, because she said nothing, but after that faint response I fell asleep quickly. I was very tired and it had comforted me.'

But here I saw, by the desperate bite on his lower lip, the quivering of his head, and the arrested uprush of one hand on his face —arrested because he was ashamed to touch his eyes before the people—that the sobs were high in his throat, and that until he could get command of himself, speech was impossible. His unshed tears were infectious, and there was a stir among the people. I saw that ·Miryam was fighting back her sobs and that Hetty McGee had a handkerchief at her mouth which she had just dabbed at her eyes. Even Jane Julia's face was softened, though she was not a woman to weep. Uncle Willy's face was sympathetic too. There was every reason why he should have sympathy with an illicit lover.

In a voice yet gentler the Coroner said, 'Take your own time. Would you like to sit down? Constable, get him a chair.'

'No, no.' Siward said it loudly and braced back his shoulders. 'I am sorry, sir. I can go on.'

'Good. Perhaps you would tell me if she had ever spoken to you about taking a sleeping draught or tablets.'

'Never to me, sir. She had only complained many times that she couldn't sleep, but I had no idea that she had consulted a doctor about this. When she went to a doctor I do not know.'

'Well, we shall shortly hear about that from the doctor herself. Now, in any conversation with you, did she ever say she wished to end her life?'

'Never, never, never.' He affirmed this more loudly than anything to which he had testified before. I could see that he was trying to convince the Coroner—and himself—beyond all doubt that the death was an accident. 'She could be warmly angry and rebellious sometimes. Even defiant, but it never lasted.'

'Would it be possible, Mr Bartleby, that in her considerable unhappiness she could have drunk much alcohol?'

'No, sir. She drank hardly ever. A little wine sometimes when we were lucky and could afford it.'

A small appreciative smile from the Coroner that was almost paternal. 'And there was no letter of any kind left for you?'

'Oh, no, no, no.'

'So you say you never had the least fear, even though her distress was very great that she might take her own life?'

'Oh, no, sir. She was terribly distressed, and it was all my fault, I know, but that she would dream of taking her life never entered my imagination, and I can't believe it now and never shall.'

The Coroner wrote slowly, taking time, I thought, for his witness to achieve some ease. Then he just asked, 'Is there anything else you can tell me?'

Siward stood thinking—racking memory for some things that would support his plea for the kinder verdict—and his hope that this would be the truth. 'I know, sir, that she went to another guest in our house and told him everything . . . and that he told her to wait and try to forgive because he was sure I should come back to her in the end. I knew that she would listen to him—' all our company, Miryam, Willy and the rest, turned to look at me as he was saying this—'and I'm sure he helped her to bear up and hold on. She would have promised him that she'd do nothing wrong.'

For a moment I feared the Coroner might call me as a witness, but apparently he thought Siward's words were evidence enough.

'And that is all you can tell me?'

'I'm afraid so, sir.'

'Well, thank you very much, Mr Bartleby. You have been very helpful.'

Siward returned to his place among us, and I was surprised but glad to see that Jane Julia, of all people, laid her hand on his in comfort or congratulation.

The second witness was the house surgeon who had admitted Terry to St Benedict's. So young he looked, as if fresh from school, and I could see that he was not without pride in the skill with which he gave his evidence and the fine technical words he used to describe their attempts at resuscitation. To most of us his jargon was learned but unintelligible. A few simple, sad words rang out at the end, 'She was in a coma, and, never regaining consciousness, died at four-thirty-three in the afternoon.'

The Coroner nodded, and his police officer called, 'Miss Dorothy Cotteril, please.'

Dorothy walked up to the witness box. I had never seen her looking more beautiful, but could I blame her for having had her autumn-tinted hair well set and given of her best to a nearly perfect face, when a public appearance was before her? Her long slender figure however was no longer arrayed in a highly coloured dress to tone with the hair, but in a dark coat suited to the occasion. She wore no hat, perhaps because it would veil too much of her hair—but who knows?

She, unlike Siward, when offered the choice of swearing by Almighty God or just affirming, proudly showed her atheism by the single word, 'affirm'; and following the officer's dictation, holding no testament, said, 'I do solemnly, sincerely, and truth-fully declare and affirm that the evidence I shall give shall be the truth, the whole truth, and nothing but the truth.'

'You are Miss Dorothy Cotteril, an Assistant Principal at the Home Office?'

'I am.'

'And you saw Mrs Bartleby the evening before her husband, from whom we have heard, found her unconscious. How did you come to meet her? Tell us in your own way.'

'I was returning home to my club and when she passed me in her little car she stopped at once and called "Dorothy" as she got out to come and talk with me.'

'You are old friends?'

'Oh, no, just acquaintances. I don't think I've met her more than half-a-dozen times.'

'And yet she wanted to talk with you. What did you judge her state of mind to be in this sudden meeting?'

'Well, I could detect that she was gravely troubled about some-thing, and that she was trying to hide it.'

'How did the trouble manifest itself to you?'

'By the stumblings in her speech and the restless movements of her hands and by an exaggerated pretence of goodwill towards me which was a little difficult to understand. I judged it to be a brave effort on her part.'

'Miss Cotteril, I'm afraid I must ask you this question : it was you, was it not, of whom she might have had some cause to be jealous?'

I observed a tremble at her mouth but she carried her head high as she answered simply, 'Yes.'

Once again a stir among all in the room, and I guessed that many, especially the women, were thinking that jealousy was more than likely to rise around a creature so lovely; and were wondering how far it had caused a tragedy. The women probably not wanting in disapproval.

The Coroner may have noticed the stir but he acted an indif-ference and continued calmly, 'Your suggestion is that she was determined not to show this jealousy?'

'Yes, I feel that is true. I repeat that I thought it a brave effort.'

'Well now; tell me : did she say anything about her sleepless nights and the tablets she was taking?'

'Oh yes, she said much. She poured out a lot about it, as people generally do about their doctors and their medicine.'

To this the Coroner, himself a doctor, accorded a tight brief smile. 'Can you tell us anything further about that?'

'Only that she said the tablets hadn't worked at all and she remained awake throughout the night, or so it seemed to her. I tried to comfort her by saying that she probably slept more than she knew.'

'And you were probably right. . . . Miss Cotteril, was there anything in her state that you would have called abnormal? You have said that she seemed troubled. Was it your opinion that it was even more than this?'

'No, I don't think so because she was always excessively demonstrative. I did think it strange when she said she was just driving meaninglessly around.'

'Did she use any words that you thought unusual?'

Dorothy, like Siward before her, stood thinking; and the Coroner, tapping his pen on his manuscript, but not impatiently, left her to think. At last she spoke. 'Yes, there were two things I found unusual. After she'd said that she'd just go on driving round and round, she turned towards her car, and then turned back to me and said, "Wish me luck".'

'What did you think she meant by that?'

'I didn't know. I couldn't see what it meant. Perhaps it meant "Wish me luck with my tablets tonight".'

'And the other thing that seemed unusual?'

'When she was back in the car with its door shut, she suddenly leant out of its window, lifted her hand, and said, "Good-bye".'

'Why did that seem unusual?'

'Simply because it was never a customary phrase with her. And its utterance seemed out of place and a little deliberate. Usually she said, "Cheerioh" or "Chin Chin"—'

But here happened the most extraordinary thing of all that morning. Who knows anyone? Which of us knows the deeps of his nearest or dearest? Siward had saved himself from a breakdown in the box; this tall girl, apparently proud and tough and self-assured, failed as she testified to these two little syllables, 'Good-bye'; her face fell into her hands and stayed there while she sobbed. The kindly policeman at the box's side put an arm around her shoulders to console her. I thanked God that no eyes were away from her, and free to look at me, with my mouth tight-lipped and trembling to hold my tears, and my body shaking with them as I remembered Terry. Terry who might have been mine. The Coroner immediately said, 'I don't think I need trouble you any more, Miss Cotteril. Thank you very much. You have told us everything.' And the portly constable from the public doorway came forward, and as gently as any police matron took Dorothy, with her face still buried in her hands, and his comforting arm about her back, to a separate room, closing its door.

Then to the surprise of all our party, the policeman called an unfamiliar name.

'Miss Audrey Mackenna, please.'

And another girl walked to take Dorothy's place in the box. She looked to be in her early twenties. From the Coroner's questions it appeared that Terry, in her wild driving around, had met her, an old school friend, somewhere in the Brompton Road and, as with Dorothy, stopped her car to get out and talk with her. The girl's story was similar to Dorothy's. Terry had come quickly to her overriding subject, the craving for sleep, and her manner throughout, though over-intense, over-impetuous, was, in the girl's view, characteristic rather than abnormal. 'I have known her many years and she was always like that.'

'Then your impression was that her mind was distressed and distracted but not unbalanced?'

'Yes, I think that is right.'

'Thank you, Miss Mackenna.'

'Doctor Marion Lessingham, please.'

I had met Dr Lessingham before this official day, and could feel for her nothing but liking and admiration. She was small, unexpectedly young, with an attractive face and a voice soft but inspiring. As she gave her evidence I thought her an embodiment of goodwill and good sense.

'She said she was sleeping hardly at all at night and as a result felt completely drained and exhausted in the daytime. She begged me for a sleeping draught and a powerful one, but I tried at first to dissuade her from any such course. She told me the whole story of the matter that was troubling her, and I could see that she was very, very unhappy. So at last, after exacting a firm promise from her that she would act only as I counselled her, I gave her a prescription for some Sophronyl tablets, instructing her that she might take two at bed-time, and perhaps one more—but I hoped not—four hours later. I begged her to remember all I had said——'

It was at this moment and these words, that I guessed what had happened. 'Remember every word I have said.' Had not the doctor said, 'I'm not saying that more than two can be lethal,' and 'If you were twice the size and weight I might let you take more. The larger the patient, the more he can absorb safely'—and Terry, desperate for sleep, had gambled in her impetuous way on taking a large dose and absorbing it safely. And perhaps in her impatience, when even this seemed to be failing her, repeated the impetuous and rash adventure.

Dr Lessingham, continuing her evidence, convinced me that I was guessing aright.

'Sophronyl is usually a very effective hypnotic with prolonged action, but it is always possible that if the disturbances in the patient's mind are many and great, it may fail of its purpose. She gave me her promise again and again, but one must accept that she may not have been able to keep it in a state of grave distraction.'

Before the usual, 'Thank you, Doctor' the Coroner surprised us all by looking towards Siward and asking, 'Mr Bartleby, is there any question you would wish to put to Dr Lessingham? You may ask her any question you like, but—' here again the tight little smile—'you cannot make any speech or address the court.'

Siward rose from my side but did not speak at once. There was an empty pause, while the voices of happy children now playing in the public garden shrilled outside, and their ball impertinently (in both meanings of the word) struck the wall of the court. The Coroner looked at the window as if he were in the mood to order one of his officers to rebuke them, but he thought better of this and looked again at Siward. 'Yes, Mr Bartleby?'

Siward said, 'I can think of no question to ask the doctor, sir, but I hope I may be allowed to thank her for all she tried to do for my wife.'

And the kindly-smiling Coroner said, 'Well, I think I can regard that as a question and I am sure the doctor will have been glad to hear it.'

So Siward sat down, and again Jane Julia laid her compassionate hand on his. The Coroner turned his face towards Terry's father. 'Archdeacon, is there anything you would wish to say?'

The Archdeacon rose, at once the cynosure of all eyes. Too skilled in the formalities to phrase his words as other than a question, he opened subtly, 'Thank you, sir. I would only ask if it is legitimate for me to associate myself with the grateful words of my son-in-law, and also, if I may, to express my deep sympathy with him and with the young lady, Miss—' he hesitated over the name—'Miss Cotteril, who has recently given us her evidence.'

As he said these words I drooped my head. I could do no other in reverence for them. Here was a senior priest of my Church, and Terry's father, discharging his duty by expressing before all of us Christianity at its noblest. (*Neither do I condemn thee.*)

Visibly impressed, the Coroner said, 'Thank you, Archdeacon,' and, dismissing the doctor, 'Thank you, Dr Lessingham.'

§

Now the great and famous pathologist, Dr Daniel Tullet. Documents in hand, he walked to the box with the ease of one who had been accustomed, week after week, to visiting it, for years past. Excited and delighted, the officious little expositor at my side touched my thigh with the edge of his hand and murmured, 'Now you'll really hear something.'

'Yes, yes,' I said impatiently, for I was thinking, as the pathologist stepped into the box, 'Here is the man with the decision in his hands. The Coroner will pronounce the verdict, Misadventure or Suicide, but this is the voice that will determine it.' The small element of doubt clutched my heart. I stole a glance at Siward and saw him staring at this handsome man with mouth slightly open in fear or doubt. My heart beat in sympathy with him.

The pressmen leaned to the notepads on their table, or, lounging away from it, poised their pencils over the pads on their knees.

Dr Tullet laid his documents on the desk and without a glance at the constable stretched out a hand to receive the testament from him, held it and, needing no dictation, rattled off the oath, rearranging his papers the while.

To this familiar witness the Coroner said only, 'You conducted the examination, Dr Tullet; will you——' but before he could say any more Dr Tullet picked him up with a quick 'Yes, sir,' and with his face looking down upon his papers rattled off his story as he had rattled off the oath, rather as if he were thinking, the sooner this sorrowful business was over, the better for everyone. He testified that he had seen the capsules which were in the bedroom of the deceased; that each capsule contained about one and a half grains of phenobarbital; and that, while the exact poisonous dose could not be defined with any certainty, because it must vary with weight, the medical history, and the alcoholic intake of the deceased, he would regard ten capsules, or fifteen grains, dangerous, and twenty, in the case of a small light woman, as almost certainly a fatal dose, but there had not been so many as twenty available. So there seemed to be a picture of a small overdose of the drug followed by a much larger one taken in a state of distraction for want of sleep. There was no evidence of a lethal dose having been taken; there was no evidence of natural disease; and in his opinion death was caused by a fairly large dose and a softening of the brain for a while which deprived it of oxygen. 'We do not know at what hour in the night this dangerous dose was taken, but we do know that narcotics can vary in their danger according to the varying physiological time-scale in people.' Looking not at the Coroner but only at his papers on the desk, he ended with the abrupt statement, 'I give phenobarbital poisoning as the cause of death.'

With that, knowing that the Coroner would ask him no more questions, he reassembled his papers, stepped from the box, and, a tall man, strode quietly across the room and out of it.

It was now for the Coroner to declare his verdict. All waited while he looked through the notes he had written, and arranged them in chronological order. Then he spoke.

'The only question before me is the manner and nature of this poor young woman's death. Let me say at once, that, in my view, Dr Marion Lessingham who ministered to the greatly distressed young woman has nothing whatever to reproach herself with; nor does any blame attach to the doctors who received her into the hospital of St Benedict. They did everything that was right and proper in their attempts to save a valuable—and at one time an exceedingly bright—young life. Whether any blame attaches elsewhere it is not for me to pronounce, since, in the familiar phrase, this is not a court of morals. What seems adequately proved to me by the evidence is that this was a very intelligent young woman in the prime of her life; and accordingly I must say, first, that it seems inconceivable to me that if she had wished to disguise suicide as accidental she would not have set about doing so; and secondly, that, had she really intended to take her own life, she would have taken a dose of the drug that would have ensured the safe accomplishment of her task. This she certainly did not do; there were not tablets enough. So instead of this we have the picture of a dangerous but barely a lethal dose. She left no evidence, overt or covert, of a suicidal intention; nor has there been any history of previous self-destructive attempts. In the absence then of any evidence of intent I record a verdict that she died of phenobarbital poisoning administered by her own hand, but only in a distracted desire to secure sleep, and that her death was accidental.'

He folded the papers dealing with this case. The policeman called, 'All manner of persons engaged in this last case may now leave the court and take their ease.' All of us from Christian Street went out together. I supposed Dorothy to be still sitting in the room to which the portly policeman had led her, but I learned later that he had said to this proud girl, in the goodness of his heart but the poorness of his grammar, 'Now you just go home, ducks, and have a nice lay down. You've given your evidence beautifully.' As we went out through the door, and as the policeman called the first witness for the next case, I picked up Siward's hand for a moment, receiving a faint but hopeless pressure in return.

18

De Profundis Clamavi.
Ad Te, Domine

Within the hall of our house I again picked up Siward's hand, whose face was white as a waxen deathmask, and said, 'Come upstairs to my room and have a brandy. I'm not really a secret drinker there, but I keep my flask of cognac for occasional use—why not?' I was not trying to sound funny, but I had to say something, and perhaps lightness was best.

We went up to my room, and I think that, to both of us, this large upper room seemed empty, bleak and lonely, where so often three of us had been together, one sitting on the floor.

I put him into my easy chair, and poured for him a strong brandy, and he accepted it. I offered him a cigarette, but he only said blankly, 'No, no, no.' Then I waited, standing and wondering what words to use. I looked away from him because I could see the tears which he had withheld from the Coroner's view streaming from his eyes. Oh, what could I do for him? What to do? God, give me something to *do!*

Before I could say a word, and after he had sipped the brandy, he spoke. 'What the Coroner said doesn't matter. It didn't matter one way or the other. Whether it was an accident . . . or the other thing. I killed her.'

'No, Siward. It was a cruel mischance. You're never to think anything else.' I shook my head vigorously. 'No, no—please.'

'Yes, yes. I killed her. I killed her, and I shall believe it to my dying day. And may that day come as soon as it likes. It's useless your saying anything else. She said, "It's killing me." Those were her words. Oh, *God. . . .'*

I paced the floor and stood facing him again. 'Siward, do you remember telling me once, long ago, that she used to lull herself to sleep by repeating loving words you had said to her when she'd been in your arms?'

'Yes, yes, don't torment me with that.' His face fell into his hands as Dorothy's had done and stayed there, his head trembling. 'Not that. Not that.'

'There's comfort in it, Siward; not torment. Remember the last words she heard from you.'

'What last words?'

'You told me how on that last night you took her into your arms in the dark and said, "I love you as I love no one else." And you felt a moment of response as if she were trying to clasp you to her again. I am sure she heard you—' of course I am not sure but I declared firmly that I was— 'and isn't it comforting to think that the last words she heard as she sank back to sleep were of your love? And that they gave her some happiness?'

Siward, with his hands now dropped from his face, exclaimed, 'Oh God, let me think so. Say that all again, padre.'

I gave him his own words again. 'You said, "I love you as I love no one else." And you told me she used to repeat your words over and over to herself before going to sleep.'

But the agony of his remorse resumed its command. He shook his head. 'I killed her. She said to me on that night we quarrelled, "It's killing me. It's all killing me." *God!* And she looked so beautiful lying dead. So young. Oh, God, God, God.'

I shook my head again. 'No, no; think that she only wanted to sleep so as to wake again and find you loving her.'

But it was no good : I could not force my way through his armour of remorse. 'I killed her, padre; yes, I killed her, and I know that I loved her better than anything else on earth. . . . Heavens, heavens, I know it now.'

'It could be that she too knows it now.'

'Oh, tell me anything that could make me think that. I used to be proud of believing in nothing. Now I long to believe in something. You're a padre. Tell me something. Everything.'

Useless to offer any facile answers to this boy whose intelligence was with him even in the depths. I said only, 'I can't pretend to know what life after death may be like, but I stand with all the greatest in my Church who've said that it'll probably be entirely different from anything we can foresee, but it'll be there.'

'And Terry and I'll meet again?'

'Siward, I can only state my beliefs like this. Whatever it may be, it'll be something beyond any dreams or fancies of which we are capable. It always seems to me that its inconceivability to mortal men makes it easier to accept. After all, the idea's no less strange and miraculous than that two infinitesimal, invisible seeds should meet and grow into Shakespeare or Leonardo or Isaac Newton. I can only say I feel sure—quite sure—you can believe the best.'

'How I wish I could think it. But I seem able to believe only the worst. I'd give my soul to believe in something like that now.'

Inevitably, dutifully but haltingly and stumbling, I told him as I had told him often before, that belief in a God was not an emotional escape for me but a rational need. To me an accidental and purposeless Creation was inconceivable. I told him, as I had told Dorothy, dancing with her in the darkness of a night-club, that I believed God was Goodness too, not because any Church, fallible or infallible, ordered me to do so, but simply because, without a God who was Goodness and Love I couldn't understand the invincible impulse towards self-giving love and self-sacrifice in the saints or the heroes of history, and the invincible drive in all of us, even the worst, to bow down before and belaud all such heroic self-sacrifice. I used my old argument, 'Water cannot flow uphill unless the hill from which it springs is higher.'

He listened with interest but said nothing.

I tried to make it all easier for him by explaining that the God of the wisest teachers was beyond understanding; parable and poetry might attempt to suggest him; fatherhood, a kingdom, and power and glory we might speak of as his; but no intellectual conception could encompass him; he was forever an ineffable Mystery before whom one could but bow. 'You must give yourself to the Mystery; that is all. And intellectually it's just as simple to give oneself to the age-old fashion of worshipping this Mystery, with the demands it makes upon us, as it is to give oneself to the current fashion of worshipping a Freedom that demands no disciplines at all and usually leads to nothing in the end, except perhaps disaster.'

I didn't know how much impression I had made. He just sat there without answering, head bent, fingers fumbling together; but I didn't think all was lost on him; perhaps seeds were sown which would flower one day.

When he spoke it was only to return to the ruthless self-accusation. 'It makes no odds to me how she came to die. I was the cause of it, whatever she did. Oh, my God, my God, I shall never forgive myself till I die.'

I tried comfort again. 'This will pass. No torment like this endures for ever. Especially when it's not justified. Her death was an accident.'

He would not take it. With a speechless shake of the head he refused it.

I then suggested that perhaps in a year or two, he and Dorothy, who was plainly suffering from her part in it too, might come together in love—but he interrupted harshly, 'Don't talk about it. All that has gone sour on me. I seem to have lost the power to love anyone. I don't know if there's such a thing as absolute emotional bankruptcy, padre, but that's what I feel. I feel I shall never love anything but the memory of Terry, and that memory'll be loaded with pain for ever.'

'The child?' I ventured. 'Dorothy's child?'

'There'll be no child. We know that now. And God be praised for this at least. How could I have ever loved it? I never want any children at all now. A child of Terry's would have had all my heart. Lord, how I'd have loved it. Secretly I used to dream and long for it. . . . Never to be now. . . . Never to be now. . . .'

§

This was the moment when the great thing happened. I was suddenly possessed by an overwhelming love and pity for this suffering and deeply penitent boy, even though his deeds and his creeds had brought about the death of the girl who had captured all my heart and my desire; and whom, against these warm desires, I had been labouring to help. The total love and pity were like a dazzling flash of knowledge in which head and heart were conjoined; and it was accompanied by a sudden unspeakable bliss. I doubt if it occupied more than a measure of seconds, I doubt if the clock on the mantelpiece ticked twice before it was gone, and life was the same as it had been before—except that it has never been the same again. There has remained for ever the memory of that bliss.

I do not know how to describe it. It was knowledge; it was certainty. The knowledge and the certainty may have been illusory, but in the moment of experiencing them this was impossible, it was nonsense, to think. It was as nonsensical as to deny my body and my breathing.

My mind leapt back to that day with Perce and his friend Oliver (Perce of all people), who had talked of Edward Carpenter's illumination and quoted from Pascal, Oliver telling me about the piece of folded paper found sewn in Pascal's doublet after his death. Clearly it had been worn there near to his heart but hidden from the world. It opened with the year, the day, the hour of an overwhelming experience: 1654, Monday, the 23rd November, about half past ten. Then alone, in heavy letters, as for a title, the single word Fire. *'FEU . . . Certitude, certitude, sentiment, joye, paix. . . . Grandeur de l'âme humaine. . . . Joye, joye, et pleurs de joye. . . . Seul vrai Dieu et Celui que tu as envoyé, Jésus-christ. Jésus-christ, Jésus-christ. . . . Reconciliation totale et douce. . . .'*

It leapt back to Oliver quoting from Carpenter's *Towards Democracy.* 'That day—the day of deliverance—shall come to you in what place you know not. . . . In the pulpit while you are preaching—' and was I not preaching now?— 'Suddenly the ties and bands shall drop off . . . in the field with the plow and the chain-harrow; by the side of your horse in the stall. . . . It shall duly, at the appointed hour, come.' And in an article Carpenter almost echoed Pascal, whether or not he knew about that paper sewn in the doublet: 'Defects, accomplishments, limitations or what not—appeared of no importance whatever—an absolute freedom from mortality, accompanied by an undescribable calm and joy.'

Certitude? Knowledge? Knowledge of what? Certitude of what? Well, in this transient second of what I can only call a lightning flash, while Siward, sunk in his remorse and loss, sat in my big chair beside me, I saw with a perfect clarity that the flood of love for him which had flowed into me was akin, however humbly, to the love offered to all, no matter what their sins, by the Founder of Christianity. Dimly I had seen this before, but with no such instantaneous brightness as now. Because the experience was so momentary and so instantly gone I have always thought of it as a disc of clear light.

That such an experience could strike suddenly I knew from much reading in the lives of the great contemplatives and, after all, I had been a humble sort of contemplative for a decade. I knew that it came like something given from without, usually as a flash of revelation. I knew that it came, in its swift moment, after a time of much stress and suffering. It could spring from a darkness of deep sorrow and loss, and in the total silence of a soul's defeat. '*Jésus-christ*'. I remembered how someone, long centuries ago, in an attempt to approach the nearest possible definition of an indefinable God, had described him as 'that than which nothing greater can be conceived'. And instantly in this moment I saw that, if my feeling of love and pity for a youth lost in the misery of his sins, and (let me remember) the Archdeacon's refusal in the face of all accusers to cast one stone at two young penitents taken in adultery; if these were—as compared with God's Infinite Love—like poor human tapers compared with the full fierce light of the sun—then the Incarnation had to be. Infinite Love could have done nothing less. It had to come from the Timeless into time and history, and it did not come out thence till, in Christ's own words, it had 'paid the uttermost farthing' in identification with the erring, the outcast, the unlovable, the lost. One could conceive nothing greater than this. And no other religion in the world offered this. Therefore nothing on earth except the whole Christian answer could now satisfy my measurement of God.

§

The Passion had become as right and true for me as the Incarnation. 'I, if I be lifted up from the earth, will draw all men unto me,' Christ had said; and clearly it was only on a Cross that he could reveal to a suffering world what was a limitless and invincible love; and, so doing, draw all men unto him.

All this was now right and true for me; not for others perhaps, not for the great majority perhaps; but for me acceptable and undeniable for ever.

And together with this 'certitude and joy' had come a glimpse (I think)—no more than a glimmer—of Carpenter's universal or cosmic consciousness, on which Perce and Oliver had discoursed that day. Cosmic consciousnesss, they had said, was as far above normal self-consciousness as that was above the simple consciousness of the animals. It was an inner sense of the whole cosmic unity and of one's being part of it and eternal with it—an inner sense which transcended bodily sight as far as sight transcended touch. It seemed to make clear in its momentary flash that Space and Time were but illusions of our limited spatio-temporal minds;

and that beyond, behind, and beneath all the dark and puzzling things of our present order lie goodness and joy. It seemed another moment of vision, almost Timeless and impossible ever to forget or (for me) ever to deny.

Everything was now in place for me. I was ready, I was longing, to return to my Church and serve it again. I had suddenly a love and admiration for it, despite its many failings, and a vocation which was far larger and more certain than anything I had felt when first, twenty years before, I had offered myself as one of its ordinands. 'I settled all that for myself before I was nineteen' Dorothy had said to me, dancing in the old Forty-Three. But of a surety it may be years and years before the full gift of faith is vouchsafed : God takes his own time. One must render oneself ready and fit and worthy, it seems, for his gift, and then wait. Now at last I had, like a birth-labour pressing and swelling within me, the climax of my book which had eluded me so long. I craved to be sitting at the desk and writing it down. I felt as if I could complete it in days. I would write all day and every day. And maybe into the night. There are few joys in this life more exhilarating than to see, ahead of you at last, the summit-cairn of your mountain—or of your book.

A wilderness of wandering and troubled loneliness was for ever behind me. I could not believe I would seek that solitude again.

All was returned to me in safety : my Church's age-old ceremonials, laden with their haunting history; Bach's great Passions, his Easter and Christmas Oratorios; Mendelssohn's Oratorios; Bruckner's Mass in F minor; and every exultant gloria in Handel's *Messiah*. All were safe again.

Tomorrow I would help my vicar further. Tommorow I would mount the pulpit stairs again. Tomorrow I would have all to give.

Such were the outcomes of that brief, swift moment of insight, and they had been won for me by the vicarious sufferings of two dear children. Truly He is mysterious in his plotting. What was in it for them? Perhaps the promise of something when Siward, unspoken to, because I was lost in my dreams, said, 'I wonder if I could ever believe in all you've been saying. I don't suppose so. But at least I know I've learned something.'

Siward went far from Miryam's guest house, as I did too when, after some success of my book in the religious world, I was given a rectory in South Devon, so I saw little of him in later years, though I did learn once that he was giving much of his time, voluntarily, to lecturing and helping at Letherby Hall, an institution for poor and striving students in Liverpool slums. I doubt if he was ever able to accept the whole Christian creed, but at least it would seem that some of the Christian ethic was now lodged in his heart.

§

Who knows anything? As a Christian I can but believe, without the assent of many or most (though which of them know one jot more than I do) that the dead live on, and I sometimes dare to wonder—a fond wonder, maybe, but a dear one nonetheless— whether Terry, child of a religious home and more open to a faith than she liked to pretend, may have been allowed, because she loved us both, on that morning after the King's Inquiry, when Siward and I were talking together in my 'prophet's chamber on the wall'—to be, not far away from us, but near, and helping us to see.